3 0063 00252 7663

"Would you call that a brotherly kiss, Alice?"

And then he let out a harsh laugh that Alice could only interpret as triumphant. As if that kiss was only a means to teach her a lesson, which she supposed she deserved. Apparently she had wounded his pride when she'd compared his kiss to a brotherly peck and he had used all his talents to prove her wrong.

"Hardly," she said, taking a shaking breath. "It was nothing like any kiss I've experienced." There, she'd put him in his place, implying with her tone that she'd not been altogether pleased with the kiss and reminding him that she had been kissed—and more than once. Why she felt the need to gain the upper hand, she couldn't say. Perhaps it was because she was standing there with knees still shaking, with a dull throb between her legs, and he was standing there, arms crossed casually across his chest, smiling at her. His eyes flickered at her words, but then his smile widened.

"I do apologize. I am used to kissing women who have, let us say, a bit more experience."

"Please do spare me your false apology. You were trying to teach me a lesson and nothing more."

"Perhaps. You did seem in need of one."

Alice put her hands on her hips, outraged. "You needn't be so smug. It wasn't that good."

His burst of laughter was even more annoying than his smugness. "Of course it was." He waggled his eyebrows. "But I have done better."

DISCAF

More Historical Romance from Jane Goodger

Published by Kensington Publishing Corporation

DAVENPORT PUBLIC LIBRARY
321 MAIN STREET
DAVENPORT, IOWA 52801-1490

The Bad Luck Bride

The Brides of St. Ives

Jane Goodger

LYRICAL PRESS
Kensington Publishing Corp.
www.kensingtonbooks.com

To the extent that the image or images on the cover of this book depict a person or persons, such person or persons are merely models, and are not intended to portray any character or characters featured in the book.

LYRICAL PRESS BOOKS are published by

Kensington Publishing Corp.
119 West 40th Street
New York, NY 10018

Copyright © 2017 by Jane Goodger

All rights reserved. No part of this book may be reproduced in any form or by any means without the prior written consent of the Publisher, excepting brief quotes used in reviews.

All Kensington titles, imprints, and distributed lines are available at special quantity discounts for bulk purchases for sales promotion, premiums, fund-raising, educational, or institutional use.

Special book excerpts or customized printings can also be created to fit specific needs. For details, write or phone the office of the Kensington Sales Manager: Kensington Publishing Corp., 119 West 40th Street, New York, NY 10018. Attn. Sales Department. Phone: 1-800-221-2647.

Lyrical Press and Lyrical Press logo Reg. U.S. Pat. & TM Off.

First Electronic Edition: June 2017
eISBN-13: 978-1-5161-0151-1
eISBN-10: 1-5161-0151-0

First Print Edition: June 2017
ISBN-13: 978-1-5161-0152-8
ISBN-10: 1-5161-0152-9

Printed in the United States of America

Chapter 1

If only her fiancé had died five minutes *after* the ceremony instead of five minutes *before*, Alice wouldn't be in her current, unfathomable, situation.

A terrible thought, yes, but there was never a truer sentiment to go through her mind.

He was late. Her current and very much alive fiancé was terribly, horribly, embarrassingly late, and the vicar was giving her sad looks and the congregation was whispering, and Alice felt like she might scream for them all to just shut up. Harvey Reginald Heddingford III, Viscount Northrup, whom she actually liked (the first of her three fiancés whom she actually *had* liked) had apparently grown ice cold feet.

It wasn't much of a surprise, actually.

The night before he'd seemed…off. Distracted. Overly nice. *Guilty.* That's when the first niggling feeling of doubt touched her but she forced herself to ignore it. Certainly *three* men couldn't leave her at the altar. Though to be fair, Bertram Russell, her second ill-fated fiancé, was ousted by her enraged father long before she'd set foot in the church. Bertram had been found out—not one week before their planned nuptials—to be a complete fraud. He made ordinary fortune hunters seem like innocent children dabbling at seducing marriage out of highly placed, rich women.

One dead. One fraud. One very, very late.

This could not be happening again. She stood in the vestibule with her father and sister, dread slowly wrapping around her like a toxic fog, making it almost impossible to breathe. As she waited for her groom to make an appearance, knowing he would not, Alice vowed she would never, *ever*, be put in this position again. When she saw Vicar Jamison coming toward the spot where she stood with her father, Alice knew it was over. She couldn't seem to gather the energy to cry and in fact had the terrible urge to laugh, something she sometimes did at the worst possible moment. Actually, other than feeling a bit off kilter and extremely humiliated, she felt nothing at all. Certainly not heartbroken.

"Lord Hubbard," the vicar said, giving her father a small bow. "It may be time to address the congregation."

Her dear, dear, papa looked at her, his eyes filled with sorrow. "I think I must."

Alice nodded and pressed her hands, still holding her silly bouquet, into her stomach. *God, the humiliation.* This was far worse than Bertram and, well, poor Lord Livingston was deemed a tragedy, not a humiliation. People at least felt sorry for her when her first ill-fated husband-to-be dropped dead waiting for her to walk down the aisle. Just five more minutes and she might have been a widow, and a widow was a far better thing to be than a jilted bride.

It was all her sister's fault. Christina had been fussing with her gown, fixing something in the bustle, insisting that Alice would never get the chance to be a bride again (what a lark) and everything must be absolutely perfect for that most important day when Alice would have become a baroness. And then Lord Livingston died, right then, right as he walked toward the front of the church. Dropped like a stone without warning and was dead before he hit the hard marble floor with a sickening thud.

Instead of Lady Livingston or Lady Northrup, she was still Miss Hubbard and it looked like she would be Miss Hubbard for the rest of her days.

Christina stood, eyes wide with horror, as their father walked slowly to the front of the church. The large room became deathly quiet, and Alice turned, grabbed her sister's arm, and walked out the front door of the church. She couldn't bear to see the pity in their eyes, nor the tears in her mother's. Certainly Mama had never suspected her eldest daughter would once again be abandoned by her groom. Thank God they'd decided to get married in London and not St. Ives, where the villagers would have likely gathered to celebrate her marriage. No one was about except for the normal crowds.

"I'll murder him," Christina said feelingly when they reached their carriage. The startled footman hurriedly dropped the steps and then handed the sisters into the carriage, which was meant to carry the happy couple to their wedding breakfast.

Alice tore off her veil then gave her ferocious sister a weak smile. "I think he was in love with Patricia Flemings."

"No!" Christina said with the conviction of someone who cannot accept the fact that anyone could choose a Flemings over a Hubbard. Their father, Lord Richard Hubbard, was the third son of the fifth Duke of Warwick, and though he held no title, his connection to the great duke had put their family firmly in the lofty realm of the ton. Christina adored working "my grandfather, the Duke of Warwick" into as many conversations as possible, no matter what the topic. At eighteen, Christina was looking forward to her first season and was no doubt wondering how this latest wedding debacle with her sister would hurt her chances of making a good match.

Alice realized she was officially a hopeless case, and would no doubt become the terrible punch line to jokes told from Nottinghamshire to Cornwall. *You've heard of Alice Hubbard—or is it Miss Havisham?* Charles Dickens had done her no favor by portraying a jilted bride as such a bitterly tragic character. Alice didn't feel bitter, at least not at the moment, but she suspected she could not escape the label of 'tragic.'

Now she would have to hide away for a time at their country estate in St. Ives, which wasn't such a sacrifice, as St. Ives was her favorite place in all the world. Perhaps in her elder years she could be chaperone to her sister's beautiful daughters. She would be known by them as "my poor spinster aunt who never found love."

Three fiancés and she had hardly tolerated any of them, never mind loved them. She'd only loved one man in her life but he, of course, did not love her. And that, perhaps, was the most humiliating thing of all. Henderson Southwell, entirely inappropriate and devastatingly handsome. She called him Henny, which irritated him hugely, and that, of course, was why she did it. To say he was her one love was a bit of an exaggeration, for she now recognized her feelings for what they had been: youthful infatuation. But goodness, her heart had sped up whenever she heard his voice and nearly jumped from her chest when she actually saw him. Ah, the tall, lean, dark, handsome glory of him. She'd known Henderson for years and had fallen in love with him when she was seventeen or perhaps even before. Perhaps she'd fallen in love with him on those quiet nights when they would talk in the library while the rest of the house was sound asleep. He was her brother Joseph's closest friend, which delegated her immediately to that invisible moniker of little sister.

She hadn't seen him in four years. He'd disappeared from society and no one, not even her other brother, Oliver, had seen or heard from him in years.

"He's not the same as you remember, Allie," her brother Oliver told her when she'd asked if Henny would be invited to her wedding—the first one. "Even if I knew where he was and could invite him, I don't think he'd come."

And he hadn't; Alice hadn't even known if he'd received the invitation. Nor had he accepted her invitation for the second hastily cancelled wedding. As for this last, Alice still had no idea where Henderson was, but as this was to be a small affair, he hadn't been on the guest list at all. Just as well.

The carriage moved forward and Alice closed her eyes, relief flooding her that this day was over. When the carriage stopped with a startling jerk, she opened her eyes and gasped as Henderson Southwell, whom she hadn't seen in more than four years, burst into her carriage and sat across from her and next to her sister as if he'd been expected.

"Shall I kill him for you?" Henderson asked blandly as he settled himself into his seat and crossed his arms over his chest. His skin was tanned and she could see white lines that fanned out from his eyes from either smiling or squinting in the sun. His brown hair was nearly blond at the tips, and he was thinner than she remembered—and far handsomer.

"Henny. You weren't invited, you know." It gave her a small pleasure to not react to his completely unexpected appearance, other than that small gasp, which she wished she could have stifled.

"Wasn't I?"

"No. You were not. You were, however, invited to the first two of my weddings."

His dark brows rose as if in surprise. "You've been married twice already?"

"Oh, do stop teasing my sister, Mr. Southwell," Christina said. "Hasn't she been through enough this morning?"

Henderson turned to his right as if surprised to see someone sitting next to him. "Do not tell me this is little Christina." He looked over to Alice as if for confirmation.

Christina beamed and Alice gritted her teeth. Henderson had always been able to charm; it was his greatest talent. When she was younger, she'd heard things, unsavory things, about Henderson that an unmarried girl should not hear. Affairs with married women, with widows, opera singers, actresses. Those rumors had nearly killed her when she'd been in the deepest throes of her crush on him. More than one of her friends had been warned away from him, and not just because of his lowly birth. His mother was a member of the landed gentry who'd had the misfortune of getting pregnant without the benefit of a marriage. This small fact had been quite titillating when Alice was a girl.

"I was just a child when we last saw you..." Christina's voice drifted off as she realized when that was—her brother Joseph's funeral. It was a terrible reminder of a dreadful time. The eldest of the four Hubbard children, Joseph had been the light of their family, the one who would sing loudly and purposely badly in the morning to wake everyone up. One couldn't get angry with Joseph. In fact, the only time Alice had ever gotten angry with Joseph was after he'd died. Why had he been so reckless? Why had he left them alone?

Four children, two boys, two girls, Joseph the first born. The three younger children adored Joseph to the point of hero worship. When he died, falling off the roof of a school chum's carriage house when Alice was just seventeen, he'd left an endless hole in the Hubbard family. Nothing had been the same ever since. Joseph used to play the piano, make his mother stand by his side to sing a duet. The joy in their house, the music, all ended the day Joseph died. Her father, his face filled with fathomless pain, had the piano removed from their home the day after his funeral.

Looking at Henderson made Alice's heart hurt, for the two young men had been inseparable—except for that faithful night. Even though Alice had been wretched the day of her brother's funeral, when she'd looked up and saw Henderson, eyes red-rimmed and staring blinding at the casket, she knew he was feeling the same pain as she. And then he'd disappeared. Until now.

Henderson shifted, the light in his striking blue eyes dimming momentarily before he grinned at her again. "You didn't answer my question. Shall I kill Northrup or just make him suffer?"

Alice sighed. "Neither, I'm afraid." She looked out the window at the row of elegant and neat houses that told her she was nearing her father's home on St. James Square. "He was following his heart and I can hardly blame him for that."

"Of course you can," Christina said, and Alice gave her a grateful look. "Besides, his heart should have led him directly to you, not that miserable girl. Honestly, Alice, you cannot just let people take complete advantage of you."

Alice stared at her sister until Christina began to squirm. "I simply do not inspire men to love. I have come to accept this. As for Northrup's actions today? Yes, they were unforgivable and humiliating, but how would I have felt years from now knowing he loved another all along? Better a few moments of humiliation than a lifetime of regret." She nodded her head to make her point, and was exceedingly annoyed when Henderson laughed aloud.

"I fail to see anything amusing in what I said."

"Had you no feeling for this man at all?"

Alice gave him a level look. "Should I have?"

He seemed stunned by her words, and inside Alice felt a small bit of discomfort. She should love the man she would marry. She wanted to, but life had shown her a different path, or perhaps she had just meandered onto the wrong path. Her first fiancé, the baron, was kind and handsome and seemed to truly enjoy her company. Spending time with him had been mostly tolerable and the man had seemed to delight in everything she said—to an annoying degree. She'd been just nineteen years old and, frankly, flattered by an older man's admiration and attention. So she basked in the novelty of having a man court her, was gratified that her parents seemed so pleased with the match and were smiling as they hadn't since Joseph's death. Here was something good, something that could make her parents happy. Somehow it hadn't mattered that he was in his fifties; he hadn't acted old nor seemed a man ready to keel over and die. When he did die, Alice had felt oddly devoid of emotion. Though sad, she hadn't cried, hadn't truly felt much of anything until, when standing by his casket at his funeral, she looked up and saw real grief in the eyes of the baron's children. They had clearly adored their father, and she'd felt like a fraud, unworthy even to be standing at his graveside. When she'd finally cried, it had been from a deep and cutting shame.

Her second fiancé was an unmitigated mistake, a man with about as much substance as a wisp of smoke. Charming, flamboyant, and the finest actor Alice had ever seen, Bertram had fooled nearly everyone he met. He claimed to be distantly related to the Queen herself, third cousin twice removed or some such stuff. Dressing and acting like a man of means, moving with ease among the ton, Bertram hardly caused suspicion. It wasn't until Papa insisted on meeting his relatives that it all fell apart. Just six days before their wedding, he was gone, leaving behind a note that said, "Sorry, love. I think it would have been grand."

Alice hadn't crumpled the note, hadn't cried. She'd laid the note on the small rosewood table that she used for all her correspondence and sighed, thinking only that her poor parents would be terribly upset to realize they'd wasted money on yet another engagement ball. Part of her realized she should feel something more; she even tried to make herself cry, then gave up, laughing at her own foolishness. Since her brother's death, Alice had changed, she realized. Joseph's dying had scarred her in ways she hadn't realized until recently. I should feel *something*, she thought, having just been jilted at the altar.

Now, sitting in the carriage after her third failed wedding, that hollowness grew until there was no room for anything else. The giddy feeling she used to get when Henderson walked in the room was missing. *Everything* was missing.

Henderson tilted his head and studied her as if he were trying to determine whether or not she was joking, wondering, perhaps, how it was possible a woman who'd just been jilted could sit in a carriage dry-eyed and perfectly calm. Had he thought she'd be in hysterics?

"I suppose I'm a romantic," Henderson said finally, off-handedly. "I actually thought girls *liked* to be in love when they married."

Alice gave him a stare, then turned to look out the window again just as the carriage stopped in front of their home. As soon as the step was lowered and the door opened, Alice stood and offered her hand to the footman. Christina followed, but turned to Henderson and said, "She may not show her emotions, sir, but I know she is terribly hurt."

Alice heard her sister and stifled the retort that hung on the tip of her tongue. Oddly, she was not hurt. She knew she should be…something. Outraged, angered, distraught. But the only emotion she seemed to feel at the moment was humiliation. Her pride had been hurt, not her heart. And as her grandmamma always said, pride goeth before a fall.

* * *

Henderson *hated* that look in Alice's eyes, that cool emptiness. As illogical as it was, he blamed himself for everything that had befallen her, including her brother's death. That night, that terrible night when everything in his life stopped and irrevocably changed, Joseph had wanted him to join their Oxford friends for a house party. Henderson had been at their home in St. Ives, where he spent nearly all his free time. So much so, that he seemed a part of the family. As an only child, Henderson, especially when he was younger, had imagined he *was* part of the family. To a boy who lived alone with a mother who rarely spoke to him directly and a father of unknown origins, the Hubbard household seemed perfect.

"My God, Joseph, have you *seen* Mrs. Patterson?" Henderson had said to Joseph that night. Mrs. Patterson was a willing widow, and in Henderson's experience, nothing trumped that.

Joseph had given him a look of disgust. "It'll be a lark, Southie. Plus, he's got one of the finest race horses in all of England and I'd like to see it.

Come on, you can see your widow any old night. I really want you there."

No one called him Southie, short for Southwell, except Joseph. They'd gone to Eton together, and by the time Henderson had got there, Joseph was already well-liked with a solid group of chaps and welcomed him into their fold quickly. Alone among all the men he'd ever known, Joseph had never judged him, never faulted him for who he was. Until Henderson had looked a little too long at Alice.

He still remembered that night, every detail, vivid and awful. They'd been bantering about whether Henderson should join Joseph's friends when what Henderson truly wanted to do was climb between the legs of Mrs. Patterson. Of course Joseph knew what Henderson's plans had been that night, and Joseph didn't mind telling Henderson he was rather disgusted with his seemingly indiscriminate taste in women. Henderson was unapologetic about his affairs. He never seduced an innocent, never made promises he had no intention of keeping, never allowed his emotions to enter into his encounters. Pure pleasure and plenty of it.

"Just because you're afraid of women doesn't mean I have to pretend to be," Henderson had teased. That's when Alice had walked by. He hadn't meant to look at her overlong, hadn't thought to school his features. He'd been more than a bit in love with her for about two years now, but he'd never been stupid enough to let his emotions show. But in that moment, she was purely beautiful, with womanly curves, and by God, she was glorious. Walking past the pair as they talked in the library, she smiled at him and that smile, well, it did something to his heart. It always had, even though she was far too young for him to even contemplate.

"Southie." His name, low and hard, and Henderson inwardly shook himself and tore his gaze away from Alice. "Do not ever look that way at my sister again."

Henderson could feel his cheeks heat. He found he couldn't meet his friend's eyes and was deeply hurt that Joseph would get so angry over a simple gaze. "I wasn't—"

"You were," Joseph said, his tone sharp. "Promise me you will never touch my sister. Promise."

"God, Joseph, of course. Of course, I promise on my life. I will never touch your sister." He hadn't meant that promise, though his words had been spoken fervently. He thought he'd have years to court Alice properly, to get Joseph to understand that he was more than a little in love with her, that she would never be like those other women he only used to ease the ache in his body. Henderson knew when Joseph realized how much he loved Alice, he'd come around. He may not have known who his father was, but he was an Oxford man now with a promising future. Alice was far too young, wouldn't even come out for another year. He'd be patient and in the meantime, could see her any time he wanted. Could dance with her and laugh with her and make her love him as much as he loved her. He'd thought he'd have all the time in the world to convince Joseph to allow him to break that promise.

But that night, Joseph died.

Chapter 2

Alice tried to ignore Mr. Owens's shocked face when she entered the front door, still in her bride's dress.

"Miss?"

"My groom was absent," she said, and was touched when he flinched, as if her words had caused him pain.

"I am very sorry, miss." Dear Mr. Owens had volunteered to stay behind whilst the rest of the staff had attended the wedding. He was likely glad he had.

"It's all right, Mr. Owens. I shall live. My only regret is that you all will likely be stuck with me in perpetuity."

"Hardly a sacrifice, miss."

She gave him a tight smile and stiffened when she heard her sister and Henderson come up behind her. Giving Henderson a pointed look, she pulled off her gloves and handed them to Mr. Owens, who took them and bowed. "Tea in the parlor, miss?"

"That would be perfect. For two."

"Three, Mr. Owens. There's a good man. Miss Hubbard is so upset, she forgot I was here."

Alice narrowed her eyes at him and for some reason found herself suppressing a smile. It wouldn't do to give him any encouragement. It was difficult enough to maintain her dignity when he was grinning at her like a fool. The thing was, it was wonderful to see Henderson, and had it been any other occasion, she might have forgotten herself and fallen into his arms. Knowing he had witnessed this ultimate humiliation was, well, humiliating. Why, after being absent for four years, had he decided to come to her wedding, of all things?

He had changed a bit, grown older, of course, but though he smiled and acted as he always had, she sensed an underlying seriousness. Perhaps it was his eyes. His smile didn't seem to completely fill his features as it had once. He was still tall, of course, and impossibly handsome. Debonair, one might say, with his carefully tamed dark hair and well-cut jacket, though she did notice his shoes were quite dusty, as if he'd been running in a field.

They settled, all three of them, in the parlor and waited for tea. Alice supposed she should be up in her room sobbing. Perhaps after she'd had some tea that's exactly what she would do.

"So. Three."

Christina gasped, but Alice waved her outrage away.

"Yes. Three. First Baron Livingston. Then a scoundrel. Then—"

"—another scoundrel," he finished for her. "You really do have the worst taste in men."

"Says a man who is known as one of the worst rakes in all of England."

He looked shocked and hurt. Mockingly so. "Rake? Hardly. Well, perhaps in my younger years. You have noticed, haven't you, that I've been gone out of the country these last four years."

"Were you?" She pretended to think. "Yes, I do believe I haven't seen your name in the *Tattler* in quite some time."

The look he gave her nearly made Alice shiver. For just a moment, he seemed genuinely angry with her.

Christina sat silently, but it was never an easy thing for her to do, and apparently her sister also saw that glimmer of irritation. "Alice isn't the only one who thinks you're a rake. Since your return to London, you've been in the *Tattler* several times."

Henderson raised one dark brow. Slowly. It really was quite fascinating to watch the control the man had over that muscle.

Turning to Christina, Alice said, "Has he really?"

Christina's cheeks tinged a bit pink. Their mother had forbidden the girls from reading the gossip column, but they did manage to sneak a peek at friends' houses now and then. Apparently Christina had been sneaking a peek more frequently than Alice. "Yes. Just last week there was something about a Mr. S, back from his travels, being seen with Madame L. That must mean Mr. Southwell and Madame Lavigne. She's appearing at the Vauxhall Theater, you know."

"You are mistaken," Henderson said, his voice oddly flat, and Alice gave him a sharp look.

"It must have been Thomas Southwick, Christina. Or any other number of men who've been traveling and whose last names begin with

s. Really, you should not listen to such gossip nor spread it."

Christina looked horrified and her cheeks flamed even brighter. "I do apologize, Mr. Southwell. It's just that—"

He held up a hand to stop her. "Please do not distress, Miss Hubbard. Not too long ago, that Mr. S could very well have been I. But I am a reformed man, these days. I haven't been to the theater in years."

A maid entered the room at that moment, and not far behind her came Alice's mother and father, both looking weary and worried. Hurrying over to her as if she were about to drop off a cliff, when it seemed perfectly obvious to Alice that she was handling the whole jilting thing rather well, they each clutched one of her hands.

"I shall file a breach of promise immediately," her father said.

"Papa, you'll do no such thing. I don't want to bring more attention to this."

"You have been terribly wronged, Alice. If we do not file a petition, you will appear an even more tragic figure."

Alice shook her head. "I find such actions crass, and endorsed mostly by women seeking money. I have no need for money, thanks to you and grandmamma, and no stomach for the proceeding."

"I agree," Henderson said, causing her parents to turn toward him.

"By God, Henderson," her father said. "I didn't realize you were back in England." Richard strode over to Henderson and clasped his hand warmly. "It is so good to see you."

Alice felt her throat close painfully. Her parents had loved Henderson like a son; everyone had loved Henderson in their family and everyone had felt his loss, paired as it was with Joseph's death. It was almost like getting a tiny bit of Joseph back, bittersweet as it was.

Her mother also went over to Henderson, who had stood upon their entering, and gave him a warm embrace. "Where have you been? We have all missed you. Haven't we, Alice?"

"Of course."

"I've been in India working with a physician, a Dr. Cornish. The famine, you see."

"Oh, yes, those poor people. Florence Nightingale has written several passionate letters to the *Times* about it." Alice was not a regular reader of the *Times*, but she read it frequently enough to have known about a famine. "The drought must have been terrible."

Henderson gave her a tight smile. "It was. I only wish the drought was the worst of it."

Alice looked to her father, who shook his head. Apparently he wasn't certain what Henderson meant either.

"I hope to return there soon," Henderson said. "I'm here to gather support for relief."

"Of course we should help, shouldn't we, Papa?"

"Yes. But I'm afraid my influence with the politicians is not particularly widespread. We can talk later about this and see what I can do to rally support."

Henderson seemed hugely relieved. "Thank you, sir. We've been getting an astounding amount of resistance, you see. People are dying from starvation. I've seen it with my own eyes. You cannot imagine the horror of it."

Richard gave an uncomfortable cough. "Yes, I can see you are passionate about this, Henderson, but I do not think this is a topic to be discussed at the moment."

Henderson shot a look to Alice and nodded. "Yes, sir. My apologies. I seem to have lost a bit of my polish in the last few years."

"Think nothing of it, my dear boy. India is so far from British society as to be on another planet."

"Indeed, India is very different from England," Henderson said.

Oliver came into the room at that moment, and her brother was looking thunderous. "I couldn't find the lout."

"Oh, Oliver, please do tell me you haven't been scouring London looking for Lord Northrup."

"Of course I have, I—" He stopped, bringing back his head in shock. "Henderson! By God, we all thought you'd never set foot on English soil again." Oliver went to his old friend and gave him a hearty handshake.

"He was just about to tell us about his time in India," Christina said. She sat forward, looking as if she were near to bursting to involve herself in the conversation, and Alice found herself oddly relieved. It seemed, suddenly, such an effort to converse about anything. Perhaps she should have immediately gone to her room and had herself a good cry. "Please do tell us about India. I've heard such wonderful tales about it," Christina continued.

Henderson gave her younger sister an indulgent smile before he winked at Oliver. "I'll fill you in later, shall I?" he said to his old friend before turning back to Christina. "What would you like to know?"

"Do elephants walk in the streets? Are there truly man-eating tigers roaming about? And I've heard it's dreadfully hot there. Oh, and the palaces. I've heard there are the most fantastical palaces, exotic and marvelous. Have you ever been in one? And was there really a party where sixty thousand people were invited?"

Henderson laughed. "So many questions, Miss Hubbard. Where shall I begin?"

"With the elephants," Alice said, finding herself caught up in her sister's enthusiasm. The only elephant she'd seen, of course, had been in the zoo.

"Then, yes, there are elephants, though they're not as big as our Jumbo. The natives use them to help farm and move things. They are highly trained and wonderful creatures. I rode upon one when I first arrived."

"Did you?" Christina gushed.

"I did. And I have to say I'd much rather ride a horse any day of the week. It's rather disconcerting how very high up you are when on an elephant and they are not nearly as easy to steer. Still, they are magnificent creatures."

"And the tigers?"

"I saw no tigers. Only dogs. Hundreds of them. Very fat and well-fed."

Something about the way Henderson said this last gave Alice pause. He seemed very nearly angry about the well-fed canines.

"If you'd rather not talk about India…" Christina must have heard the same thing in his tone.

Henderson smiled, and Alice found herself relaxing slightly, for at that moment, he looked like the man she remembered, that teasing, happy-go-lucky boy she'd found herself infatuated with as a girl. Now thinking about how her heart had fluttered when she'd go into the library and see him there, book in hand, reading the sort of novels her mother would never allow her to read, she felt only embarrassment. No doubt Henderson had been annoyed with her constant presence, but he'd never let on. He would always put his book aside, or read a particularly titillating passage (he adored reading adventure novels) so he could laugh at her shocked expression. He once read *Robinson Crusoe* to her, but the book was far too short. She'd loved listening to him, his soft baritone, the way he made it seem as if he were the narrator. On the evenings she found the library empty, she'd been dearly disappointed. In truth, she'd been devastated the way only a young girl can be when the young man she's infatuated with is likely with an older, more sophisticated woman.

"I don't mind talking about India, but I don't want to bore you."

"Oh, no," Christina said. "Please, what was it like?"

"Hot, beautiful. A study in contrasts. I've never seen people so wealthy nor so poor. The land is either lush or dead, depending on what part of the country you are in. And the people are wonderful or unbearably cruel."

He stopped. "Actually, I'd rather not talk about India at the moment, if you don't mind."

The room took on a heavy silence.

"How long have you been in England?" Alice asked before taking a delicate sip of tea.

"Surely you cannot be ready to have a polite intercourse on my travels when you have just returned from your wedding sans husband."

"What else shall we talk about? The weather? I'm already dreadfully bored thinking about what occurred this morning. So, please, sir, do tell us how long you've been home."

Henderson narrowed his eyes, but his lips turned up in a smile. "As a matter of fact, I arrived in London just this morning and haven't even been to visit my grandparents." He laughed aloud at what Alice knew must be a shocked expression.

"And you hurried over to a wedding, to which you had not been invited, before even going to see your own family? Whatever possessed you?" Alice asked.

Henderson looked at each person in the room before replying succinctly, "I'd hoped to stop the wedding."

Chapter 3

The Hubbards' reaction to his pronouncement that he'd arrived that morning hoping to stop the wedding was not at all what Henderson expected. He'd thought perhaps a gasp or two. A shocked look, particularly on Alice's face. Anger, for suggesting something that would have likely turned into a terrible scandal. But to a one, they all burst out laughing. He supposed the man he'd been four years ago *would* have been joking about such a thing. There was nothing to do but join in and ignore the little stab in his heart that Alice was nearly in tears from mirth.

She sobered rather quickly, though it was clear she was still trying not to laugh, and said, "Of course you did." She turned to her mother. "Mother, my reputation is saved."

"I, for one, do think it's rather callous of Mr. Southwell to be making a jest of things so early," Christina said, and Alice was touched by her sister's fierce loyalty.

"I apologize," Henderson said, giving Alice a small bow. From the narrowing of her eyes, she knew he was mocking her, and to be perfectly honest, at that moment, when his heart had just taken a small beating, he did not care.

Oliver gave him a long look, which Henderson pointedly ignored. "You were joking, weren't you, Henderson?"

"What sort of a man would show up after four years and do such a thing?" It was not an answer but no one pointed that out, for which Henderson was grateful.

The group was silent for a few beats before Mrs. Hubbard suggested they not waste the fine breakfast the cook had prepared in anticipatory celebration of the bridal party returning to their home. Looking over at

Alice, Henderson noted her color was high, no doubt caused by the small reminder of the expense her parents had once again undertaken.

"I'm not very hungry, Mama. If you don't mind, I think I will go up to my room to change. Have the staff returned from the church yet?"

Henderson tried not to look at her, but it was nearly impossible. He wanted, more than anything, to draw her into his arms and take away the pain that she was so clearly trying to hide. She might not be heartbroken, but the fact that she'd been left at the altar—again—had to be devastating.

"Of course. I think I heard someone moving about downstairs." Her mother pulled on a velvet cord and moments later Mr. Owens appeared, his face even more solemn than usual.

"Yes, ma'am."

"Could you have Hazel go up to Miss Hubbard's rooms?"

After Mr. Owens left to find Alice's maid, Alice kissed her mother's cheek, then her father's.

"Are you certain you don't want me to find him and pummel him?" Oliver asked, and Alice let out a small laugh.

"I am certain." She swallowed and before she turned to leave the room, Henderson was sure her eyes filled with tears. He took a step toward her but stopped abruptly, realizing how strange that would seem. It didn't matter that he'd thought about her every day since he'd left; it was clear she hadn't thought of him. Then again, what had he expected? That she would wait for him when he hadn't even had the courage to ask her to?

He'd left without a word, without even a letter of explanation, thinking it was better. Everything was so raw, so horribly, horribly wrong after Joseph's death. When that first wedding invitation reached him, two weeks after the supposed event, Henderson had felt something shift in his heart. He'd lost her because he'd been too ashamed, too filled with guilt and remorse and that awful promise he'd made to Joseph. And he'd lost her. Word that her fiancé had died before the wedding gave him a small amount of hope—until the second invitation reached him just a year later.

That was the last he knew until one of his grandmother's infrequent letters reached him and mentioned Alice and her third attempt at matrimony. Apparently, it was unusual enough to spark even his grandmother's interest. Something came over him in that moment as he held his grandmother's letter in his hand, something fierce and raw. It was almost as if God were up in heaven giving him chance after chance and Henderson was simply too stupid to take a hint. Or perhaps it was Joseph manipulating things down on Earth so that his best friend could finally be with the only woman he'd ever loved. It was a fanciful thought, but it began to grow and grow until it was a physical thing inside him, this need to leave India, to return home and stop Alice from marrying again. A miracle happened then. Dr. Cornish, sanitary commissioner for Madras, urged him to return to England, to rally support for famine relief, to give first-hand accounts of what was happening, to try to use any influence he had to get someone, anyone, interested in the millions of lives that were being lost.

Henderson had left that meeting with a feeling of inevitability, and as he'd looked up at the gray sky over Madras, he'd smiled. "Thanks, Joseph." He could picture his friend up there, rolling his eyes, and saying, "It's about time, Southie, you stubborn fool."

Four weeks later—a week after his original arrival date thanks to several delays—he was stepping off a ship, his heart pounding like mad. Alice was getting married in one hour. A hack was waiting, as if for him, and Henderson climbed aboard, feeling his heart swell with what he recognized as hope. It bloomed inside him, nearly felling him. He'd rehearsed on his journey home what he was going to say, but as he approached the church, his brain got all muddled and the only thing he knew was that he had to stop it. Had to. Then, disaster struck. The hack's wheel shattered, leaving it listing far to one side on a crowded London street. Pulling out his watch, he realized with sick dread that he was going to be late. He jumped from the hack, throwing the driver a coin, and began frantically looking about for another. Nothing. The streets were clogged with traffic, the noise suddenly unbearable. And so he began to run, knowing even as he did that he would be late. After four bloody years of pining away for her and doing nothing, he was going to lose his one chance to act, to make her his.

Somewhere in the distance, a church bell rang, nine loud peals, each one causing more and more pain in his heart. The wedding had started and he was still several long minutes away from the church. He stopped, breathing hard, sweat dripping from his forehead, his hands on his knees, failure gripping him. It hit him then that perhaps Joseph hadn't been helping him all these years but rather torturing him. She's getting married. Suffer. She didn't get married. Relief! Again and again. Until this day when he'd been so very close to finally at least trying to do something, only to have fate step in again. Or Joseph, who was no doubt up in heaven wearing a satisfied smirk on his face. *If you had been there that night, I wouldn't be dead.* It was nothing but the truth.

After that, he'd walked with slow purpose toward the church as a punishment of sorts. For if he hadn't left England, she might be his wife even now. Surely he could have convinced Lord Hubbard that he was worthy of her. He'd gone quietly into a side door at the church and slipped into a pew toward the back. And waited. When the vicar started to make his way to the back of the church, Henderson walked out the way he'd come in and waited until Alice and her sister emerged from the church. She looked pale and distraught, but all he could think was, *I still have a chance.*

* * *

Alice settled in front of her mirror as Hazel, clucking her tongue in sympathy, removed her veil and started unpinning her hair. It was the second time in three years that she'd sat in this very spot, her throat thick, her eyes dry, wondering what would become of her.

"A terrible thing, miss," Hazel said. "Everyone downstairs is so upset for you."

"Thank you, Hazel." After first removing her wedding dress, Hazel had swiftly, and unceremoniously, put the garment away and out of sight before focusing on her veil and hair. No doubt her mother would donate the dress to charity. Perhaps the League of Impoverished Women Who Were Actually Getting Married. She sighed, staring at herself and promising with every fiber of her being to say no the next time someone proposed.

At least her friends from St. Ives hadn't made the trip this time. They had wanted to come, of course, but Alice told them it was to be a small ceremony. The truth was, most of her friends could hardly spare the expense of attending yet another wedding. Alice wondered if she'd had a feeling even weeks ago that this wedding would never occur. Looking back, she tried to see if she'd missed something, a sign that Lord Northrup was lying to her. He'd told her several times that he adored her, that he was looking forward to their life together. All along, he'd been in love with someone else, somehow realizing she was not nearly the catch he'd thought she was.

Just the idea of going home to St. Ives, still Miss Hubbard when everyone in that little seaside village thought she'd be Lady Northrup, made a fresh rush of humiliation flood her. Although Alice had never put too much stock in attaining a titled husband, she had indulged in writing her name over and over: Lady Alice Heddingford, Viscountess Northrup.

"Shall I brush out your hair, miss?"

"No, thank you, Hazel," Alice said, taking the brush from her maid's hands and setting it on the vanity in front of her.

It wasn't until Hazel had softly closed the door behind her that Alice gave in to the tears pressing painfully against her eyes, and for that moment she fervently wished that her small group of friends were with her. They were all a bit younger than Alice, all unmarried, and all her champions. Except, perhaps, for Eliza, who had always been a bit jealous of the fact that Alice had gotten engaged three times when she'd never even had a serious beau. Still, she knew Eliza would drop everything to be with her. They all would: Eliza, Harriet, and Rebecca. They had spent endless hours together since they were still in short skirts. Alice wondered if the four of them were cursed, because though the women were all attractive, all intelligent (some less than others, but still), and all of marriageable age, each remained steadfastly single.

A soft knock on the door had her quickly dabbing her eyes and casting a quick look in the mirror to make sure she didn't look quite as devastated as she felt.

"Come in," she called, hastily rising and pulling on her wrap just in case it was her brother. But it was her mother, her face filled with concern, who came into her room, still wearing the dress she'd worn in the church.

"How are you really?" she asked.

"Awful," Alice said with a watery laugh. Her mother hurried to her and gave her a warm hug. Just feeling her mother's arms wrap around her, with her familiar mother-smell, made Alice want to weep all the more.

"I daresay I don't know what words to tell you to make this better. It is unbelievable that this has happened to you."

"Again."

"Again." Her mother let out a sigh and stepped back so she could peer into Alice's eyes. "Are you certain you don't want to take any legal action against him? What he did is unconscionable. Why not tell you last evening? Or any other time? He certainly had plenty of opportunity to call things off."

"I believe he meant to see it through; I could tell something was wrong yesterday evening. I thought perhaps he was just nervous about the wedding. I know what he did was wrong, Mama, believe me I do. But I just want it over. I want to forget it happened. I want everyone to forget that it happened."

Elda walked to the window and looked out. "Henderson is leaving." She sounded unaccountably sad, and Alice understood that her mother felt very much the same way she did when she saw him. Joseph and he had been so inseparable; one could hardly think of Joseph without thinking of Henderson. "Odd that he's shown up now, today, after all these years."

"Very odd." Alice looked in the mirror to make certain the flush she felt wasn't showing on her cheeks. It had always been that way, ever since she was fifteen years old and Henderson had come to stay for the summer. Her infatuation with him was a secret she held close to her heart; no one knew, especially not the man himself.

"It does make one wonder if he really did come to stop the wedding."

Alice laughed, unable to stop herself. "Mama, he's just got off the boat this morning. He must have heard about the wedding somehow and thought he'd peek in to see everyone. And on what grounds would he have done such a thing? Lord Northrup is a fine man with a good reputation. It wasn't like the last time, with Mr. Russell. I could believe someone trying to stop *that* wedding."

"I am sure you are correct," Elda said, dropping the curtain and walking back to where Alice sat. "Besides, as much as I adore Henderson, he's probably the last man I'd want for you."

"Mama, what a snob you are!"

A small sigh escaped her mother's lips. "His birth has nothing do with my feelings toward Henderson, you know that. It's that he's known as a bit of a rake, my dear. I can't imagine he's changed all that much in four years."

Pressing her lips together to stop from smiling, Alice nodded. "I'd heard."

"You had?"

"I may not read the *Tattler*, but my friends do. Before Henderson left he was tied to no fewer than three actresses and an opera singer. And he was only twenty-one. It used to vex Joseph terribly when my friends and I quoted from the gossip columns."

Elda's expression grew wistful. "It did. Joseph was fiercely loyal to everyone he loved. Why, I remember he got into a terrible row with Julian Giles when he said something unflattering about you. Your father had to go and apologize to old Mr. Giles for the violence done to his son."

A smile bloomed on Alice's face. "He did? Why didn't I know about this?"

"We didn't want you to be upset about what Julian said or what Joseph did." She leaned forward conspiratorially. "Your father was secretly proud."

Alice laughed. "What on earth did Julian say?"

"He said you were the homeliest girl in St. Ives."

Alice was truly shocked, for she'd always liked Julian and the two of them had been friends when they were children. "He did? How old was I? Perhaps I *was* the homeliest."

Shaking her head, Elda said, "No. You were never the homeliest. I think he said that terrible thing because he didn't want the other boys to know how much he liked you."

"That makes more sense," Alice said, laughing. It wasn't that she was vain, but she did have a certain appreciation of the fact that she wasn't ugly. She let out a sigh. "It's nice to talk about Joseph. Sometimes I feel as if he never existed, as if we want to forget him."

Her mother's eyes instantly misted. "It's just so painful. Your father, he cannot bear to think about it. You have no idea how devastated he was, and still is."

"We all are," Alice said, gazing at her hands. "It's just that talking about Joseph makes him less gone. Do you know what I mean? And seeing Henderson…"

"I know," her mother said, reaching over and placing one hand on Alice's knee. "It seems like it was just yesterday. Maybe because Henderson left right after the funeral."

"I still get angry with Joseph, you know. I picture him with his mates, climbing that stupid roof, taking that insane chance. What was he thinking?"

"He was no doubt thinking what all young men think, that they will never die."

Alice's eyes filled with tears. "I hope he wasn't frightened." It was something she'd thought about for years, a thought that tortured her, and it felt oddly comforting to say it aloud.

Her mother smiled sadly. "I have a feeling that even in mid-air, our Joseph was thinking how grand it was to fly and that he'd likely bounce off the ground like a rubber ball."

Alice laughed at the image. Her mother was right, that was exactly what Joseph would have been thinking.

Elda stood, looking uncertain, as if she were wondering if her daughter was truly as *un*heartbroken as she appeared to be. "Is there anything I can get you?"

"No, Mama. And lest you think I'm heartbroken, I am not. I am sad, yes. And embarrassed and mortified and angry. More than anything, I want to go home and never set foot in London again."

Elda laughed, bringing her daughter back in for another embrace. "At least until next season."

Alice pulled away. "No, Mama. Never again. I'm not going to allow anyone to court me and I'm never, ever going to wear a bridal gown again." "Oh, Alice, don't say such things. This too shall pass."

Alice hugged her arms around herself and fingered the embroidery on the sleeve of her wrap. This would not pass. This would be the defining moment of her life, the day Alice Hubbard vowed never to marry.

* * *

Henderson stepped down from his hack onto Albermarle Street and looked up at the façade of Brown's Hotel, his home for at least the next week. It felt strange to be back in London after the grit and poverty of India. Strange and good. He hadn't known how much he'd missed the city until now. His mad dash from the ship hadn't afforded him much of a chance to look about, and now that he had the opportunity, he realized how dear the old place was. Every corner, every street, held a memory. It was home. The accents, the smell of roses, the sound of horses on the cobblestoned streets.

He entered the hotel, his feet sinking into the almost decadent carpet that covered much of the gleaming marble beneath, and breathed in the scent of beeswax and fine food. A small bit of guilt hit him, that he should enjoy such sensations when so many millions were suffering back in India. His mission was not to bask in creature comforts, but to enlist the help of powerful men to push the House of Lords into providing funding and support for relief. Dr. Cornish was not optimistic about his mission, but Henderson believed passionately that it was every Englishman's duty to help the poor. Yes, they had run into opposition again and again in India, but that was only because the people back in England did not fully understand the scope of what was happening. When he left England to return to India, everyone would know.

As he waited for the clerk to determine which rooms were available, Henderson pulled out his well-worn list of men who held in their well-manicured hands the power to save the millions of starving people. Eight men who could change the world, who could literally save lives, simply by allowing England's massive stockpiles of grain to be used by the starving people of India rather than shipped to well-fed citizens of Britain.

"Room four twenty-one, Mr. Southwell," the clerk said. "If you need anything, please do not hesitate to ask. We'll have your bags delivered to your room shortly."

"And a bottle of brandy."

"Of course, sir."

After a day such as he'd had, a bottle of brandy was just the ticket.

Mrs. Henderson Southwell. Alice Southwell.

Alice could still remember giggling at her scribblings, then crumpling them up quickly when she heard her brother's voice right outside her door. The very last thing she needed was for Joseph to discover that she was madly in love with his best friend. She was just fifteen then, and Henderson was already in university.

It happened quite quickly, and was far different from anything she'd ever felt for a boy. For one thing, Henderson Southwell was a man. Or close enough to one. He was tall and handsome and his smile, it was enough to make her heart pound madly in her chest every time she saw it. She fell in love that first night when Henderson had come into the library and spied her there reading. Instead of apologizing and leaving, he had settled into a chair opposite, his own book in hand, and said, "I find reading late at night, when the house is quiet and dark, allows me to enter the author's world more readily. Don't you?"

Her heart had stuttered to a stop. This man had actually spoken to her as if she were an intelligent, thoughtful person. Which she was. But no one had ever done so before, at least no man. Her father would have sent her to bed, her brothers would have teased her about what she was reading. But Henderson had asked her opinion, and that was the instant she fell in love.

Of course, no one could ever know, least of all Henderson. Having witnessed the discovery and humiliation of a girl in the throes of a terrible crush, Alice had been adamant that no one, not even her good friend Harriet, would know. It was Harriet's sister, Clara, who had made a cake of herself over Earnest Franklin, a dashing young man from a well-placed family. He was a bit of a rake, always throwing compliments at girls whether they were homely, pretty, fat, or whisper thin. A single dance with Clara at her come-out and she lost her mind over him. She mooned after him during balls, tried to manipulate seating assignments so she was seated next to him at dinners, and generally was about as discreet with her feelings as a peacock showing its feathers. Alice and Harriet would spy on Clara as she tracked Earnest the way a hound tracks a fox, leaving the two younger girls doubled over in laughter. It all came to a terrible head when Clara snuck into Earnest's room during a house party and waited in his room. Naked. Earnest, being an honorable man, took one look at Clara in all her glory, and ran down the hall to fetch the girl's mother, who immediately sent Clara to live with a maiden aunt on the border of Scotland for two years. Thankfully, the Anderson family was able to keep the incident under wraps. Harriet had sworn Alice to secrecy when imparting this scandalous end to Clara's infatuation, and as far as anyone knew, no one had ever spoken of the event. Not even Earnest.

Alice had never wanted to be laughed at or pitied, and so she kept her wildly beating heart to herself and tried with all her might not to look up and stare each time Henderson walked into a room. Those nights in the library, with just the two of them reading or talking, were the most difficult but she was quite certain she never let on how much those evenings meant to her. How she would wait in anticipation for the rest of the house to go to bed and fly on slippered feet down to the library, breathless and excited. Tucking her feet beneath her dressing gown, Alice would pretend to read, her entire body singing with expectation. And on those nights when Henderson joined her, she would give him a slight look of annoyance for interrupting her reading, sigh, and put her book aside reluctantly to wish him a good evening, while inside she was a jumble of happy nerves. She believed with all her heart that if Henderson had even the smallest inkling that she was in love with him, he would stop coming to the library. And so, she made very sure he was none the wiser.

Chapter 4

Lord Alfred Bellingham was first on the list. He'd met the baron at a summer party he had attended with the Hubbards years ago, and remembered only that he seemed a stern and austere man, one whom Richard Hubbard had disliked, though Henderson had never learned why. Lord Hubbard was one of those gentlemen who seemed to like everyone, and the fact he found Bellingham disagreeable was quite telling. Dr. Cornish had added Lord Bellingham as an afterthought, warning Henderson that it was highly unlikely he would find an ally for his relief efforts in the man. But Henderson had to try. His list of eight, from most likely to support his cause to least likely, was deemed the List of Lost Hopes by Dr. Cornish, who had grown cynical over the years. Every effort the doctor made to save the starving masses was met by resistance from Lord Lytton, the viceroy in India. Cornish had argued passionately that the rations given to those in the work relief camps were hardly adequate to sustain life, but Lytton refused to authorize an increase until pressured to do so. Even then, the rations were hardly adequate and only half of what Cornish had recommended.

Bellingham, who had spent several years in India, was seen as someone who might very well be sympathetic to the plight of the starving. Henderson refused to believe that when confronted with the facts of the tragedy, anyone could deny him.

Lord Bellingham's London home was located in Berkeley Square in Mayfair, whose gardens featured a nymph and whose homes held some of the more influential men in London. Henderson knew enough to make an appointment with the gentleman, and was frankly surprised that Bellingham had accommodated him so quickly, given it was a certainty that the peer would not know who he was. It boded well, he thought, and with a decided bounce in his step, he walked toward the home, an ornate building with intricate carvings above an oversized entrance. The sun shone fully on the mansion's façade, and Henderson chose to see this as another positive sign.

Henderson was ushered into the home by an ancient butler, so stooped over he didn't get a good look at the man's face. He waved away the man's request to take his hat and coat, for he knew he would not have the patience to wait for his items should things go badly. Shuffling slowly down a long hall, the butler bade Henderson to follow with a wave of his bony hand, finally stopping outside a heavily carved door.

"Mr. Henderson Southwell, my lord," he intoned with a surprisingly strong voice.

"Yes, I am expecting him, Johnson."

Henderson hadn't seen Bellingham in years, but he looked much the same. Perhaps his jowls hung a bit more loosely and the bags beneath his eyes were a bit more pronounced. As Bellingham looked him over, Henderson had the ridiculous urge to suppress a shudder, for his dark, expressionless eyes reminded him of the dead-eyed stare of a marsh crocodile he'd seen once in India. It was somehow predatory, that look, as if Bellingham was sizing up an opponent and finding him unworthy of his attention. Bellingham did not stand when Henderson entered, nor did he hold out his hand in greeting, and Henderson's earlier optimism took a decided turn.

"Thank you for meeting with me, sir," Henderson said, laying his coat and hat on one of two chairs positioned in front of Bellingham's large and meticulously organized desk. He felt rather like a boy confronting a school master and was unsure whether he should sit or remain standing. Choosing the former, Henderson sat on the edge of the room's other chair. After exchanging awkward niceties about the Hubbards, their single mutual acquaintance, Henderson got to the point. "I understand you lived in India for several years."

"Yes. Foul place," Bellingham said.

Ah. This did not bode well at all. "Yes, I've just come from India myself. Are you aware of the famine, sir?"

The older man's eyes narrowed to the point Henderson wondered if he could see at all. "You're not one of those fools looking for relief, are you?"

Henderson could feel his cheeks heat—with anger. He smiled tightly. "As a matter of fact, I am. And I believe if you had been in India these past two years, you would feel very much the way I do."

Bellingham folded his hands on his desk with exaggerated care. "I would not." His words were succinct and brooked no misinterpretation. "Are you familiar with Charles Darwin?"

It was all Henderson could do to keep his temper in check. He had heard this argument before—the aristocrats, including Lord Lytton himself, invoked the name of Charles Darwin as an excuse not to save starving people. Survival of the fittest. A way of culling the weak from the herd. What these men seemed not to understand was that they were talking about people, people with children, people who had lost everything, including their humanity, in a desperate attempt to survive.

"I am very much familiar with his teachings, but I hardly think they pertain to men. Or children."

Bellingham let out a low, mean laugh. "Are you going to tell me that it is up to the British Empire to make certain every human being on this planet who is starving is fed? There are droughts all over the world. Shall we send our funds and our citizens to feed them? If we were to do this, sir, it would spell the end of the empire."

Henderson could feel his heart beating thickly, his face heating, his fists clenching, so he forced himself to relax, to try to talk sense into this man even though he knew it was likely a lost cause. But faced with such ignorance, he could not stop himself. "I am not suggesting we feed all the world's hungry and poor, but I am suggesting that we take care of a people that the British Empire helped to starve."

Bellingham's face tightened. "How dare you."

"How dare I? How dare England allow millions of people starve to death when there are mountains of grain being guarded and then shipped to our shores so that we may have our bread at breakfast?"

"You tread very close to treason, Southwell. I would watch what you say."

Henderson swallowed, willed himself to calm. "If you had seen what I have. People begging the soldiers guarding the grain for just one pot of rice. Mothers selling themselves so they can buy food for their children. They die within feet of a mountain of rice that they themselves might have helped to grow." He could feel his throat tighten and was horrified at the emotion he'd allowed into his voice.

"People too lazy to grow their own food," Bellingham said, with a dismissive wave of his hand.

"No, sir. These people worked in fields, grew the crops, which was then put on trains and rails we constructed to ship here. Before we came and built the rails, villages kept their grain, sold it to the people for a price they could afford. But now they ship all the grain here for profit and what food is available is priced so high, very few can buy it."

"Is there something wrong with profit?" Bellingham asked loudly, his tone belittling.

"I see you will be of no help."

"Let them help themselves. What will they learn if we feed them and clothe them? They will come to rely on us and they will never do anything for themselves. They will become like children, dependent on us for everything they need. And where will it stop? No, sir. That kind of policy would ruin this country. If they die, they die too lazy to do anything about their lot. I pity fools like you, Southwell, I truly do. You will spend your life defending the rights of those people and it is meaningless. In the end, those who are meant to die will die, and there is nothing you or I can do about it."

Henderson stood and took up his coat and hat, glad he'd had the foresight to keep the articles with him. It had, indeed, gone very badly. "I thank you for your time, sir. Good day."

He had about reached the door when Bellingham called out. "Take some advice, son. Don't waste your time asking others for help. No one cares whether a bunch of blacks die. No one."

Henderson stopped and turned slowly. "There you are wrong. I care."

When he reached the street, Henderson pressed the heels of his palms hard into this eyes. He'd known it would be difficult; he'd faced such prejudice and ignorance in India, from the British and the wealthy Indians. But he'd convinced himself that his impassioned words could sway hard men. He'd been wrong. At least with Bellingham.

Taking out his well-worn list, Henderson looked at the names, mentally scratching out most of them. And these were purported to be the men who would be most sympathetic? Dr. Cornish must have been too long away from England if he thought these men would have even an ounce of sympathy.

Without thinking about where he was going, Henderson started to walk until he realized with a start that he was standing in front of the Hubbard home. As a youth, he hadn't spent very much time in the Hubbards' London home, but it still seemed like a haven to him. A home, when all he had ever had was a house filled with bitter disappointment. He wasn't aware of how long he stood there, and so was a bit embarrassed when Mrs. Hubbard opened the door and stepped out onto the stoop.

"Would you like to come in, Henderson?" she asked, a knowing smile on her face.

Henderson grinned. "I would, actually. Is Oliver about? I thought we might go to Pratt's."

Elda looked down the square toward the gentleman's club and frowned. "It's nearly tea time. Why don't you come in and join us? Alice is leaving tomorrow for St. Ives and I'm certain she'd like to say good-bye before you go back to India."

"Yes. I'll only be in London a few weeks before I return and I hardly think I'll have time to go to St. Ives to say good-bye."

Her smile faltered just a bit before she stepped back, like a well-trained butler, and ushered him inside.

* * *

The moment her sister walked into the room clutching the *Town Talk* newspaper, Alice knew something terrible had happened. It was silly to think no one would have commented on the fact that the granddaughter of the Duke of Warwick had been jilted—again—but Alice had hoped. As society weddings went, Alice's wedding to Lord Northrup was a small affair and one of little note. Her first wedding had been a theatrical event, with articles written in advance detailing nearly every aspect of the ceremony, from the design of her gown to the flowers her mother chose for the church. A throng of Londoners had gathered outside St. Paul's Cathedral waiting for the bride and groom to make their appearance. But for her wedding to Lord Northrup, no one lined the streets and the gossip columns held nary a mention. Thank goodness.

So Alice had hoped a non-wedding might be of as little consequence as the actual wedding.

She closed her eyes briefly as Christina, her eyes livid and her mouth tight, held the paper in a hand that trembled.

"I thought you should know," Christina said as she handed over the paper.

Alice quickly scanned the column, her green eyes darting back and forth until she stopped, recognizing instantly the small part that was about her. Two sentences. Two sentences that sealed her humiliation like a blob of wax on the letter of her life.

Poor Miss H has failed again to say her wedding vows. The bad luck bride, indeed.

"It's of little consequence," Alice said, even as she felt her entire body burn with humiliation. It was almost worse than the moment the reverend began walking toward the end of the church to tell them there would be no wedding ceremony that day.

"Oh, Alice," Christina said, throwing herself into Alice's arms.

"I'm so glad to be going home," Alice said fiercely. "I've never wanted to go home more in my life. And I'm never, ever leaving. I loathe London." Christina leaned back, her mouth open in shock. "But you mustn't stay away from London forever. Mother said I could have my season next year and I have to have you with me. I could never do it without you by my side."

Alice pulled away and continued to place items in her trunk for the journey. "I think you must consider that I will not be an asset, Christina." She looked up and immediately realized Christina hadn't considered what it meant to be the younger sister of the bad luck bride. It was a clever little moniker that would no doubt stick to her for the rest of her life.

Shaking her head, Christina said, "No one would hold that against me." And then in a smaller voice, "Would they?"

"I only know that the *ton* can be unforgiving," she said, placing her jewelry box in her trunk before turning to face her sister. "I wouldn't want to do anything that could hurt your chances of wedding a fine gentleman. It would break my heart, Christina, if I thought..." Her throat closed up, but she swallowed hard. "I don't want to come back to London at any rate." Forcing a smile, she said, "Goodness, no one knows London society better than Mama. You're in very good hands, you know. Heavens, she found me three husbands when some girls can't find one!" The two laughed, and Alice felt infinitely better.

Christina turned to go but hesitated. "Was it right that I showed you the article?"

"Yes. It would have been far worse if someone said something to me about it and I didn't know. Now I can prepare several witty remarks that show I have not a care what a silly paper like the *Town Talk* has to say about me."

Christina smiled, obviously relieved, and left Alice to prepare for her journey home. She looked about her room and realized she was very nearly done packing. Alice placed her most prized possession, her portable rosewood writing desk, into her trunk, nestled between her riding habit and her light cloak. The desk had been a gift from her late grandmother, the duchess, given to her with the admonition to write at least monthly. Alice, then fifteen, thought it such a grown-up sort of gift and had religiously written to her grandmother twice per month until the old lady's death. No one was allowed to use it or even open it, and Alice kept its key either on a chain she wore around her neck or in the desk's secret compartment at all times.

Christina used to beg to see what was inside, but Alice never relented. It was here that she hid away her true thoughts, her life after Joseph died. And after Henderson went away. Though she never let him know of her infatuation with him, hidden away in her writing desk were nearly fifty letters never sent. How could she have sent them when she didn't know where Henderson had gone? She didn't want to take the chance of sending them to his mother for fear she would read them. And so Alice kept them, those heartfelt outpourings of grief and loneliness. When she'd begun packing to return to St. Ives, Alice considered throwing them away. What was the purpose of them now? She could never show them to Henderson. Instead, when she closed the top with its intricate brass inlay and turned the lock, the letters remained inside.

Alice looked around her room, wondering if she'd ever return to their London home. St. Ives was the home of her heart, and she was fiercely glad to be returning there—even carrying the baggage of humiliation with her. She missed the smell of the sea, the constant racket of seagulls, even the smell of bait fish that the fishermen used.

"Nearly ready, I see." Alice turned to see her mother standing at her bedroom door. Ever since she'd been jilted at the altar, her mother's face had held an expression Alice could only describe as pensive.

"It will be good to get home."

"Have you written the girls?"

The girls, as they had been called in her home since Alice was ten years old, were her small group of friends. "Only Harriet. She loves being the bearer of bad news." Her mother chuckled at the truth of those words. Harriet read the *London Times* each morning, clipping out the articles she knew would shock the most, murder being her favorite topic (the more macabre the better), followed closely by executions. Though Harriet was one of her dearest friends, ruination and jiltings were also a favorite topic, friend or no. In a perverse way, Alice almost wished she was there when Harriet imparted the news from her letter.

"Henderson is here. I found him standing outside the house. Or rather pacing. He's come to say good-bye."

Funny how the words "Henderson is here" made her heart speed up and "he's come to say good-bye" caused it to tumble to her feet.

"Hazel, will you be able to finish on your own?" Her maid smiled as she placed a box filled with her embroidery materials into the trunk.

"Yes, miss."

"Good. Then I shall say good-bye," Alice announced, as if saying good-bye was something she was looking forward to. As she walked toward the door where her mother stood, Alice resisted the urge to look in the mirror, knowing her mother would notice. When she'd been young, it had taken a great deal of fortitude to keep her feelings to herself; she'd done such a fine job of it that even Oliver never teased her. "I wonder when he'll be returning to India."

"He mentioned he was going back in three weeks," her mother said, moving down the hall. Behind her, Alice quickly pinched her cheeks before smoothing her hair.

Alice ignored the way her stomach fell. She might very well never see Henderson again. Not that it mattered, or rather, not that it *should* matter. For some reason, it did. "My goodness, he's hardly arrived and he'll be going back so soon. I do hope he takes the time to visit his grandparents; I'm sure they've missed him." Alice thought back on the small bit of information she knew about Henderson and his family. He'd rarely talked of them, even when their conversations had turned away from books and toward more personal topics. "I would think he would at least visit for a time. Can you imagine how you would feel if Oliver had gone abroad for four years, returned to England, and didn't bother saying hello?"

"I think your father would hunt Oliver down and drag him home," Elda said as they walked into the main parlor.

"What has Oliver done now?" asked Henderson, who rose from his seat when the two women entered the room.

"I was just telling Mama how very vexed she would be if Oliver were gone for four years but didn't bother to visit before leaving again."

"Ah. I'm being chastised for not being a good grandson," Henderson said pleasantly. "Neither of my grandparents cares much for visitors."

"You're hardly a visitor, you know. You're their grandson."

"A visitor, none-the-less."

"Mama says you've come to say good-bye. That was very thoughtful of you."

Henderson looked a bit discomfited. "I was in the neighborhood. Or rather, not far. I had a meeting in Mayfair with Lord Bellingham. Charming fellow." It was clear from Henderson's tone that he was being sardonic.

Alice knew Lord Bellingham and his insipid son and knew they were anything but charming. "I take it your meeting did not go well?"

"It did not."

"Bellingham is the last sort of fellow who would help any cause that did not involve lining his pockets," Elda said. She was drawn to a flower arrangement and proceeded to pluck a few dead blooms from their moorings. "Is this about famine relief?"

Henderson stared at the discarded blooms, lined up neatly on the well-polished table, as if he found them somehow repulsive. He snapped his attention to Elda, apparently realizing his distraction. "It is. I have a list of men I plan to appeal to."

Elda held out her hand. "May I see it?"

"Of course," he said, pulling a folded piece of paper from his jacket pocket. "A colleague in India helped me to create it, but I fear he's been away from England so long, he is a bit out of touch."

He handed over the list and Alice watched her mother curiously; she hadn't thought her mother was interested in the famine relief cause. Elda read down the list, her eyes widening just slightly, before handing it back. "I'm afraid I can be of no help," she said. "I'm familiar with many men on the list, but I don't know their politics."

"I fear this may be a lost cause," Henderson said with a weary note. "Bellingham actually accused me of treason, or very nearly so."

"What did you say to him?" Alice asked, horrified. She couldn't imagine Henderson saying anything so controversial to be interpreted as treasonous.

Henderson let out a humorless laugh. "I may have implied that the famine was caused by England and our greed and not entirely by the drought, which seems to be the commonly held belief."

"Oh." Alice could not imagine Henderson, who had always seemed so *laissez-faire*, inciting someone to such an accusation.

"I was forewarned by my associate in India, a Dr. Cornish, but I suppose I thought my impassioned speech could sway any man."

"Ego," Alice blurted, then felt her cheeks warm when Henderson looked at her rather oddly. "Men and their egos. You should have told him that everyone who supports the cause will get a statue of themselves erected. Or some such thing." The way Henderson looked at her made Alice want to squirm. It was as if he were weighing each of her words, then rearranging them to see if they made sense. "It's just that with men like Bellingham, you cannot appeal to their moral integrity. I doubt…" She let her voice trail off because he was still staring at her.

A smile slowly grew on Henderson's face, and for just a moment, Alice found it difficult to draw in a breath. She'd forgotten how handsome he was, how he affected her.

"You should come with me." Alice shook her head, rather vigorously, but Henderson persisted. "I get angry too quickly and the thought of stroking someone's ego does not appeal in the least. You could be a young Florence Nightingale."

"I'm returning to St. Ives tomorrow morning. And as respected as Miss Nightingale is, her entreaties about India have been mostly ignored. More to the point, I hardly think someone who is a laughingstock in London at the moment could possibly be taken seriously."

"Alice does have a point," Elda said, agreeing with her daughter so quickly, Alice was momentarily taken aback.

"Mother!"

"You said it yourself," Elda said, chuckling. "Do not get yourself all in a tizzy, Alice. But it is too soon for you to go out soliciting aid, and I suspect Henderson, given his schedule, needs to complete his task as soon as possible. And I do not want you to suffer the same fate as Miss Nightingale."

"I hardly think I could become ill urging men to become involved in famine relief."

"No, but it could end badly, just the same. It is *Miss* Nightingale, after all," Elda said, plucking another brown bloom from the arrangement. "If you have any chance of getting married, you cannot involve yourself in grand causes, my dear. It is not at all attractive."

"Perhaps I *shall* accompany you, Henny, as I have absolutely no intention of ever getting married," Alice said between gritted teeth. Sometimes her mother made her want to scream, and now was one such occasion.

"You would only slow Henderson's progress, Alice," Elda said cheerfully, as if she were completely unaware of how very annoyed Alice was.

"I'm not on a strict schedule," Henderson said, hesitantly. "Though I am concerned that the longer relief is delayed, the more people will perish."

After glaring at her mother, a completely unnoticed glare, Alice softened her features and turned toward Henderson. "Was it very terrible?" she asked. Something bleak flickered momentarily in Henderson's eyes, a darkness that inexplicably made her throat tighten.

"It was worse than that. It was beyond imagination. I'll leave it at that." He smiled, but it was his new, distant smile, the one she hadn't seen when they were younger, and suddenly Alice wished she knew what it meant, what had happened that had created that false, hard smile.

"Why don't the two of you take a turn around the garden?" Elda suggested brightly. "It's a lovely day. I'll have tea brought out to you there."

"Won't you be joining us, Mama?"

"Oh, no. I'm having tea with Mrs. Stuart, poor thing. She gets so lonely." Mrs. Stuart was their ancient neighbor whose children rarely visited her, so the Hubbard family made a point of making her part of their lives when they were in London.

Alice knew her mother was simply ending the conversation, but she allowed it. She truly had no desire to go before any of the men on Henderson's list and beg for influence in the famine relief efforts. They would be polite, they would listen, but Alice knew they would only be thinking one thing: This is the girl who tried to get married three times and failed. Perhaps she could have done it if that small piece hadn't run in the *Town Talk*, but Alice knew she was the subject of gossip and she simply couldn't bear to see the looks of sympathy, or worse, the snide remarks she knew a visit from her would elicit.

"Shall we?" Henderson said after her mother had left the room. "Or we could go to the library for old time's sake."

Alice smiled. "We never sat together in this library. Do you know I didn't go to Tregrennar's library for months and months after you left?" Henderson looked at her sharply and Alice wished she hadn't said such a thing. "The whole house felt different." His expression grew solemn, as he assumed she was speaking of Joseph's death, not his departure, when Alice had meant nothing of the sort. The library held no particular memories of Joseph for her. Indeed, it was one of the few rooms in the house that didn't remind her of her brother. Yet she still couldn't bring herself to enter a room in which she had spent so many happy hours.

The Hubbards' London garden was a neat rectangle split down the middle by a gravel path that led to a gate and the muse across a narrow lane. It was July, so the garden was in its glory. Fragrant waxflowers spilled onto the gravel, their small white blooms filling the air with sweet scent. Her mother's roses were in full blossom and the vibrant blue of sea holly stood in bright contrast.

Beside her, Henderson took a deep breath. "God, I'd forgotten how lovely London smells in the summer. At least this part of London."

As he looked around the garden, Alice took the chance to study his profile, noting the sharp line of his jaw, the way one curl tucked itself against the lobe of his ear. She closed her eyes briefly with the intent of memorizing this moment, of keeping it safe when she needed to bring it out in those times she knew she would think of him. "It is good to see you, Henderson. Are you very certain you cannot come to St. Ives before you leave? The girls would love to see you. Harriet especially." This last was said with a bit of a teasing note, a reminder of when they were young and Harriet followed him about like a small, eager puppy.

Henderson chuckled lightly, no doubt remembering how ridiculous Harriet would act whenever she was visiting and happened to see him. It had been torture to hear Harriet go on and on about Henderson when she herself had been in the throes of a terrible infatuation. "I'm surprised she's not married, pretty girl and all that."

Even now, the ugly heat of jealousy tinged Alice's cheeks. "None of us are. All old maids."

"I hardly count you old, any of you." He gave Alice a sidelong look. "Harriet, you say? Perhaps I can find time for a visit."

Suddenly, Alice was seventeen years old and dying inside all over again. She remembered distinctly talking about Harriet when they had been ensconced in the library, whispering their secrets so as not to alert anyone in the house of their conversation. Against all reason, Alice had mentioned to Henderson that Harriet had a bit of a crush on him. Perhaps it was to see his reaction or maybe elicit some sort of declaration from him—*but it's you I adore, Alice*—or some such thing. She would never forget that terrible feeling when Henderson had sat up, curiosity piqued, and had asked to hear more.

"It would be lovely if you could come to St. Ives," Alice said, wanting to kick herself all over again.

"You know, Alice, I had a bit of a crush myself back then."

Breathing had become rather an effort, so Alice sat down on a nearby bench. Henderson immediately sat next to her, even though the bench was quite small. "Then of course you should make time to visit St. Ives. Harriet is even prettier now."

He let out a small sigh. "And I am, of course, much better looking."

He was joking, she knew he was, but she couldn't stop herself from looking at him, studying his face. He *was* much better looking now. His jaw was more defined, and the shadow of his beard was showing even though it was evident he had shaved earlier that day. His hair, a deep rich chocolate, wavy on top, short on the sides and back, made her fingers itch to touch it. "You are, you know. Much better looking." She squinted her eyes to examine him, as if she were studying a specimen and her heart wasn't clamoring in her chest.

With a heart-stopping grin, he stole that bit of her heart she was trying with all her being to reserve for someone who loved her, who didn't think of her as a little sister, who wasn't leaving for India in a matter of weeks.

"Alas, my dear old friend, I cannot take the time to travel to St. Ives."

"There's a new rail, you know. Just built. You could be in St. Ives in just a day."

He tilted his head in that way she remembered that made her feel as if he was not only listening to every word she said, but was actually interested. "Is there?"

He seemed to ponder visiting for a moment. "Harriet would be so thrilled to see you." *God above, what was she doing? Trying to match her best friend with the man she loved? Was she mad?*

A small smile touched his lips and for just a moment Alice thought she'd been able to convince him. "Still, no. I really must concentrate on my mission here and remove myself to India as soon as possible. As it is, I will have been gone for nearly three months by the time I return."

"So this is truly good-bye," Alice said, unable to keep her tone light. She looked straight ahead, not wanting to look at him for fear he would see just how bereft saying good-bye left her. She could tell he was looking at her and she schooled her features into a blandness she didn't come close to feeling. How was it she still could love him when he'd been gone for so long? It was almost as if he'd never left, as if all those years of his absence, all her fiancés, all her days of feeling nothing, had disappeared. Alice pressed her lips together just slightly, irritated with herself.

"It is." Beside her he took a bracing breath. "I thought this time I might say a proper good-bye." He stood abruptly, and Alice rose as well, facing him, looking directly at him so she could recall his face, the distinct blue of his eyes. Like the sea holly that grew in a bundle behind the bench they'd just sat on. An impossible blue, and Alice was struck with the terrible thought that she would never be able to look at sea holly again without thinking of Henderson.

"Good-bye, Henderson," she said, holding out her hand for him to take.

He looked at her hand curiously before saying, "My dear girl, a shake of a hand is not a proper good-bye."

And before she could move, before she knew even what Henderson planned, he leaned toward her and all she could think was, *He's going to kiss me. He's finally going to kiss me.* Closer, closer, until his handsome face was nothing but a blur, until all she could see were those brilliant eyes. Her eyelids drifted closed and she held herself still.

"Good-bye, my dear girl," he said softly, and she could feel the puff of his breath against her lips. Then, she felt his lips. Kiss her cheek. Alice very nearly laughed aloud at her own ridiculousness. So when Henderson pulled back, she was smiling, probably looking rather maniacal. He was still standing quite close, close enough so that, had she wanted to, Alice could have stood on tiptoe and kissed Henderson where she wanted to kiss him. His eyes held some intense emotion before he smiled and it was gone. At least it was a real smile this time. Stepping back, he took a deep breath and stuffed his hands in his trouser pockets, probably having no idea how very charming and boyish he looked at the moment. He nodded, an odd sort of nod that ended with him shaking his head, and let out a small laugh.

"I'll go now. It was lovely seeing you, Alice."

Alice swallowed down the ache in her throat. "Godspeed, Henderson."

She watched him leave, fighting the urge to run after him and... And what? Beg him to stay? Beg him to see her as a woman? Beg him to kiss her properly? Instead, she simply stood there, mute, and watched him disappear into the house and out of her life.

Chapter 5

With every fiber in his being, Henderson wished he had kissed Alice. One, if he had, he would always remember how she tasted, how soft her lips were. Two, he would know for a certainty if she felt the same way about him that he felt about her. And now, he would never know either. He'd spend the rest of his life wondering. It was just as well. His promise to Joseph was ringing in his ears as he approached her, fully intending to kiss her properly, and in the end, with her looking up at him so damned innocently, he just couldn't bring himself to do it, to turn what they had into something else. For what if she'd been angry, or worse, repulsed? He would have carried that memory with him forever too. Still, now he would never know what it was like to press his lips against hers.

"You bloody idiot," Henderson said aloud as he strode from the Hubbards' home. She was leaving in the morning and he was fairly certain he would never see her again. If she stayed in St. Ives and he lived in India for years as he intended, it was almost a certainty they would not meet again. When he was gone from England and back in the hot misery that was India, he at least would have had the sweet memory of that last kiss. Now when he would think back on this kiss, it would only be with humiliation and the terrible memory of how soft and sweet her mouth looked. He supposed part of him had hoped she would melt against him and beg him to stay. As Henderson walked toward his hotel, he looked up at heaven and wondered if Joseph were having a grand ol' time looking down at him.

* * *

Over the next two weeks, Henderson, already in a foul mood, felt his mood darken exponentially following his meeting with each highly positioned gentleman. He tried pleading, flattery, and as a last and terrible resort, he brought out pictures of those poor starving souls. They looked more corpse than human. Women with sunken eyes, skulls clearly and grotesquely showing beneath a thin layer of flesh. Men, eyes empty of hope, unable to stop their children from starving to death. And worse, small children, curled up on hot, dirty streets, waiting to die. Those images, which had brought him to tears even though he had seen such atrocities with his own eyes, were looked at with either disgust or scorn. By the time he left the seventh home, he had lost his faith in humanity and was sickened by his country's apathy.

Exhausted, he climbed the shallow stone steps that led up to the arched entry of Pratt's Club. The club was a favorite among titled gentlemen, especially those who thought themselves friends of the Duke of Devonshire. He had gained admission years ago through Joseph's father, who petitioned the club for his entrance. The son of a duke held impressive power, and Henderson never forgot the gesture. The main room was nearly empty but for one table where several youngish toffs were sitting talking animatedly. Henderson recognized a few, including Mr. Thaddeus Tiddle, Belleville's obnoxious heir, so he steered clear of the group. He didn't know how often father and son talked, but he did know the very last thing he wanted was for Tiddle to mention Henderson's meeting with his father.

A thin haze of cigar smoke clung to the ceiling, where heavy, rough-hewn beams divided the room into two distinct sections—one for card playing and socializing and one for quiet reading or contemplation. Gathering up a copy of the *Times* laid out neatly on a heavily carved side table with serpents twisting up its legs, Henderson headed toward the small sitting area and waved a footman over so he could order a brandy. The brandy and cigars, not the company, made Pratt's his favorite club. Though he was always aware that he didn't quite belong there, he refused to allow himself to be intimidated by the other members who held lofty titles and vast estates. He might not have a title, but his grandfather was a wealthy, well-respected man who had never made him feel less because of his birth. Still, he felt the separation between him and the other young men sitting across the room as severely as if they were first class on a ship and he in steerage. Though he was nearly the same age as the young men talking so animatedly at the table, he felt worlds older.

Settling down into a comfortable leather chair, Henderson snapped the newspaper open, trying his best to shut out the gregarious laughing of the group of men on the other side of the room. Until he heard one say, "Bad luck bride, eh? More like lucky groom, if you ask me. I say Northrup realized what he was in for and ran for the hills."

The other men laughed, and Henderson slowly put the newspaper aside and stood up—a movement that was noticed by one of the men at the table, who shot Tiddle a warning look. Plastering a smile on his face that was by no means pleasant, Henderson walked to the table of young men and stood silently until the laughter slowly dissipated. "Do you think it is amusing that a young lady was humiliated?"

He looked from one man to the next, not bothering to hide his anger, and each had the good grace to look ashamed. Except for Tiddle. "What of you, Mr. Tiddle?"

"Everyone knows she's made of ice, Southwell. I know you're a friend of the family, but you have to admit it's a bit amusing that a girl is jilted three times." Tiddle looked over at his companions as if to make certain they were finding him amusing.

"Her first intended died moments before the ceremony. Do you find that amusing, sir?"

Tiddle had the audacity—and stupidity—to chuckle. "I suppose allowing oneself to die to escape marriage to Miss Hubbard is a bit drastic, but I must say I commend the man his determination." Nervous laughter followed, quickly stifled. The other men sitting around the table tensed, because though Tiddle was seemingly oblivious to the blinding rage that Henderson barely had in check, they were not. One of Tiddle's friends leaned toward him and whispered something Henderson could not hear, but he suspected it was something like "shut the hell up, you idiot."

Tiddle gave his friend an annoyed glance, then looked up at Henderson with an ugly smirk. "I say, Mr. Southwell, I *do* think it's amusing. Damn amusing."

Hell, Henderson had just wanted to relax, read the paper, and savor a nice snifter of brandy, and now he was going to have to beat this man to a pulp.

"She might be a nice little piece, but she's a cold bitch. I can attest—"

The rest of Tiddle's sentence was lost as Henderson moved with frightening speed to clutch the young whelp's lapels, heave him up, and slam him against the richly paneled mahogany wall behind him. The other four men stood, but none stepped forward to assist Tiddle; they stood silently, watching warily as Henderson pulled him back and slammed him against the wall again.

"Get your hands off me, Southwell. You don't even belong here, you ba—"

"If you keep talking, I'm just going to have to keep driving you into the wall until you can no longer speak. Do you understand me?"

Tiddle stared at Henderson belligerently. "I could have you arrested for laying a hand on my person."

"You are not to speak of Miss Hubbard again," Henderson said, ignoring the threat. "If I hear one whisper, I can promise you it will be the last thing you say against anyone. And please do not make the mistake of thinking I am bluffing. I would happily go to the gallows knowing I had silenced you forever."

Tiddle's eyes widened, and he looked behind Henderson to his friends. "He threatened to murder me. Did you all hear that? Murder. I say, that's a crime."

"I didn't hear him say any such thing."

Henderson jerked his head around and grinned to see Oliver standing behind the group of men. "You didn't hear anything, gentlemen, did you?" he asked. They all remained silent.

Henderson shoved Tiddle away with disgust. "Go home, Tiddle, and sober up."

Tiddle huffed and straightened his coat before grabbing up his walking stick. He clutched it, his knuckles white, and for just a moment Henderson wondered if he intended to brain him with it. Instead, he left the room walking stiffly, his back rigid.

"I hope you gentlemen will refrain from speaking ill of any lady."

The four young toffs nodded and resumed their seats as Oliver slapped him on the back. "I think it's a very good thing for Tiddle that I didn't hear what was said," he remarked, drawing Henderson toward the exit. "What did he say, anyway?"

"Did you see the piece in *Town Talk*?"

Oliver grimaced. "Who hasn't?"

"Tiddle found it amusing. More amusing than I did," Henderson said blandly. His heartbeat was just now returning to its normal rate. "It is times like this when I wish I were born in the last century so I could have called him out."

"I'm gratified that you were here to set the bastard straight. Someone needs to. Come, I'll join you for a brandy so you can tell me what you've been doing for the past four years."

* * *

By the time Henderson was back in his hotel room, he felt as if he could sleep standing. These past two weeks had been an exercise in frustration, only adding to the insidious desperation he felt each time he thought of the poor souls in India.

If he'd held a lofty title, Henderson would have the sort of influence needed to address parliament. But with no power or influence, he was lucky to get two minutes of time with the men who blithely allowed millions to die under the mantle of the crown. One name remained on his list. One.

How could he return to India with nothing to show for his efforts except pity and scorn? He sat down heavily on his bed, staring blindly at the creased piece of paper he held in his hands—the names crossed off, each a mark of failure. A darkness and self-loathing that he hadn't felt since Joseph's death made it nearly impossible to scratch Lord Thrompton, his latest failure, off his list. With no small amount of disgust Henderson realized, as he held his pencil to his battered list, that his hand trembled. Clenching his hand around the wood, he roughly drew a line through Thrompton's name, grimacing when his lead pierced the paper. One left. Frederick Lawton, Lord Berkley. He knew nothing of the man, but if he were the sort of person to bet, Henderson would wager that another door would be closed in his face. Nothing had gone right for him since his return. The one thing that had happened in his favor, Alice being left at the altar, only worked to torture him all the more. It would be better to know she was happily married. *Liar*.

* * *

Lord Berkley lived in the newly fashionable Cavendish Square. It was a neighborhood where nannies strolled with their charges, where sidewalks were well-swept and gardens well-tended. He knew nothing of Lord Berkley but that he was supposed to hold great influence over the liberal party. When he'd mentioned to Oliver at Pratt's that Berkley was on his list, Oliver had let out a low whistle and said, "That's a tough nut to crack." He should just cross the man's name off his list now and be done with it. Why go through the torture of pleading his case to someone whose belly was full of food and whose mind was full of superiority?

Feeling defeat was only a few minutes away, Henderson climbed the steps and adjusted his satchel so he could more easily grasp the large knocker, in the shape of a scowling lion, and swing it down. Momentarily, Berkley's butler opened the door and immediately stepped back to allow Henderson into a large foyer that gleamed brightly in the afternoon sun streaming down from a skylight overhead.

"May I help you, sir." The butler held out a sterling silver basket in which Henderson placed his card. He wore a black band around his sleeve, and Henderson wondered who had died. The house was not in mourning, so he assumed it was someone of little consequence.

"I would like an audience with Lord Berkley."

"I'm afraid that is quite impossible"—He looked down at his card, and for a moment Henderson thought that perhaps his lordship *was* dead—"Mr. Southwell. His lordship is not at home."

"I see," Henderson said, feeling a stab of disappointment mixed with relief that he had not committed some sort of social faux pas. He wanted this business over with. "Is his secretary here? I should like to make an appointment with his lordship."

"Lord Berkley is at one of his country estates, my lord. Costille House."

Henderson furrowed his brow, for the name of the estate was vaguely familiar. "And where is that, sir?"

"St. Ives, my lord."

Henderson blinked slowly. "St. Ives."

"Yes, my lord. Is there anything else I can do for you?"

His bark of laughter startled the butler, but Henderson couldn't stop the grin that stayed on his face. "St. Ives. St. bloody Ives. Thank you, sir."

As Henderson left Cavendish Square, his steps were decidedly lighter. "What the devil, Joseph. What are you about, old chap?" A young lady pushing a pram gave him a cautious look, probably thinking him a bit touched. "I'm going to St. Ives," he shouted, and laughed as she hurried her steps as if she were about to be attacked by a raving lunatic. "By God," he said to himself. "What are the chances?"

* * *

Harriet Anderson, Alice's oldest and dearest friend, entered the parlor cautiously as if she might be interrupting some terrible bout of tears and hysteria. She wore a plain, gray dress, not particularly unusual for Harriet, who tended to dress more like a stern governess than the daughter of a wealthy man, but this one smacked of mourning. The dress matched her friend's expression, for her moss-green eyes were looking at her as if she were walking into a sick room.

"Oh, stop, will you?" Alice said, grinning. "I am not dead, you know. Please stop looking at me as if I'm lying in my coffin. Or soon will be."

Harriet smiled and rushed to her friend, her hands outstretched. "I'm sorry, Alice, but I've been so worried about you."

Alice waved a hand, dismissing her friend's concern. "I'll live. And I'd very much appreciate it if you would never look at me that way again, not you. Unless I actually am dying, and then I would quite appreciate a sad look or two." Alice let out a gusty sigh. "Everyone is trying to be kind, tiptoeing around me as if I'm constantly on the verge of tears, and it's getting a bit tiresome."

"I shall endeavor to treat you with complete callous disregard."

"Thank you," Alice said on a laugh.

"We were all very angry with Lord Northrup. I do wish we were there. I would have hunted him down and given him a piece of my mind. The cad."

"No, it was much better that you were all here. I don't know I could have borne it if you were witness to yet another humiliation. To be honest, Harriet, it's my pride that stings more than anything. And the realization that I must abandon the future I had so carefully planned for myself."

"Don't say such things, Alice."

"It's only the truth and the sooner I come to accept my fate, the better. I hardly think any man will even look my way now. Three fiancés, Harri. Three. And not a single marriage." Alice smoothed her skirts and looked down to her lap. "Did you see *Town Talk?*"

"No one reads that drivel and if they do, they don't pay attention to anything it—" Harriet stopped abruptly when Alice jerked her head up and gave her friend a hard stare. "Oh, very well. Everyone has read it and everyone is talking about it. But it will pass, Alice. These things always do."

Alice shook her head. "No, they do not. When I am eighty years old, little children will point and say, 'there goes the bad luck bride.' Oh, I could shoot whoever wrote those words. Wasn't it bad enough that my chances are all but ruined of ever finding a husband? With those words, my fate was sealed."

Harriet was silent for a moment, and Alice realized she'd hoped that her friend would dismiss her predictions. When she did not, it made her situation somehow more real. "Then we shall be two old maids together,"

Harriet said, "for I doubt I shall ever marry, given that no one has even so much as asked me for a dance except as an act of charity."

"That's not true, Harri," Alice said fiercely. When Harriet was with her friends, she was vibrant and witty, but this was not the case during social events. She withdrew, grew quiet, and had a terrible tendency to keep her eyes lowered and averted whenever a man happened to look her way. The first time Alice had seen her friend outside of one of their group's houses, she'd been dismayed by how quiet and reserved Harriet was, as if she was an automaton that had wound itself down and could no longer move.

Harriet, who was pretty but not beautiful, who could sing but not well, who fumbled on the pianoforte and produced needlepoint that was always a bit messy, lived in the shadow of her older sister. Clara was all that Harriet was not, and it was impossible to dislike her because she truly was the loveliest girl, inside and out. Their mother, on the other hand, made no attempt to hide the fact she had no patience and little affection for her younger daughter. It had been evident from Harriet's birth. Merely the fact she had not been a boy, when Mrs. Anderson had so fervently wanted one, might have been overlooked if Harriet hadn't come short of Clara in nearly every category. Only with her friends could she be herself, could she allow her wit to shine. Seeing her outside their cocoon of friendship was devastating.

"You'll never guess who I saw," Alice said, desperate to change the subject. "Henderson."

Harriet's face lit up. "Is he in St. Ives?"

Alice tried to stop her stomach from clenching. "No. He's in London. Or perhaps already on his way back to India. He's working on famine relief and is very passionate about it."

"Oh." Harriet didn't keep the disappointment from her voice. Unlike Alice, who would have died before letting her feelings for Henderson be known, Harriet had no such compunction. In fact, it had become a bit of a joke between the girls, for Harriet fully and gleefully admitted her crush. "Is he well?"

"Yes," Alice said with the smallest bit of hesitation. "He's changed, though, become more serious. Grown up a bit, I suppose."

"We all have." Harriet furrowed her brow slightly. "Have you seen Eliza and Rebecca since your return?"

Alice shook her head. "I think they're afraid to see me, but you can assure them I am well and would love their company. I promise not to cry or fall into hysterics."

Harriet grinned. "As if you would. I know if it happened to me I'd be in bed with the curtains drawn for a year. But here you are looking as calm as ever, as if it never happened. I wish I could be so."

Alice tilted her head. "I've never seen you cry or fall into hysterics and I've known you a long time."

Her friend looked away and toyed with a bit of lace on her dress before lifting her head and smiling impishly. "You do know my mother forbids any show of emotion. Particularly joy or happiness."

Alice laughed, even though she knew this to be true, for the times all four girls had been in the Anderson home, her mother had looked at them sourly whenever they burst into laughter, as if the sound somehow offended her. It would be horrible, indeed, if Harriet couldn't escape her mother by marrying someone who adored her as she should be adored.

"The John Knill celebration is next week, you know. Do you think you'll be up to going?"

Everyone in town would be there for the historic celebration, and Alice wasn't sure she wanted to be the object of pity or scrutiny, so she wrinkled her nose.

"You must go. It's only every five years and you'll create more gossip by not going than by attending."

Alice gave her friend a skeptical look. "Very well. Perhaps I will wear Tragedy as a mask at this year's ball, even if it's not a masquerade."

"Or a horse shoe around your neck," Harriet said.

"Ah. Good luck for the bad luck bride? Perhaps a wreath of four leaf clovers?"

Harriet shook her head. "Too difficult to find that many." She snapped her fingers. "A black cat on a leash. Oh, perfect!"

Laughing, Alice said, "You are the meanest of all my friends."

"And the only one who you know will tell you the truth at all times."

"What is my truth, then?"

Harriet looked her over as if taking her question seriously. "The reason you haven't gotten married is simply because you haven't fallen in love."

Alice couldn't help but feel a small bit of anger. Love had nothing to do with her ill-fated weddings. She could have very well been in love with all three of her fiancés, and would have been a far more tragic figure. It would have been unbearable to lose even one man she loved.

Some of her anger must have shown, for Harriet leaned forward, her expression stricken. "I didn't mean to hurt you. I suppose I meant that if your fiancés loved you—except for Lord Livingston; he couldn't help that he died—you would have been married by now. Normally, when one loves a man, they love you in return."

"Not necessarily," Alice said softly.

* * *

Two weeks after Henderson believed he was saying good-bye to Alice possibly forever, he flung open his mullioned window, its warped glass distorting the lovely view outside, and breathed in the sweet smell of the sea, tinged only a bit with the less sweet smell of fish. It was a gloriously pretty day, the kind that seemed common when he was a youth exploring the beaches and hills with Joseph and the other local lads. Unlike the northern coast of England, the water here was warm and stunning blue-green. Though he'd never been, he'd heard it compared to the waters in the Caribbean. He knew the narrow, cobbled streets of St. Ives better than his own village, and couldn't help but think of it as home. And yet, it was strange to be here in St. Ives knowing that Joseph was not. Stranger still to know Alice was less than a twenty-minute walk away and he couldn't gather the courage to visit. It wasn't as if she had thrown herself into his arms and proclaimed her undying love. For God's sake, she had talked about Harriet, as if she might play matchmaker between them. If anything, Alice had seemed rather cool and reserved, as if their friendship had not been the grand thing he remembered. Perhaps it was not. Perhaps he was looking at the past through the damaged lens of time. Nothing would be worse than letting Alice know how he felt and having her look at him with pity or surprise. She would be kind, and he simply couldn't bear it if she gently explained to him that she thought of him as a brother and that the idea of marrying him was the furthest thing from her mind. After all, she had been engaged three times since he'd left. In those four years, he may not have been celibate, but every time he'd even begun to consider a girl to marry, he would remember Alice and that would be that.

A seagull carrying a live crab in its mouth wheeled wildly in the sky in an attempt to get away from another gull that screeched in its wake. Henderson followed the gulls' progress, trying to determine whether he was rooting for the seagull with the crab or the one who was trying to steal its meal. It was better to consider such a mundane event rather than think about his own life.

"I should have kissed her," he said aloud, glaring at the seagull in the lead as it dropped its meal and the other bird followed the crab down to the streets below. He was in St. Ives and she was just twenty minutes away. If he were going to kiss her, he would have to do so in the next few days. Henderson pushed away from the window to stare bleakly as his small, neatly made bed, his valise still sitting atop it packed. With efficient movements, he unfastened the leather straps and opened his valise to take out his writing materials. First, he would write a letter to Lord Berkley requesting a meeting. He considered writing to Alice and letting her know he was in St. Ives. But what if that letter did not immediately elicit an invitation to Tregrennar? Perhaps he should simply show up at her doorstep, a happy surprise. He had to find out before he left for India if she felt even a little of what he did. After all, how could he know how she would react to a kiss unless he kissed her?

Chapter 6

One of the things Alice loved about St. Ives was its light. She wasn't certain whether it was the proximity to the ocean, the endless blue skies, or simply because she was happier there than anywhere else, but the light was divine. The renowned painter JMW Turner had discovered St. Ives in the forties, and his prestigious presence had drawn even more artists, who came to paint the sea, the quaint architecture, and its stunning vistas. Of course, Alice didn't count herself among the artists, but she was pleased with her current work. She stood in their main parlor painting a watercolor of a vase of flowers, trying to capture the glorious way the sun was shining through a translucent blue vase overflowing with Irises, some of which were beginning to whither in a rather lovely way. Her mother was behind her going through her correspondence and commenting now and again about some news from friends and relatives, many of whom were still in London. Alice was quite certain, given the long pauses between sentences, that her mother was editing out any words of concern or sympathy having to do with Alice being jilted.

Christina was off laying flowers on the graves of veterans in St. Ives Parish Church's cemetery, though Alice knew the real reason she and her friends had gone there was to get a glimpse of the new vicar, who was purportedly a fine-looking young man from an excellent family. Christina had begged Alice not to mention anything to her mother, though Alice suspected Elda most certainly knew why Christina and her friends had suddenly become so altruistic. They expected her back any minute, and so Alice was not surprised when she heard the rustle of her sister's skirts behind her.

"How was your outing?" Elda asked.

"Uneventful." Alice could almost see her sister's pout. No doubt the handsome vicar had not been seen. "But the cemetery does look nice with the new flowers."

"Which was the reason for your trip," her mother pointed out.

Alice turned and gave her sister an impish smile before going back to her painting.

"I do have news, however," Christina said as she sat down next to her mother. "Mr. Southwell is in the village."

Alice stilled momentarily, unable to complete the delicate blue she was applying to one of her Irises, and she prayed neither her mother nor Christina noticed her brief inability to breathe. A sudden and fierce smile touched her lips and her heart hammered in her chest. Pressing her lips together and schooling her features, she turned and said (as if the news that Henderson had come to St. Ives was of little consequence), "Oh?"

"Yes. He didn't see me. We were in the Downalong coming back from the cemetery and he was going into the new bookstore."

"A new bookstore?" Alice asked. "How wonderful." *Henderson is here. Henderson is here!*

"At any rate, he's here. We should visit the bookstore tomorrow," Christina said. "Would you like to go?"

"We should all go," Elda said. "I wonder if they have the newest *New Quarterly*. It hadn't been published yet when we were in London."

Alice turned back to her painting, her heart singing with the knowledge that Henderson was so close. What was he doing in St. Ives? She furrowed her brow trying to think of one thing, other than he wanted to visit with the Hubbards, and perhaps particularly her, that could have drawn him to the village. Could it be possible he had been here for days and yet hadn't written to let them know? Her heart, beating so happily not one minute before, slowed to a painful tempo. What if he had no intention of calling on them? What if his visit to St. Ives had nothing at all to do with her?

Squeezing her eyes shut, Alice had to accept that it was quite possible Henderson had absolutely no intention of seeing her, that his visit to St. Ives had nothing to do with her. That he hadn't been close to kissing her when he'd left that day in England as she had so foolishly thought. She began frantically searching her mind for an excuse to go into the village immediately.

"Is something amiss, Alice?" her mother asked.

Alice realized with a start that she had been staring blindly at her painting, her brush drying in her hand, lost in her thoughts. "I'm having trouble with this bloom," she said, locking her eyes on the painting. "Something is wrong with the perspective, I think."

Christina came up next to her and studied the half-finished painting. "It's lovely, Alice. I wish I could paint half as well."

Alice laughed. "And I wish I could play the violin half as well as you." "Your voice is better." Christina gave her a cheeky grin. "But I'm better at needlepoint. Are we finished?"

"No. I'm better at penmanship and you are better at archery."

"Girls, stop," Elda said, laughing. "You are both well accomplished in your own ways." She set aside her correspondence as she looked at her daughters. "I wonder why Mr. Southwell hasn't stopped by. I'm sure he knows he is welcome. And I don't know why he would stay in one of the village's little inns when he would be far more comfortable here."

Alice turned her attention back to her painting. "He hasn't been back since Joseph's funeral. He was his particular friend and perhaps he feels a bit awkward staying here now."

"Still, if we do see him, I shall issue an invitation. With your father and Oliver still in London, it would be nice to have a man in the house."

"To protect us from all the evil forces in St. Ives?" Alice asked with a smile, for St. Ives was perhaps the most tranquil place in all of England.

"No, dear, we need a baritone."

For some reason, that struck Alice as terribly funny, and she bent over with laughter and was soon joined by her mother and sister.

"We need a little music in this house," Elda said when she'd calmed. "I think having Henderson about would make all the difference."

* * *

"I'm sorry, sir, but Lord Berkley is not at home." Henderson eyed the black crepe tied on the door knocker before turning his attention back to the solemn-faced butler, and remembered the earl's Cavendish Square butler had been wearing a black band. When he'd seen the obvious sign of mourning, he'd nearly turned around and left. Feeling a bit like a cad, he'd turned the bell on the door anyway, wondering vaguely why he hadn't seen any signs of mourning at the earl's London home. When his own great-grandfather had died, they had shrouded the home in black, changing the curtains, draping the mantel in black, and hanging black wreaths even though not a single person within the home had tolerated the old man.

"I was not aware of a death in the family. Please do accept my apologies. May I leave my card and this letter?"

"Of course, Mr. Southwell," the butler said, quickly reading his card.

"I'm staying at the White Hart Inn in the village if Lord Berkley would like to reach me."

The butler bowed and shut the door, leaving Henderson feeling a bit at odds. If the man was in deep mourning, the last thing he would want to do was discuss the deaths in India when his own grief was still raw. He mounted his rented horse, grimacing a bit as he did so; it had been weeks since he had been astride and his muscles were feeling the pain. Before turning the horse back down the long, curving drive, he looked back at Costille House, a medieval home, with a massive stone tower and tiny arched windows built for the archer's bow. Nothing had been done to modernize the hulking home that overlooked St. Ives Bay and he could almost imagine himself wearing knight's armor. The home was visible from the Porthmeor Beach, a large expanse of soft white sand where he and Joseph would sometimes fish, a mystical and somehow comforting presence on the cliff above them. He would like to see the inside and hoped to hear from Lord Berkley soon.

As he headed down the long drive, he wondered what to do with the rest of his day. He suspected most of the men he'd spent time with as a lad were in London for the season.

Pulling out his watch, he noted it was about half an hour before tea. And it was also about a half hour's ride to Tregrennar and Alice. He rode along a narrow dirt-paved road lined with stone walls covered by some sweet-smelling flowering vine. Trees made a canopy overhead, the air cool in the shadows. Abruptly, the road gave way to brilliant sun and the heartbreaking blue of the sea to his right and the charming village of St. Ives in the distance.

St. Ives was known by some as the Naples of Cornwall, due to the large, curving bay and its temperate climate. It never got very hot, nor very cold, and few locals could recall ever seeing a snowflake fall even in the deepest part of winter. A narrow isthmus connected the village to a peninsula, known by locals as the Island, for once it had been separated from the mainland. He and Joseph, and occasionally Alice, had explored the Island and its Cornish ruins, imagining what it must have been like when the isthmus had been used by smugglers to bring in their wares. From his vantage point, St. Ives, with its centuries-old gray buildings constructed in a hodge-podge, looked more European than English, and Henderson guessed that was part of its charm. It looked as if it had always been there, tucked between the sea and the heather-covered hills. The harbor below was clogged with fishing boats and small schooners, the beach dotted with smaller boats, hauled up on the beach and above high tide. Tall hedgerows nearly obscured the water from time to time, but Henderson didn't care. He could still smell the sea, and hear it crashing ashore on the beach below. Perhaps when he was done with India he could buy a little cottage and just gaze out over the ocean for hours. His grandfather's own country estate held little appeal to him; he hadn't been back in more than four years and had no desire to see its stark walls again. He missed his grandparents, but his mother's toxic presence was enough to keep him away.

When he reached the intersection that would either bring him to the Downalong and its rows of tightly packed homes and his hotel or up to Tregrennar, he stopped. Just above the cabbage trees, he could see the very top of Tregrennar's roof. At that moment, his stomach grumbled and he pulled the horse slightly to the left, toward Tregrennar, feeling as if he were somehow sealing his fate—whatever that might be.

* * *

The wind coming up from the bay whipped at Alice's skirts and threatened to pull her well-anchored bonnet from her head. If it hadn't been so very windy, it would have been quite warm, though not nearly as warm as London was in mid-July. Gathering her wool coat around her, Alice looked out over the white-capped bay, taking in the sights and sounds of her childhood home. Truly, it was a good thing Northrup hadn't showed up to the church. He lived in Manchester and Alice didn't care much for that section of Britain; too cold in the winter and hardly warm at all in the summer. St. Ives never got too hot and never too cold and in the summer it seemed as if it were gloriously sunny all the time. It wasn't true, of course, for the storms that raged ashore from the Atlantic could be fearsome, but whenever Alice thought back on her childhood it was always sunny. And from the time she was fifteen, her summers had been filled with Henderson.

When she entered the part of the path lined with tall and ancient hedgerows, most of the wind was blocked, and it became a silent world but for the sounds of nature. Bees flew lazily and the cry of seagulls was nearly always present. She heard the sound of an approaching horse long before she saw it, and pressed close to the side in the event the rider did not see her. Alice and her friends had nearly been trampled more than once by a rider heading to Tregrennar—including her own father. This rider, however, seemed to be in no hurry, for every once in a while the horse would stop, then start, until finally the rider came into view. Her entire body went briefly rigid when she recognized Henderson's tall form riding toward her.

"Henderson. Hello," Alice called, wishing her heart wouldn't speed up quite so much every time she saw him. He smiled, and something in that smile made her heart pound, it was just that beautiful. "Christina mentioned that she saw you in the Downalong going into the new bookstore."

He dismounted and held the reins loosely in his hands, giving her a small bow of greeting. "Miss Hubbard, a pleasure. Why didn't your sister say hello?"

"She said she saw you from a distance and didn't want to shout." Alice couldn't stop her smile, couldn't stop the hope that caused her chest to hurt. Henderson was not only in St. Ives, he was very obviously heading to Tregrennar. When she was sixteen years old, she'd come across Joseph and Henderson walking on this very path; she'd been heading to the overlook and they'd been coming from town. Henderson had slung an arm around her shoulders for exactly ten steps, a brotherly gesture that didn't even garner a raised brow from her protective brother. Ten steps of feeling that heavy arm around her, of having him so near she could feel the heat of him, his manly scent of horse, cigar, and sea. She wished fervently that he was still so comfortable around her that he would do the same, throw his arm around her so that she might just one more time know what it was like. "Why didn't you write to say you were coming to St. Ives?"

"There wasn't time. I'm here to see Lord Berkley. You know him?"

Disappointment pierced her, a sharp little slice that made it difficult to maintain her pleasant smile. "Lord Berkley died just this past week," Alice said, keeping her voice even.

"Well, apparently there's another Lord Berkley in residence."

Alice stopped walking and looked at Henderson in surprise. "Not Augustus. I thought he'd gone to Australia or some such thing. America? There were some terrible rumors about him two years ago when his wife died. At any rate, no one has seen him in St. Ives for years. I've never met him, actually." Alice willed herself to stop speaking as she tended to babble overlong when she was nervous. "Is this about famine relief?"

"It is, though I fear I shall be disappointed again. Apparently, his father was the one with great influence in the House of Lords. I doubt if Berkley has even taken his father's seat. From what I understand, the old Lord Berkley was a man to be reckoned with, but I have no idea if the son holds any influence."

"I'm afraid I cannot help you there. I know nothing of the man. Perhaps Mother can be of some assistance. Have you had any success thus far?" A shadow crossed over his features before he answered. "No, I have not. Otherwise I would not be here wasting my time."

Of course, Henderson hadn't meant to be so cruel; he didn't know she was in love with him, didn't know her heart sang every time she looked at him, every time his beautiful blue eyes looked at her. How could he know? To say such a thing, however, only brought home how ridiculous her feelings were. Alice forced a laugh and prayed it sounded sincere. "And here I was thinking you'd come to St. Ives to have some of Cook's cherry tarts." *Or to see me.*

"My God, Mrs. Godfrey is still with you?'

"Indeed, she is. And I know when she learns you're in St. Ives, she'll be sure to make you your favorites."

"Then the trip was worth it," he said, sounding like his old self and looking down at her with real fondness. Yes, Henderson was fond of her. Like he was fond of cherry tarts.

Alice stopped and glared up at him with mock anger. "Mr. Southwell, I have just realized it is very close to tea time. Is it possible you planned your visit accordingly?"

He threw back his head and laughed. "Indeed I have, Miss Hubbard, although I hadn't thought there would be even a small chance of tasting Mrs. Godfrey's cherry charts. My God—" His hand threw out to stop her mid-step. "An adder, Alice. Don't move." With his hand still pressed against her stomach, he pushed her back slightly, slowly, and Alice wasn't certain whether it was the venomous viper that was making her heart thud in her chest or the feeling of his strong hand against her.

Beside them, the horse had also sensed the danger of the adder, which lay in the sun, basking on a section of soft sand in the very middle of the path. "I didn't see it," Alice said, her voice shaking slightly. Though adders were not deadly in most cases, being bitten by one was exceedingly unpleasant. "I would have stepped directly on it."

The small brown snake flicked its tongue before moving off beneath the hedgerow, and Alice let out a sigh of relief.

Grinning, Alice threw her hands over her heart dramatically and said, "Sirrah, you have saved my life. However shall I repay you?"

"A kiss."

Chapter 7

A kiss?

Alice, her heart nearly leaping out of her chest, her skin going instantly clammy, smiled almost maniacally and had to stop the sudden urge to throw herself into his arms. *Oh, finally, finally!* "Very well," she managed to say lightly. "I have been engaged three times, after all." Alice knew she sounded calm enough, but inside she was such a jumble nerves she sincerely doubted she'd be able to take a step without keeling over. How many times had she wondered what it would be like to kiss Henderson? Those nights lying in bed, pressing the back of her hand against her lips and imaging she was pressing her mouth against his.

Except that Henderson was standing there in front of her, arms crossed casually, looking for all the world as if he'd just asked to shake her hand. A thrush flew overhead and he was momentarily distracted, and when he turned back, he looked at her expectantly, with an almost bored look on his handsome face. He gave her a quick smile. "Perhaps not."

"Oh, no, that would be fine. A fair exchange for saving my life," Alice said, knowing she was grandly overstating the matter. Although people *had* died of adder bites. Sick people. Small children.

"Very well." He looked as if he'd wished he'd never claimed such a reward, but Alice refused to give up on what might very well be the only time she'd ever get to kiss him.

He took two steps, his blue eyes moving from her green ones down to her lips. He placed one hand on each upper arm, holding her gently. *Henderson Southwell is going to kiss me. Now. Oh God!* He was so near, she could see his beard starting to grow, the way his upper lip seemed sharply carved, but his lower fuller. With her knees knocking beneath her skirts and her heart beating madly in her chest, Alice leaned forward just a bit, and closed her eyes, her entire body focused on her lips and the touch that would soon be on them.

There. Oh, yes.

And then, to her horror, Alice burst out laughing. It was something she'd done all her life. She'd nearly laughed at her first fiancé's funeral and had laughed standing in the vestibule waiting for Lord Northrup to show up. And she laughed now, even as her heart broke. How she hated herself at that moment, for Henderson immediately withdrew and Alice opened her eyes to see him looking down at her with an expression of puzzled bemusement.

"I'm so sorry, Henny," Alice said, still laughing, still dying inside. How could she explain her laughter? How could she tell him that she'd been dreaming of his kiss since she was fifteen years old and the thought that this moment had finally come had sent her into such a nervous state she could hardly stand? She couldn't. And so she said the first thing that came into her head, the first thing that didn't seem ridiculous. "It's just that it's almost like kissing Oliver."

He narrowed his eyes and let out a small answering laugh before dropping his hands and stepping back, and Alice felt so very cold at that moment, missing the warmth and strength of his hands on her arms.

"Well, then." He jammed his hands into his pockets and looked down the path.

Alice truly felt like crying. She would never get another chance to kiss the one man she loved. Lord Northrup was a nice enough fellow and she did hold him in great affection, but she hadn't loved him. Hadn't nearly swooned when he'd kissed her, though the two times he had gathered enough courage to do so, it was mildly pleasant. Kissing Henderson had to be better than that, and now she would never find out.

"I think we should have another go of it," she said, with almost desperate nonchalance. "That hardly counted as a kiss."

His head whipped around and his eyes took on the strangest glint. "You have surprised me, Alice Hubbard."

"Have I?"

"Indeed you have. All right then, another kiss. And if you tell me that it's like kissing your brother, I'm afraid I'll have to bring your brother before the magistrate."

His words sent a thrill of anticipation down her spine, knowing she was about to be thoroughly kissed by a man who knew how to kiss a woman—if the rumors about him had been true.

This time, there was no warning, no gentle hold on her upper arms. This time, he stepped forward, placed one hand behind her neck, and pulled her forward, flush against him so she could feel the hard plane of his body. Then he bent his head and she was being kissed, kissed as she had never been in her entire life. With three engagements and three near-marriages, no one had consumed her the way Henderson did at that moment. His was not the gentle kiss of a man courting a woman, his was the kiss of a man who wanted something more. Alice let out a startled cry, then a muffled moan when she felt his tongue invade her mouth and brush against her own, caressing, capturing, making her feel things no man had ever made her feel. A shock of sensation between her legs nearly had her knees buckling beneath her and she wanted, *needed*, something more. When she pressed against him with almost frantic need, throwing her arms around him in abandon, she felt his arousal and stiffened. Even though she had never felt a man's part before, she knew what it was pressing hot against the juncture of her thighs, knew what it meant that it was hard and long.

Letting out a low sound more growl than moan, Henderson stepped back, his eyes fierce and dark as Alice swayed toward him, as if her body was not ready to release him. Alice lifted a trembling hand to her mouth. What had just happened? Was that the way all kisses were supposed to feel?

"Would you call that a brotherly kiss, Alice?" And then he let out a harsh laugh that Alice could only interpret as triumphant. As if that kiss was only a means to teach her a lesson, which she supposed she deserved. Apparently she had wounded his pride when she'd compared his kiss to a brotherly peck and he had used all his talents to prove her wrong.

"Hardly," she said, taking a shaking breath. "It was nothing like any kiss I've experienced." There, she'd put him in his place, implying with her tone that she'd not been altogether pleased with the kiss and reminding him that she had been kissed—and more than once. Why she felt the need to gain the upper hand, she couldn't say. Perhaps it was because she was standing there with knees still shaking, with a dull throb between her legs, and he was standing there, arms crossed casually across his chest, smiling at her. His eyes flickered at her words, but then his smile widened.

"I do apologize. I am used to kissing women who have, let us say, a bit more experience."

"Please do spare me your false apology. You were trying to teach me a lesson and nothing more."

"Perhaps. You did seem in need of one."

Alice put her hands on her hips, outraged. "You needn't be so smug. It wasn't that good."

His burst of laughter was even more annoying than his smugness. "Of course it was." He waggled his eyebrows. "But I have done better."

Alice wrinkled her nose. "I suppose it was passable. And certainly nothing I would like repeated."

Henderson took up the reins of his horse, which had been happily munching on the grass at the side of the road, and pulled out his watch. "We're still on time for tea," he said happily, and Alice shot him another look of annoyance. Food. How could he think about food when they'd just kissed...like that? With tongues and bodies and moans? Then he stopped and leaned toward her. "I don't understand what you are in such a huff about. The prize was your idea, if you recall."

Alice's cheeks flushed instantly, because in truth, that was what she'd been hinting at, though she would die before admitting such.

"You are utterly conceited if you think that ever in a hundred years I would have guessed you would ask for a kiss," she said with a toss of her head.

"And utterly correct."

* * *

Alice walked ahead of him, still in a snit, and he stared at her back, angrier with himself than he had ever been. He hadn't meant for that kiss to be so carnal, but when she'd likened kissing him to kissing her brother, it had driven him a bit mad. Now he knew what she tasted like, how soft her lips where, the way she sounded when he pleased her. It was only a small leap to picture her beneath him, naked, looking up at him, her eyes drowsy with desire. The way her eyes had looked when he'd pulled away, like a woman who was aroused and wanted more, would haunt him this night and all the nights to come.

Oh, God, how would he ever get that image out of his head?

"Are your father and brother in residence?" he asked, being careful to keep his tone neutral.

"No. They both stayed in London. Why?" She paused on the path and looked up at him from beneath the brim of her bonnet, her cheeks flushed, her lips rosy and slightly swollen. His cock, which had finally begun to grow small, jumped to life and he tugged on his jacket to make certain he was covered.

"I should like to go fishing whilst I'm in St. Ives," he said with a shrug. *And I plan to ask your father for permission to court you. To marry you.*

And after that, he wasn't sure what he would do. Henderson was still committed to helping those starving in India, but he wasn't certain he would be able to leave Alice behind even for a few months. He would never make that mistake again. Once she was his...God, that was a beautiful thought.

Feeling as if the steel band that had been surrounding his heart for four years had loosened, Henderson started lightly whistling a Gilbert and Sullivan song, and Alice cast him a small smile. Apparently he had been forgiven.

"My mother will likely insist you stay at Tregrennar, you know."

Henderson instantly decided that would be a bad idea. It was difficult enough to be in the same town as Alice; living in the same house would be far too dangerous. No doubt Alice would want to continue their talks in the library, but he was not a young man anymore and she was not fifteen. She was a woman and he wanted her more with every breath he took. Sitting in the library, late at night, with her in her night rail—oh God, he was not strong enough to resist trying to touch her, not now, now when he knew how responsive she was. He would have to talk to her father immediately, for it suddenly became imperative that he stake his claim on her now before she went and got herself engaged again.

Just then, they left the path and there it was, Tregrennar, looking gloriously familiar. "The old girl looks exactly the same," he said, hearing the wistful note in his own voice. No, he could not stay at Tregrennar, not with echoes of Joseph still there. His heart tore as if it were only yesterday when he'd heard the terrible news that Joseph was dead.

That night, after he'd left Joseph to find other amusements between the soft thighs of a local widow, he hadn't given his friend another thought. He'd spent a pleasant evening with Mrs. Patterson, slaking his lust in the way only a young man can—with enthusiasm and little finesse. He was on his way back to Tregrennar when he decided to stop in the White Hart for a pint before making the rest of the walk back, and was surprised to find one of the lads Joseph had been planning to see that evening sitting at a table.

When Gerald Grant had looked up, Henderson knew immediately that something was wrong. His friend's eyes were red-rimmed, the hands that held the tin mug in front him shaking as he took a sip. Worse still, Gerald could not look him in the eye. "Where's Joseph?" he asked, and somehow knew before he answered that something terrible had happened to his friend.

Gerald motioned for him to sit, and Henderson pulled out a chair, lowering himself into it cautiously, as if taking care with such a mundane movement would somehow make whatever he was about to tell him untrue.

"He's dead, Henderson," Gerald said, his voice breaking. "Fell off the damned stable roof."

"My God." Henderson sat back, stunned, a burning lead ball growing in his chest. It couldn't be true. He'd just seen Joseph. He wanted to tell him about his evening, about how Mrs. Patterson's cat had leapt on the bed just as things were getting exciting. They were supposed to have laughed about it, and then Joseph was supposed to have looked at him with disappointment and a little bit of disgust for having sex with the pretty widow.

"He didn't just *fall*," Gerald had said, his eyes bleak as he stared unseeingly at his pint.

"What are you saying? What happened?"

Gerald looked about to speak, but then shook his head, unable to say a word as his throat convulsed. "Damn it, Gerald, what happened?" Henderson had asked, trying not to reach over the table and shake the other man.

"I'm not really sure what happened. We were having a grand time. It was Joseph's idea to get on the stable roof. Said he wanted to see the stars better. So I hauled out a ladder and we all climbed up. You know the place, where it's flat, the overhang where we bring the cattle in. We all sat there, talking about nothing. And then Joseph got up and started climbing. We all laughed." He paused and stared at Henderson for a long moment. "He was always doing things like that. We thought it was a lark. Then he stood at the very end, at the peak, and turned toward us." Gerald swallowed heavily. "We told him to come down, we did. It was bloody dark and all we could see was his silhouette and that roof is steep. Stupid, bloody idiot." He choked down a sob and banged a fist lightly against the worn wood of the table.

"What happened?" Henderson could feel his eyes burning, his throat aching, his heart tearing in his chest. It couldn't be true, it could not. His mind rebelled and his heart felt as if it had been ripped from his chest. Nothing had ever felt like this, nothing had hurt him to the point of agony. He could still hear Joseph begging him to go with him. *Come on, you can see your widow any old night. I really want you there.*

Gerald paused, giving Henderson a tortured look, and Henderson wanted to bash his head against the table so he would just finish the story.

"He stood there for the longest time, and then he said…God, Henderson, I'm so sorry. He said 'Tell Southie I'm sorry.' And then he fell back, just like that, the way you would if you were falling back onto a feather mattress. Not a sound, nothing, until he hit."

That night had been the worst of his life, for his dearest friend had died.

Now, he had to live not only with the knowledge that Joseph had taken his own life, but also the memory that Henderson had promised never to touch Alice. Well, it was too bloody late for that, and now he'd have to live with the guilt of happily breaking that promise. As they walked toward Tregrennar, memories assailed him; it was almost cruel how he felt as if he were coming home.

* * *

The first time he'd gone to Tregrennar, he and Joseph were just nineteen, freshly graduated from Eton and looking forward to Oxford.

"My parents won't mind, really. I've written them and it's all set. And you don't want to spend a dreary summer dodging your mother, do you?" Joseph gave Henderson's shoulder a nudge. "We have the best trout stream in Cornwall running right through our property."

Henderson stared at his suitcase, stuffed full of what he'd need for his summer holiday, and felt a longing in his stomach so strong he nearly felt ill from it. No, he did not want to go home to Chelmsford and spend his entire summer with his grandparents and mother. He'd written dutifully to his mother and she'd responded with the same apathy he'd been subject to his entire life. Indeed, he was surprised she'd responded at all, for he'd written many letters over the years that had been ignored.

Eton had been his haven, a place he could be with chaps his own age, who liked an adventure as much as he did, who somehow overlooked the fact he was illegitimate—overlooked because Joseph had insisted they all do so.

And it was so blasted, bloody boring in Chelmsford.

Cornwall was the warm sea, trout fishing, and living in a home with a family, a lively, boisterous family, if the stories Joseph told him were true. Joseph had been begging him to spend the summer with his family for years. Now that they had graduated from Eton and were heading to university next year, it might be the very last time he'd get a chance.

"I'll go," he said, suddenly feeling a weight lifted from him. His mother would not even notice his absence. She hardly acknowledged him when he was home. The last few summers, he'd thought he might go out of his head from boredom.

"Excellent. I only hope you don't mind my little sisters, Alice and Christina. They're both tolerable, I supposed, but Alice can be a bit of a rascal. She's not too bad once you get to know her."

"She's twelve?"

Joseph paused. "Good God, she's fifteen. Cripes, didn't realize. She'll be coming out in just three years, two if she has her way. I keep thinking about her as if she was a little girl. You'll like my sisters, though. Everyone does."

Truth be told, Henderson was a bit nervous about spending any time with a girl. He'd grown up quite alone and spent most of his time at school. He could hardly even recall having a conversation with a female his own age. To him, they were a foreign and beautiful mystery. All that hair and lace and creamy skin.

"Come on, then, the carriage is waiting," Joseph said, hauling up his overstuffed bag. He stopped, his brown eyes shining with excitement. "This is going to be the best summer."

* * *

Henderson had been given the room next to Joseph and one that overlooked the garden. Through the trees at the edge of the property, he could see the brilliant blue-green of the sea. It had touched him that they had put him in the family wing rather than where guests might normally stay. The Hubbards puzzled him, to be honest, welcoming a complete stranger into their home. Richard was the son of a duke, thus the reason he was called "Lord" Hubbard instead of "Mr." Hubbard, and they were part of a world Henderson had never even hoped to have a glimpse of, never mind be welcomed into as if part of the family. His own mother detested him, though his grandparents did try to make up for that with their love. Both Hubbard boys insisted he stay in the family wing, saying he was more a brother to them than anything else. Indeed, the Hubbards and their easy ways had immediately made him feel comfortable.

The first morning he took his cup of strong, black coffee and stepped out onto the balcony to greet the day. Sunlight streamed into his room, and when he swung open the French doors, a strong scent of the sea rushed in, carrying with it the sounds of summer—birds, a gardener clipping shrubbery, a squirrel chattering angrily at a massive tabby cat that sat beneath a tree. God, he loved it here.

He'd taken his first sip when he spied a woman in the gardens below him, and he paused, the cup held suspended, as he watched her. Though he hadn't been exposed to many women in his nineteen years, he realized he was staring at pure female perfection. Had anyone been standing next to him, it would have been painfully obvious that he'd become almost instantly smitten. She was the loveliest thing he'd ever seen. She was strolling in the garden, wearing a wide-brimmed hat trimmed with sky-blue ribbon and a dress that matched the ribbon perfectly. His eyes drifted down her form, stopping briefly at the swell of her breasts, the curve of her waist. As he watched, she bent to take a closer look at a rose and the smile that came to her face made him feel a rush of lust so strong, he found himself gripping the railing, his knuckles white from the strain, and he let out a small sound.

Straightening suddenly, she whirled about and looked up directly at him, one hand shielding her eyes from the bright sun. "Hello. You must be Henderson."

Odd, how would she know—*Oh, God. No.*

Walking toward the house, a breeze causing a few stray strands of her light hair to escape her hat, she looked up and smiled. "I'm Alice, Joseph's sister." He stood there, mute, horrified. "Don't tell me Joseph didn't tell you he had a sister. Two, actually, though Christina is off with Aunt Gladys this summer. It would be something he would do just to vex me." She laughed, as if the idea of her brother pulling such a trick was great fun.

"No. I, that is to say, Joseph told me he had a sister. Two sisters." Alice was supposed to be a fifteen-year-old child. Not this...this woman who stood before him, all luscious curves and sparkling eyes.

Henderson shook his head and let out a near-silent chuckle, frankly horrified that his body had such a violent reaction to Joseph's little sister. God, he was depraved. Then again, he hadn't known he was looking at Alice. In his mind, she was a child.

She seemed disappointed to learn he had known of her existence and a bit uncertain what to say.

"I'll see you at breakfast, then," she said cheerfully.

"Oh, yes. Breakfast."

"It's a meal in the morning where one breaks one's fast." She smiled and tilted her head, then turned around, her skirts flying about, and headed back to the garden.

"Yes, I'll see you there," Henderson called out, feeling foolish. She didn't turn around again, merely waved her hand in acknowledgment, which made him feel as if he were a gauche boy, not a man about to enter university.

Giving himself a mental shake, he returned to his room, wishing with all his being that he had known whom he was looking at before seeing her in the garden. Joseph's sister might look like a woman, have a woman's curves, but she was still just fifteen. Swallowing heavily, he made a promise to himself to stay away from Alice, to never let her know where his thoughts had gone.

A quiet knock on the door pulled him away from his thoughts. "Enter." Joseph's valet came into the room and wished him a brisk good morning.

"Lord Hubbard has asked that you meet him for breakfast after your shave, sir."

Henderson laughed, bringing his hand up to touch his jaw, which was covered with three days' growth. Shaving was one of his least favorite activities, even under the care of an excellent valet. If it were up to him, he would let his beard grow, but neither his mother nor Joseph would allow it. "You look like an American mountain man," Joseph had said more than once. Henderson didn't much care how he looked, so he forced himself to shave if only to shut Joseph up.

"If you insist, Mr. Boxter."

"I do, sir."

Once he was freshly shaved and his cravat straightened rather forcefully by Boxter, Henderson headed down the stairs, already feeling quite at home in the grand old place. Joseph's parents and younger brother had met Henderson enthusiastically, claiming they had heard so much about him from Joseph they felt they knew him already. With them, he hadn't experienced the awkwardness he usually did when dining with strangers. Now, though, ready to face the third Hubbard sibling, Henderson felt his stomach twist with nervousness. He hadn't thought much about her absence thus far, assuming she was off visiting a relative or some such thing.

When he entered the breakfast room, a warm place with sun streaming through floor-to-ceiling windows, every member of the Hubbard family but for Christina was already there—including the elder daughter. Alice looked up and gave him a little smile, as if the two of them shared some sort of grand secret.

"Good morning," he said, before going to the sideboard and filling his plate until it was heavy in his hand. Henderson had always had a healthy appetite, and since he was naturally lean, he never bothered to limit his meals. He sat next to Joseph, who was nearly done with his meal, and looked across to Alice, who eyed his plate with unreserved amusement.

Joseph reached over and stole a scone.

"Joseph, that's rude," his mother, Elda, said, but Henderson could tell she wasn't truly angry.

Joseph immediately put the scone, minus one large bite, back on his plate and apologized exuberantly to his mother, who looked as if she was on the verge of laughter. It was this sort of simple exchange that Henderson so loved about this family and had been missing for his entire life. Family dinners were subdued and, looking back, rather miserable affairs, with his mother pointedly not engaging with him. There had been no laughter or joy in his house and he realized now that a soul needed laughter and joy.

"What are you two up to today?" Lord Hubbard asked.

"Thaddeus's bitch just had a litter and I thought we could take a look." Before his father could object, he added, "I'm not getting one, Father, just looking."

Lord Hubbard sighed and looked at his wife. "Do we have room for another dog, Ellie?"

"Only if he's got a lovely pup, Father," Joseph had said. "Fritz is getting a bit old and—"

"Fritz is only three, Joseph," Alice said. "And I don't think he'd care for another dog running about."

"It'd be a friend to him," Joseph said. "And to me. Fritz is your dog. And Scat is yours too." He turned to Henderson. "That's the big tom you've seen about the house. Menace to all our song birds."

"He can't help it if he's a good hunter," Alice said. "He's merely doing what cats do."

"Tell that to Cook. She found a half-eaten sparrow on the back step yesterday."

Alice grinned. "A present."

"At any rate, I'll be home this summer and I'll have time to make him mine."

"I thought you just told your father you weren't getting a puppy," Elda said. "And you know you wouldn't be able to bring him to university. It'll be left to us to care for him."

Henderson thought the banter was all in good fun until he noticed how fiercely Joseph was digging his hands into his leg. "I just want something of my own," he said.

"He'll be home on holidays and summer." When all eyes turned toward Henderson, he could feel his face heat.

His lordship threw down his napkin, symbolically throwing in the towel. "Very well, Joseph, you may have your pup."

"Oh, Richard, really?" Elda's expression was a mixture of love and disbelief.

"Really. That's settled, then." With those words, Lord Hubbard rose from the table and left the room, but not before putting a hand on his older son's shoulder and giving it a squeeze.

"You always were his favorite. Oldest and heir and all that," Alice said, with just the smallest bit of resentment in her tone.

Joseph grinned at his younger sister. "It's only that I know how to get my way."

"Not all the time," Elda said sternly, but Joseph just laughed.

"I've an idea. We'll let Henderson name the pup," Joseph said. "That way it'll have a respectable name." He winked at his sister and she made a face at her big brother before looking over to Henderson.

"Do you realize the import of this?" she asked, her blue eyes steady on him. "It means you're officially one of us."

Henderson smiled and tried not to show how ridiculously happy those words made him.

* * *

"It is out of the question that you stay in the village, Henderson. I won't hear of it."

Alice suppressed a smile. She'd known her mother would be adamant and would not take no for an answer. The minute she'd seen Henderson walk through the door, Elda had called to two footmen to fetch Henderson's things from the inn. Alice recognized the moment he realized that continuing to argue would only hurt her mother's feelings and so he relented, giving her a look of resigned bemusement. Inside, her stomach was a tight swirl of happiness followed quickly by almost nauseating trepidation.

"How is your mother?" Elda asked once they had all settled in the main parlor for tea. Henderson had just popped a cherry tart into his mouth and grimaced—not from the tart, as they were his favorite, but from the question. Though Henderson had never spoken at length about his family, Alice knew he didn't like to discuss his home life. She sensed he loved his grandparents but his relationship with his mother was particularly strained. She had gleaned this information during one of their long talks, and it had seemed like a gift to Alice at the time, a tiny piece of Henderson that he so rarely gave away.

"I have no idea," he said after swallowing the confection. "As far as I know, she's still wallowing in bitter disappointment," he said with irony. Henderson had been an only—and very lonely—child, Alice guessed, with a mother who could hardly look at him without letting her feelings of disgust show. It had been Henderson's grandmother who had insisted they keep him rather than send him to one of the foundling homes where so many bastard children ended up. He'd often said his grandmother's heart was too soft, but he'd been glad of it.

"And your grandparents?"

Alice gave her mother a telling look, which her mother ignored. "Well. I write to them regularly. It was my grandmother who wrote to say Miss Hubbard's wedding was imminent. That's when I immediately found a ship and headed home to stop the wedding." Henderson grinned and Elda laughed.

"I thought it must be something like that," Elda said, a twinkle in her eye that told Henderson she knew he was jesting.

"If it puts your mind at ease, I have been dutifully writing my grandparents since the day I left England, and they have dutifully responded."

Alice had often wondered what it had been like for Henderson to grow up in such a home. Yes, he had been sent away to school since he was seven (still another thought that drew sympathy from her), but when he was younger he had been home for summers and holidays. Whom had he talked to? Played with? In the Hubbard home, there had always been someone to talk to, play a game with. Joseph had been a wonderfully indulgent brother and Alice had taken advantage of his kind heart and giving nature. He had set the tone for the Hubbard children, who loved each other and were uncommonly close. The remaining Hubbard children were still close, of course, but there was always a feeling that a large part was missing and would never be replaced, no matter how much time passed. At least she had wonderful memories of Joseph and their happy childhood. What did Henderson have?

"His mother blames Henderson for the fact she never married and—" Her mother gave her a sharp look and nodded subtly in Christina's direction, and Alice stopped abruptly.

"It's all right, Mama, I know all about Mr. Southwell's birth," Christina said, giving Henderson an apologetic look.

"Alice, really." Elda always seemed surprised that her daughters shared so much information. "Christina is only eighteen."

"I knew when I was eighteen," Alice said logically, and Elda let out a small puff of exasperation.

Henderson let out a low chuckle. "Yes, she knows about my mother and her fall from grace."

"Do you ever wonder where your father is? If I were your grandmother, I would have hunted him down," Christina said, grabbing up the last tart, "and made things right. Your mother must have been so hurt."

"I doubt my mother could garner the energy to feel such strong emotion," Henderson said, laughing lightly.

"I'm sure she feels emotion—she simply does not put it on display," Christina argued.

"Perhaps," he said, a hollow note in his tone.

"*We* love you," Elda said.

Henderson's eyes flickered briefly to Alice before he smiled at her mother. "That is very kind, Lady Hubbard."

"I was not being kind, young man. I was stating a fact."

* * *

Alice and her sister and mother gathered each evening before a fire even in the summertime, for the nights in St. Ives could be quite chilly. Unless they were attending an entertainment, the family kept early hours, dining at seven and turning in for the evening by ten. Elda was perpetually knitting socks and sending them off to a veterans' home in London and this evening was no different. After an early supper of ham, potatoes, and beet salad, Henderson had gone back to the village to meet up with some friends he hadn't seen in four years, promising to return before midnight.

"I suppose a house full of women isn't much fun for a young man," Elda said, laughing, while Alice tried not to feel too disappointed. Her thoughts of the day's events mingled with the soft clacking of her mother's knitting needles and the occasional rustle of a page from the book her sister was reading. A book sat on Alice's lap as well, but it was impossible to read with her thoughts whirling about her head.

"You seem distracted this evening, Alice," her mother said, looking up from her knitting.

She glanced down at her book. "Oh, no. Just tired." *Liar.*

"It's the fresh sea air," Elda said. "There is something about being close to the sea that is so fatiguing."

"It's a good sort of fatigue. That's why I'm living here forever," Alice said feelingly. "There is nothing like St. Ives."

"Alice, you cannot live here forever, you silly goose. What will you do when Mama and Papa are no longer here?" Christina cast a look of apology to their mother. "Oliver will eventually get married, for all his protestations to the contrary. And I doubt he'd like to have his sister hanging about."

Alice hated when her younger sister was more practical than she.

"I'll live with you."

Christina laughed. "I'm afraid His Grace and I will not have room in our castle."

"You're marrying a duke, are you?"

"Why not? My grandfather is a duke," Christina said predictably. "I don't know why you didn't have higher aspirations."

Alice shot her little sister a look of disbelief. "I was engaged to marry a baron and a viscount. And a pretend earl. I hardly call that having low aspirations."

Elda looked between her daughters, an indulgent smile on her face. "If you want to marry a duke and Alice wants to marry a baron, that's fine with me."

"I'm not getting married to anyone," Alice announced, and was surprised when her mother and her sister both laughed. "I'm not," she insisted. "Don't you think it highly unlikely at this point that anyone will want to marry me? The bad luck bride?"

Elda furrowed her brow. "Christina, you didn't."

"Someone had to tell her. Really, Mother, did you think she wouldn't find out?"

Alice quickly interjected before her mother got truly angry with Christina. "Mother, it's far better that I know than not. This way when someone says something—and they will—I shall be prepared. Harriet told me already at any rate, so you cannot place sole blame on Christina."

"That silly moniker will not prevent you from marrying," Elda said firmly. "I'm certain most people have already forgotten it or haven't read that awful piece in the first place."

"Maybe we can bribe someone to marry her," Christina said cheerfully.

"What about Mr. Southwell?"

Alice immediately felt her face heat. "That's just silly. He's far too good a friend to subject him to having you as a sister-in-law."

Christina stuck out her tongue and Elda tsked. "Girls, that is enough. No one is marrying anyone in the foreseeable future."

"I might marry next year," Christina said. "I've made a list of potential suitors already." She giggled. "Would you like to know who is at the top of the list?"

Alice struggled not to roll her eyes. "I know very well who is at the top of your list. It might as well be Prince Edward."

"He's married," Christina quipped. "And Prince Napoleon is living in England now, you know."

"Yes, I know. It's all you can speak of. You do know there is talk of him marrying Princess Beatrice."

Christina made a face. "Have you seen her nose?"

"Christina!" Elda looked at her daughter, shocked.

"Well, have you?"

Alice tried her best to stifle her laughter but found it nearly impossible. "You are terrible. The princess is really a lovely person." Christina picked up her book pointedly and began to read, effectively ending the conversation and leaving Alice to her own thoughts again, which immediately returned to the path to Tregrennar and Henderson.

And that kiss.

Forever it would be sealed in her memory. She wished it had never happened, that she hadn't teased him about his kiss being brotherly. It would be far better to have never experienced Henderson's skilled caresses. The thought of a man's tongue in her mouth would have repulsed her just one day before. Truthfully, the thought of any man's tongue other than Henderson's made her feel slightly queasy. With that one, scorching, life-altering kiss, Henderson had completely changed the way she thought of him. While her heart had always stepped up a beat whenever he walked in a room, now it seemed ready to explode out of her body just at the thought of him. She felt odd and faint and not at all herself. And she didn't like it one bit, because she had a terrible feeling that after he'd done kissing her and stepped back, he hadn't given another thought to how wonderful it had been. All her friends had insisted that men felt differently about kissing than did women. For a woman to kiss, it was far more emotional, held far more meaning. Men went around kissing girls all the time if they could get away with it. Four years ago, even as sheltered as she'd been, she'd heard the rumors about Henderson being quite the ladies' man.

For him it had been a kiss. For her it had been *the* kiss.

The kiss that changed her life. Now she was even more certain that she would never marry. For what man could she possibly marry who could make her forget she wasn't in the arms of the man she loved?

Chapter 8

Henderson returned, as promised, just before midnight. He'd been in the Downalong, the very old center of St. Ives, sharing drinks and stories with one of the chaps Joseph and he used to see when they were in school. Percy Taylor was the son of a local squire and was one of the most intelligent men Henderson had ever known. Unfortunately, Percy also had a tendency to think of all others who didn't share his intelligence as lesser beings. Still, he was sharp-witted and a nice distraction—and he had mellowed in the past four years since his marriage and the birth of his daughter. The last time Henderson had seen Percy was at Joseph's funeral, a common theme since his return to England. They studiously avoided talking about Joseph, to Henderson's great relief. It was difficult enough staying at Tregrennar with all its ghosts without discussing Joseph with every man he met who had known of their friendship. Like Henderson, Percy had not been there the night Joseph died.

Instead they talked about Percy's life, politics, the weather, and India, though Henderson did not go into detail about the famine. The truth was, Henderson wanted to forget about the suffering for a time. A note had been forwarded to him with his luggage from Lord Berkley, setting up a meeting the following day. He would save his thoughts of India for that meeting; this night was for drinking and laughing with an old friend.

He had said a good night to Percy and was about to walk through the door when Sebastian Turner—one of the men who had been there that fateful night—entered the pub. Henderson recognized him immediately and was tempted to pretend he didn't see him, but Sebastian, after a double take, greeted him with far more enthusiasm than Henderson felt.

"My God, Henderson. What are you doing in St. Ives? Come sit and catch up."

The two men sat at the very same table Henderson had just vacated, and after giving the other man a brief accounting of his time in St. Ives, Sebastian sat back and shook his head in wonder. "I cannot believe you are here. How long has it..." His voice trailed off as he realized precisely how long it had been. "Ah, that night."

Sebastian stared at his tankard of beer for a long moment. "A hellish time, wasn't it? Tristan is dead, you know. Two years ago. Hunting accident, apparently."

"No, I didn't know." Tristan had been part of their small group, and had been Sebastian's closest friend. But the five of them—Joseph, Henderson, Tristan, Sebastian, and Gerald—had spent a lot of time together at Oxford, carousing and generally raising hell. Now, two of their group were dead. It was difficult to comprehend. "I'm sorry."

Sebastian shrugged, but Henderson saw a deep pain in the other man's eyes before he took a long drink of his beer. "I was wondering," he said, staring into his beer, "did Joseph ever mention a Mr. Stewart?"

Henderson thought back and couldn't recall such a conversation. "I don't believe so, but he may have."

An odd smile crossed Sebastian's face. "You would have remembered. Just wondering."

The conversation turned to other things, their exploits, the women, and they drew more than one patron's attention with their laughter.

"We'll get together again before I leave for India, shall we? I'm staying at the Hubbards'—Lady Hubbard insisted—and I dare not be too late." Henderson stood and shook the other man's hand. "It was good to see you, Sebastian."

"Likewise." He grinned suddenly. "I'm getting married, you know. In November. Do you remember Cecelia Whitemore?"

"Of course. Congratulations. I haven't gone down that road yet."

"I am running down that road, Mr. Southwell."

Henderson let out a chuckle. "So it's like that, is it?"

His grin widened. "It is."

Henderson left the pub feeling a bit melancholy. It has been grand seeing Sebastian, even though talking with him brought back painful memories, but it had also been shocking to hear another of his friends had died. Though he was feeling a bit of the effects of alcohol, by the time he reached Tregrennar, he was quite sober—a good thing, too, for the minute he walked in the door he noticed a dim light showing beneath the library door, which could mean only one thing: Alice was waiting for him.

"Hell," he whispered, staring at the thin bit of light. Just seeing it, knowing she was there curled up in a chair with a book, probably wearing her nightgown and a robe, was enough to make him ache. God, he wanted her.

To subject himself to the torture of being in the same room as Alice, knowing the only thing that separated him from her naked flesh was two thin layers of fabric, was enough to drive him mad. He stood there, hearing only his breath and the soft clicking of a hall clock, and stared at that light, feeling the heavy weight of his arousal. Suddenly the light was doused, and he was caught in the middle of the wide hallway with nowhere to go and certainly not enough time to make his escape before the door opened and...

She appeared before his muddled mind could decide whether he should run or hide, and so he was left standing there stupidly. "Alice."

She let out a sound. "My goodness, Henderson, I didn't see you there."

"I thought not, and I didn't want to startle you. But it seems I did in any case." He grinned, even knowing it was too dark for her to see.

"I was going to retire. Are you just getting home?"

"I am. I saw the light and...well..." He bent his head, feeling foolish. "I was trying to decide whether or not I should go in."

Even in the darkness, he could see her tilt her head. "Was it such a difficult decision?"

"I'm tired and I know how you can talk," he said, teasing her because he certainly couldn't tell her the truth. *I couldn't go in because if I did I knew I would do something very foolish. And very wonderful.*

"Come on, then. I need to tell you about the last four years and it may take a while." She turned around and walked back into the library, sure he would follow. And after the smallest hesitation, he did, vowing he would *not* do what he wanted to do even if it killed him.

He nearly groaned aloud when she lit a small lamp, for her hair was in a thick braid down her back, and she was, indeed, wearing only a nightgown and robe. And why not? She thought of him as a brother. It irked him, to be honest, that she could be so naïve as to think he didn't want to ravish her, didn't realize it took a hellish effort not to go up behind her and draw her against him so she could feel just how aroused he was.

She settled on a large, deep sofa and curled her legs up beneath her while he threw himself on an oversized chair opposite; the same spots they had sat four years earlier.

"What would you like to know?" She drew her knees up and rested her chin on them, looking adorable and desirable. Henderson crossed his legs and winced.

"Tell me about your betrotheds. Is that a word? Can you make betrothed plural?"

She narrowed her eyes at him. "Yes, you can. Is that what you really want to know?"

"I suppose what I really want to know is why you didn't write."

Her eyes flew wide and she laughed. "I did. All the time. I just didn't send the letters. I didn't know where you were and I couldn't send them to your grandparents. What if they read what I'd written?"

Something sharp hit his heart. "You wrote?"

"I did. I still have the letters."

He was completely taken aback. "May I see them?"

"Never," she said with an adamant shake of her head. "Never, ever. Once I realized I would never actually send them, they became a diary of sorts. Those letters helped me with what happened to Joseph." She was silent for a few beats. "Why didn't you write? You certainly knew how to reach me."

Henderson looked toward the fire, which still held a few glowing embers. "I did," he said softly. At her soft gasp, he shook his head. "I didn't send my letters either. I burned them. Every time."

"Why?"

Henderson shrugged, unwilling to tell her the real reason. They had been far too intimate. Far too honest. He had poured out his heart in those letters, about Joseph. About her. He thanked God every day for burning them. "They were silly, inconsequential things. I'm not much of a writer."

Alice gave him a skeptical look but let it go. "All right then. I'll tell you about all three of my betrotheds." And she did. It wasn't until the east was seeing the first glow of the sunrise that they stopped talking. It had been the most fun Henderson had had, well, since the last time he'd spent hours in the library with Alice. God, he'd missed her, more than he'd even realized.

When conversation lulled and the fire, which Henderson had stoked at some point in the evening, had again turned to coals, Alice stood and stretched. Her robe had opened, just enough so that when she arched her back, her lovely dusky nipples, hard from the cold, were clearly visible, and his mouth went dry. In that split second, the control that Henderson had kept well in check nearly cracked. Snapping his gaze down, he took a deep breath. And again.

"Henderson?" She stood in front on him, so damned innocent, her breasts clearly showing through the thin material.

"Cover yourself, Alice. For God's sake."

* * *

Alice felt her face burn and knew she had turned a brilliant red. Drawing the robe tightly around her, she said, "Sorry, I didn't realize."

Henderson let out a gusty sigh. "I know you think of me as a brother, Alice, but I am not. I'm a man and when a man has a half-dressed woman in front of him, well, it can be difficult."

"Difficult?"

"Difficult for the man not to touch—" He snapped his mouth shut and Alice's eyes grew wide. She couldn't help it, she smiled.

"You think I'm pretty." It was a statement.

"God, Alice, more than pretty. I can hardly keep my hands from you." She furrowed her brow. "Truly?"

"Yes, truly." Henderson sounded angry, but Alice sensed it was directed more toward himself than at her. "It was that bloody kiss. It never should have happened. I never should have kissed you that way."

"Oh." Alice pulled in her lips, uncertain what to say, how to act. She'd always been so comfortable with Henderson and she didn't much like this awful tension between them. Yes, she'd had a crush on him when she was a girl, but she was no longer a girl. And what she was feeling, that dense throbbing between her legs, was no crush. It was desire. Feeling a bit startled and more than a little frightened—of herself, not Henderson—she took a step back. "Yes, you are right. I…" Again she pulled in her lips, and Henderson's gaze dropped from her eyes to her mouth. The terrible throbbing got worse.

"I think I'll retire now, before I do something I'll regret even more," Henderson said gravely. "I don't think it is a good idea for us to meet here anymore. We probably never should have in the first place, now that I think of it."

Alice nodded. "You are right. But I shall miss our talks."

"We can still talk, you goose," Henderson said on a laugh. "But perhaps we should do so when the sun is shining and with people about."

Alice frowned. "That won't nearly be as much fun, will it?"

"Perhaps not. But we cannot get in trouble. You do realize that if anyone discovered us, it would be disastrous."

Disastrous. Yes, it would. But Alice couldn't stop the stab of disappointment that Henderson thought the idea of being compromised would have disastrous consequences. It somehow didn't matter that she had vowed never to marry. "I suppose I never thought of that. Truly, Henderson, if my mother walked down right this minute, I don't think she'd say a thing. She knows you are practically family."

"Perhaps. But perhaps not. And neither of us wants to take that chance."

"So our first kiss is our last kiss," Alice said, her stomach tumbling at the thought.

"I'm afraid so."

No. The word exploded in her head. She had to have one more kiss. "Before you leave for good, would you kiss me one more time, Henny? For old time's sake?" He stiffened, and Alice immediately regretted her words. "Just a kiss on the cheek," she said with forced cheer. "Right here." She dimpled her cheeks and pressed an index finger into the small indent.

Henderson took a step toward her and she held her breath. Slowly he brought one hand up, index finger extended. He hesitated before placing the pad of his finger gently against her lower lip. Alice looked up into his eyes, but he was concentrating on where he pressed that finger against her, his eyes dark and hooded. "Or I could kiss you here. Now."

Alice swallowed. "Henny," she whispered.

He drew her lip slowly down, his body so close to her she could feel the heat of him, feel his light, brandy-tinged breath against her face. His expression grew hard, the muscles along his jaw bunching, and Alice swore she'd never seen him look so handsome. Her body swayed slightly, bringing them closer, putting a bit more pressure on her lip, and the very tip of his finger slipped into her mouth. Alice couldn't have said why, but she touched her tongue against his flesh, and he drew in a quick, harsh breath. "God, Alice."

He slowly trailed that finger from her lip, down her chin and to her sensitive neck, stopping at the white lace of her nightgown. For one breathless moment she thought he would push further, but instead he brought his hand behind her neck and pulled her toward him until their lips were nearly touching. And then he was kissing her, tasting her, and Alice brought her hands up to his shoulders, clinging, for she wasn't certain her legs could hold her. His breathing was harsh against her cheek and it seemed as though every inch of her body was filled with the need for something she didn't fully understand. She only knew she wanted more and more and more. Her breasts ached, and it felt so good to press against him, to relieve some of the tension that was building. When his hand moved from her back to brush lightly against one breast, she moaned and he deepened the kiss. Lost was any cognizant thought that what they were doing was wrong. The only thing she could think was *Yes, this is what I want. This is how I want to feel.*

He pulled at her erect nipple, and Alice felt a flood of heat and warmth between her legs. His clever tongue began a subtle rhythm against her own. It seemed the most natural thing in the world to press her center against the hard ridge of his arousal, seeking to take away the edge of her desire, to do something to give her body relief. And so when he abruptly pulled away, stepping back four full paces, she stumbled toward him before she realized with every step she took, he retreated.

"Alice, if we don't stop now, I don't know if I'll be able," Henderson said harshly.

"I'm sorry."

He shook his head. "No, don't be. This was my fault. I should have just gone upstairs and gone to bed. I knew... I knew I shouldn't have kissed you."

"Why?"

Henderson dipped his head and stared at the floor. "I have no right to touch you, not like that."

* * *

At breakfast the next morning, Henderson found he could hardly look at Alice. He feared everyone at the table, including Mrs. Hubbard, would know he was thinking not so pure thoughts about the elder Hubbard daughter. It was difficult enough to hide his love for Alice; he would likely be even less adept at hiding his lust. He was thankful, then, when a footman quietly delivered a note scrawled on thick vellum bearing the Berkley crest. Saying a silent prayer, he opened the note and smiled grimly. The new Lord Berkley would see him that afternoon. If the meeting was successful, something he had little hope for, he would work with Berkley to gather more support. If it was not, Henderson had no idea what he would do. Without someone like Berkley behind him, he had little influence over the great men who could make a difference. He knew he'd been lucky even to gain an audience with all eight men on his list.

"Good news, I hope," Elda said, before taking a sip of their very fine tea.

"Indeed it is, Mrs. Hubbard. I have gained an audience with the new Lord Berkley."

"Ah. Alice did mention something about him being at Costille. Of course I knew the old earl quite well, but his son is a stranger to me. He hasn't been in St. Ives in years, from what I gather."

Christina put her fork down, and Henderson had a feeling she was about to impart some great gossip. "Isn't he the one who murdered his wife? Threw her from the castle's tower?" Her eyes lit up as if murder were the most wonderful breakfast topic.

"Christina, really," Elda said, frowning heavily at her younger daughter, who had the good grace to dip her head, though Henderson had a feeling she didn't feel particularly contrite about spreading such gossip.

"The truth of the matter is," Elda said, sliding her gaze to Henderson, "that his wife did die from a fall during a house party. Several witnesses vouched that Lord Berkley was in an entirely different part of the castle when she died."

"Suicide." This quiet and devastating word came from Alice, said more into her plate than to anyone at the table. She lifted her head, and a slight tinge of red marred her pale cheeks, as if she hadn't meant for everyone at the table to hear her. "They said it was suicide."

Elda shook her head. "That is not something to be repeated, Alice. The magistrate declared her death a terrible accident. Suicide. Better to be a murder than that."

Henderson cleared his throat. "At any rate, I'm meeting the man this afternoon to discuss famine relief. Do you know when the old Lord Berkley died? The butler at Cavendish Square wore a black band but I saw no other evidence of mourning at the London house. When I went to Costille, however, it was shrouded."

"I didn't know he had passed until we arrived here," Elda said. "I imagine it must have been fairly recent, though, for I don't recall reading about his death in the *Times* when we were in London. I would have said something to you when I saw your list. I fear you'll find little help in that quarter, Mr. Southwell. Lord Berkley has not been involved in politics at all; that was his father's domain. From what I gather, he has spent a great deal of time in America. Chasing cows, I think. He was a bit of a ne'er do well, an embarrassment to the old earl." Elda tsked softly as she spread marmalade on her scone.

Deeply discouraged by Lady Hubbard's words, Henderson wondered if he should keep his appointment. Even if the new Lord Berkley was amenable to trying to help, what sort of influence could he possibly have on the men who made decisions about famine relief?

* * *

"They say he murdered her and that the only people who could vouch for his whereabouts were his closest friends. The old Lord Berkley never got over the scandal of it and some say it killed him."

Sometimes when Harriet spoke so melodramatically about a murder, it was difficult for one not to roll one's eyes, Alice thought. The four of them—herself, Harriet, Eliza and Rebecca—were all together for the first time since Alice's return from London. It was so good to see them all, to gossip as they always had, to laugh. No one could brighten her day the way her friends did, and she'd missed them all dearly when she was in London. They pretended to meet to knit together, but the true purpose of their gatherings was to gossip. Harriet had it down to an art form and often led the discussion as she was this day. That's why it was so difficult to understand how someone so lively could become so subdued in social situations.

"Why would he murder her?" Eliza asked, her pale blue eyes wide. She tucked a stray curl behind her ear, a habit encouraged by the fact her wildly curly hair was often coming unsprung from whatever hairstyle her maid had attempted that day. "One must always have a motive."

Harriet shrugged. "I haven't heard anything that would inspire murder. Still."

"Still what?" Alice asked on a laugh. "Still it wouldn't be nearly as entertaining to talk about Lord Berkley if he wasn't a murderer?"

Harriet made a face, but said, "Of course."

"Didn't you tour Costille once, Harriet?" Rebecca asked. "Did you see the tower where it happened?"

Harriet nodded. She was in her element, and Alice settled in to hear a detailed accounting of the home where Lord Berkley resided. Harriet had an uncanny memory, like nothing Alice had ever witnessed before. If she saw it, read it, heard it, she remembered each detail so well, Alice had long stopped questioning her.

"We only toured the public part of the house, of course, but the Lawton family has maintained it wonderfully. We were even able to explore the dovecote, though they don't use it as such now, just back in the fifteen hundreds. Can you imagine something three centuries old?"

Eliza shuddered. "I shouldn't like to live in such an old place. Imagine all the ghosts that must be wandering about."

"Including his dead wife," Rebecca said, her brown eyes twinkling.

"Stop it, all of you," Alice said, laughing.

"You must admit, it is rather exciting that Lord Berkley is back after all these years," Harriet said. "The old lord was such a stodgy curmudgeon."

"Who's to say the new lord isn't much the same?" Alice asked. "At any rate, I hope he is not a maniac, for Mr. Southwell is on his way there today."

Harriet lifted her head at the news Henderson was in St. Ives, and Alice made an effort to keep her expression bland, even as she felt her cheeks blush remembering their kiss. Her breasts suddenly felt heavy, her nipples *ached*, and only because he was the topic of conversation. What was wrong with her?

"Mr. Southwell is in St. Ives?"

"Here we go again," Rebecca said, pressing her lips together in an obvious attempt not to laugh aloud. "You're not going to make a cake of yourself again, are you, Harriet?"

Harriet sniffed. "I was but a girl with a silly crush and can be forgiven for falling for a handsome young man. And of course I'm going to make a cake of myself. Why wouldn't I? I'm certain he would be sorely disappointed if I did not."

Alice laughed. "Henderson is not quite the flirt he was when you all last saw him. He's grown up a bit himself. He's far more serious now than he was before. In fact, the entire reason he is in St. Ives is to solicit assistance in raising awareness of the famine in India. He's quite passionate about it."

"You mean to say he's not here to see me?" Harriet asked in mock despair.

"Alas, the only reason he is in St. Ives at all is because this is where Lord Berkley is at the moment. I daresay he'd already be on his way back to India had he concluded his business in London."

Conversation lulled for a time, and the room was silent but for the clicking of their needles.

"I always thought he might have a tender for you, Alice." This from Eliza, whose quiet nature hid a sharp intelligence.

Alice let out a forced laugh, that thankfully sounded as if it were filled with genuine amusement. "Did you? Why ever would you say such a thing? I can assure you, Henderson thought of me, when he did, as an annoying little sister."

The needles clacked, but Alice could tell the others were waiting to hear why Eliza thought Henderson might have romantic feelings toward her.

"Do you remember the Smythe ball?"

Alice wrinkled her brow, trying to think back on that event nearly five years prior. She could remember nothing unusual that had happened. She couldn't even recall whether Henderson had danced with her that night, as he often did. Joseph was always making certain his friends asked her to dance, even though she'd hardly been a wallflower. "I suppose I remember it. It was like any other ball, was it not?"

"You were dancing with William Powers. The waltz. I was at the refreshment table with my mother, and I happened to look out to see you dancing with him. And then I saw Henderson. He was looking at you, too, and I shall never forget the look on his face. It was...singular."

Harriet raised an eyebrow. "Singular? Yes, I can see how you would immediately believe Henderson was in love with Alice. Really, Eliza."

Eliza pursed her lips together, obviously annoyed by Harriet's dismissal. Of all her friends, Eliza and Harriet were the least friendly to one another. Alice wondered if Harriet was actually jealous of whatever imagined look Henderson had given her. Did she actually believe herself in love with Henderson? Alice had always thought it had been a lark, a silly game, not something that involved any true feelings for him.

"Yes, Harriet, singular. It was despair and longing and fierce joy, all wrapped into that one *singular* expression," Eliza said bitingly.

Despite her vow to remain uninvolved, Alice felt her cheeks heat.

"Are you certain it wasn't indigestion?" Rebecca asked, sounding for all the world as if this was a serious inquiry. Rebecca was like that. One could overlook her, as she wasn't much of a chatterbox, but when she did speak, she was often remarkably funny.

"Quite certain," Eliza said, laughing. "At any rate, that look stayed with me." She shrugged delicately.

"I'm sure you were mistaken," Alice said. "I'd know, wouldn't I, if Mr. Southwell was in love with me? I can assure you, he was not. I think poor Mr. Southwell would be mortified by this conversation."

"Yes, we've much more important things to discuss," Harriet said, giving Alice a quelling glance. "Such as why on earth Lord Northrup is even at this moment gallivanting off to Scotland, free as a bird, when I daresay he should be strung up somewhere, perhaps dangling over a pit of venomous snakes."

"Harriet," Alice said with a note of warning.

"We are all just worried about you," Eliza said, putting aside her knitting and any pretense that the girls were there for any reason other than to find out about Lord Northrup. No doubt her three friends had already convened and discussed in detail how the events had transpired.

"There is no need for your worry. I am perfectly well and quite content to be back in St. Ives where I belong." Her friends all looked doubtful, and Alice didn't know what she could possibly do to convince them otherwise. "Truly."

"Have you heard from him?" Eliza asked softly, as if the words would somehow hurt her.

"No," Alice said, trying to keep any emotion from her voice. While she hadn't loved Lord Northrup, she had been quite fond of him, and the fact he hadn't even bothered to write her a note of apology or explanation did hurt. It was almost as if he hadn't liked her at all, that his claims of love—and he did claim to love her more than once—were completely untrue. "And I don't wish to hear from him," she lied. All three friends stared at her, clearly not believing her.

"Oh, very well. Yes. I am bothered that he hasn't written. Are you all happy?"

"Of course not," Eliza said. "We're just worried."

"One would think you'd all be used to this by now," Alice said, trying at humor. "The Bad Luck Bride strikes again." Her friends didn't laugh, and Alice let out a long sigh. "Would it make you all happy if I were to start weeping?"

"Yes," Rebecca said.

Alice shot her friend a withering look. "All right then," she said. "Boo hoo. Sob. Sniff, sniff. There, are you satisfied?"

They all laughed.

"I was upset, but I'm perfectly well now. If Lord Northrup walked through that door right now, I wouldn't even rise to greet him. My heart would not pick up a beat. My cheeks would not turn red."

"Did that ever happen?" Eliza asked.

"Yes," Alice said. But she didn't say that all those things happened when another man entirely walked in the room.

* * *

Most of Costille Castle had been built in the early seventeen hundreds, though the remnants of the original castle, a monstrous tower that seemed completely out of place in the Tudor style manse that was built around it, rose above the stone and granite, a monument to power if not grace. Henderson walked through the smaller of two towers, its stone arch unchanged in three centuries, and into a courtyard now surrounded by the more modern home. Though "modern" was not a word most would use to describe the ancient architecture. Mullioned windows, narrow and tall, had been carved into the great slabs of stone. High above, he could see the top of the main tower, and it was easy to imagine archers standing at the ready, guarding the castle from marauders.

Henderson walked to a massive oak door, its hinges made of thick iron, and pulled back on a knocker in the shape of a steed's head. Letting it drop, Henderson couldn't help but smile at the loud, echoing sound that could no doubt be heard throughout much of the house. What a marvelous place this was, he thought, looking down at the granite beneath his feet, slightly worn by centuries of footsteps. His grandfather's home was newly built, and while a grand place, it didn't hold the tangible history of this keep.

The heavy door swung open, revealing a butler with a rich shock of white hair gleaming in the shadows of the entryway.

"Mr. Southwell here to see Lord Berkley. I have an appointment." He handed over his card, which the butler took before backing up and allowing him entry. Henderson stepped into the cool interior, marveling at the thickness of the ancient walls, and stopped dead. The inside of Costille was completely unexpected. What he had expected was ancient splendor but what he saw was modern and extremely feminine furnishing. The walls were covered with flowered wallpaper, the floors were a pinkish Italian marble, the ceiling heavily carved and ornate with gold leaf accents. Everywhere he looked were embellishments and color—pink, yellow, red—a cacophony of floral décor. It was almost as if someone had gone into a hothouse, gathered up all the petals of all the flowers within, and thrown them into the air. As he followed the butler down the wood-paneled hall, he took in the ornately etched gas light fixtures, the frescoed ceiling depicting little cherubs flying in and out of puffy clouds, and was, frankly, baffled by what had been done to the old place. It resembled more of a brand new, and rather tacky, hotel than an ancient medieval keep.

The butler opened the door to a similarly decorated study, where the new Lord Berkley sat on a pink-cushioned chair behind a gold leaf desk carved with cabbage flowers. Berkley stood as Henderson entered, and his first impression of the man was that he did not fit his surroundings. He was big and burly, with hard chiseled features and dark gray eyes that one could only describe as menacing.

"Lord Berkley, a pleasure," Henderson said, looking around the room. "Interesting décor."

Lord Berkley smiled grimly. "A gift from my late wife." The irony in his tone was nearly palpable. From his tone, Henderson had a feeling it was not a welcome gift. "How can I help you, Mr. Southwell?"

"I'm not certain you can," Henderson said. "For the past four years I've been living in India, working for the sanitary commission in Madras. You are aware of the famine there?"

Berkley nodded. "I am."

As responses went, it was not the most promising answer, but something in the earl's manner gave Henderson a glimmer of hope that he'd finally found a reasonable man. From experience, Henderson had learned that glimmer could quickly be doused with a single derisive word, so he went forward with caution, gauging the other man's reaction.

"I've been back in England for nearly a month in an attempt to garner support for famine relief efforts. There has been some support, of course, but we've met with resistance from many."

Berkley tilted his head. "Why is that?"

"A variety of reasons, the largest one being the fear that the citizenry will become dependent upon handouts and will not be self-sufficient once the famine is over."

"A sound argument."

The glimmer of hope flickered like a candle in a drafty hall. "Perhaps. But the enormity of the problem makes it inhumane to ignore India's plight." Taking a bracing breath, Henderson repeated the words he'd said so many times to so many other men. The railroads, the stockpiles, the slow deaths, the children. Through his entire speech, Berkley was silent, showing little emotion, and even less interest.

Finally, feeling desperation growing, Henderson drew out his photographs and placed them with near reluctance in front of the earl. Berkley took them up, flipping through them one at a time, studying them, his face impassive. Henderson tried to read something in the man's dark eyes, but he could not. Not disgust. Not compassion. Not even curiosity. When he was done, Berkley handed the photographs to him, holding back one and laying it on his desk facing Henderson. It was a picture of a small child, lying dead in the street. Next to the child lay a dog, sleeping.

"Why is the dog so well fed? Do these people feed their animals instead of their children?"

Henderson's gaze took in the stark scene, and he clenched his jaw briefly. "The dogs, my lord, feed on the corpses of the dead." He felt the bile rise to his throat as one such horrific memory came to vivid life in his mind.

"My God." And then the most remarkable thing happened. Though Berkley's expression hardly changed, his eyes filled, and he swallowed heavily. He pushed the photograph toward Henderson with the tips of his fingers. "And no one you've seen has agreed to help?"

"No. I think part of it is that these people are seen as not quite human. The pictures I think dehumanize them, but I wanted to show the extent of the suffering. Words do little, but to see the families, the children. I thought it would move people to action, but all it has done is create disgust. I'm afraid I have failed in my mission because I failed to adequately explain what has happened. I've seen these people in real life. These are good people. They are poor and uneducated and difficult to look at."

"And they are not British." Berkley let out an angry puff of air. "My father would have felt very much the same as I. He was a great persuader, a force in the House of Lords at a time when that institution holds little power. I, on the other hand, am unknown. I have not taken up my father's seat. Rather daunting task, actually. As much as I would like to help, and I will do what I can, I fear I will have little influence."

Henderson smiled. "But you will try?"

"I will," Berkley said with a hard jerk of his head. "You're bloody right I will."

* * *

The next evening, the women were gathered in the parlor again, her mother knitting, and Alice and Christina playing Pinochle. Henderson had been gone all day, leaving Alice on pins and needle, not knowing when he would return or how he would act. She did know one thing: There could be no more kissing. She'd hardly slept at all and felt as if she were crawling out of her skin all day, an uncommon sensation she had no idea how to stop.

"Kings around," Christina said excitedly, placing four kings down triumphantly on the table.

Christina was winning—again—and Alice made a face at her sister, which only made Christina laugh. A loud, excited barking drew their attention away from the game, and the ladies all stood, smiles on their faces. The sound of Cleo's bark could mean only one thing: Richard was home. Sure enough, her father burst through the parlor door, Cleo bouncing in behind him and going to each woman for a quick hello before throwing himself next to Richard and leaning against his leg.

"My dears, just look who I have brought with me." Richard turned, his arm extended, and Alice wondered if her father had met Henderson in the village. But it wasn't Henderson at all.

It was Harvey Reginald Heddingford III, Viscount Northrup, Alice's missing fiancé.

Chapter 9

Shock could not come close to describing what Alice felt, staring at Lord Northrup, who stood there looking uncertain with a small, hopeful smile on his face.

"Richard, how could you?" Elda said, finally breaking the silence.

Richard held his hands out in supplication. "Now, now, Elda, there is an explanation. One that I found quite satisfactory, though I do not believe this man handled the situation as well as he could have." Her father gave Northrup a quelling look.

"No, sir, I did not." Lord Northrup turned to Alice. "I cannot express to you how very sorry I am that you were put through the disgrace of my having missed our wedding. But I want you to know that circumstances prevented me from appearing."

"You don't look dead," Alice said, her eyes narrowed. "Father, is this a ghost you have brought with you?"

Richard pressed his lips together in an obvious attempt not to laugh aloud at Alice's question, then gave his daughter a chastising look.

"You should know there are very few things that could have kept me from the church that day."

"You were tied up? Gagged? Unable to write? I daresay those are the only reasons I can think of for not only missing our wedding but also not contacting me and begging my forgiveness immediately. If you don't mind, I've developed a terrible headache." Alice looked around the room to gauge the others' reactions to Northrup's appearance, but her mother and Christina looked just as confused as she felt. "I believe I shall retire."

"Alice," her father said sharply. "You will hear this young man out."

Alice straightened, her eyes flashing. "Will I."

"Yes," Richard said with a snap of his head.

"Mama, this is outrageous."

Elda glanced from Alice to her husband to Lord Northrup, who still stood in the doorway, looking hopeful and uncertain. "Very well. Alice, hear Lord Northrup out. And then he can remove himself from this house."

"Yes, ma'am," Northrup said.

Everyone filed out of the room, and as Christina passed, she gave Alice's hand a squeeze.

She simply could not believe that Lord Northrup had the audacity to show his face to her and that her father had allowed it. Alice sat and stared stonily in front of her, her face set, her hands clenched tightly in her lap.

"You have every reason to be angry with me."

"Yes, I do," Alice said, finally looking at the man she'd thought would be her husband. She'd thought he was handsome and charming, but looking at him now, he appeared pale and small and not nearly as good looking as she remembered. His eyes were a dull brown, his chin was weak, his shoulders drooping and not even his outrageously expensive clothes helped him. He sat across from her, and Alice noted his knees were bony. In fact, nothing about him appealed to her, that's how angry she was, for Lord Northrup was actually a fair looking fellow—at least that's what she'd once thought.

"Mine is a terrible story and one that I hope will sway you to forgive me. And perhaps lead us toward a happier ending." He had that hopeful smile on this face again, and Alice had the terrible urge to slap him. She had her own terrible story to tell, one that began the moment the vicar made his way slowly to the back of the church to tell her there would be no wedding that day.

Alice simply glared at him, and he shifted in his seat, clearly uncomfortable. This was an Alice he had never seen before, one who was unsmiling and rigid. Perhaps he had thought she would be so grateful to see him she would forgive him instantly. He could not be more wrong, Alice thought to herself, looking at him with no small amount of distaste. Had he no idea what he had done to her? How he had ruined her life and taken away all hope of having a family and home of her own?

"You are familiar with Lester Flemings, Lord Porter."

"I am. He is Patricia Flemings's brother." The very same Patricia Flemings Lord Northrup was purported to be in love with. For a brief moment, Alice drew her brows together. She'd thought Northrup had run away and married Patricia. Obviously, she was wrong on that account.

"Porter approached me with some information about Suzy." He closed his eyes as if speaking of this information was painful to discuss. Northrup adored his younger sister and Alice knew he would move mountains in an effort to please her. Suzy was a spoiled little thing whose every whim Northrup indulged. "Our families have been close, so I had no reason to doubt him and later found what he told me was the truth. I won't bore you with the details, but suffice it to say that the information Porter had would have ruined Suzy's life." He pressed his lips together, clearly distressed. "He threatened to expose Suzy unless I agreed to marry his sister, Patricia, who had troubles of her own."

"What sort of troubles?"

"The sort that require a husband," Northrup said darkly. "At any rate, I agreed. Stupidly, I know. Porter made me swear not to say a word. He wanted everyone to believe I was in love with Patricia and forbade me to warn you about our elopement."

Even though Alice was livid, hearing those words caused the blood to drain from her head. "So you did marry her," she said softly.

"No, I did not."

"I don't understand."

Lord Northrup moved over to where she sat and knelt beside her, taking one cold hand in his. "You know I would do anything to protect Suzy. She's my sister. I was half mad knowing what you were going through and unable to do anything to stop it. You must understand, Suzy's life would have been ruined, any hope she had of marrying would have been completely eliminated. I could not let that happen. I had to choose, darling. I had to and it was the most difficult decision of my entire life."

Alice hated that she understood, for she would have done the same if Christina's life had hung in the balance. Still, it had been weeks since their planned wedding and she hadn't had a single word from him.

"Why are you here now? What happened?"

Tears filled Northrup's eyes, and despite herself, Alice felt pity for him. She had been fond of him, after all, and it wasn't easy to see him so distraught.

"It was all for nothing. You see, Porter was going to expose Suzy's affair with the piano master. I don't know how he found out, but Suzy didn't deny it." He closed his eyes briefly, forcing the tears down his cheek. "She ran off and married him. Suzy eloped with the bloody piano master."

"Oh my goodness, my lord, no." It was terrible news indeed, and despite everything, Alice knew how tragic such an event would be to his family. "When?"

"The day you and I were to be married. I found out that night, thankfully before I hied off to Scotland with Miss Flemings. You cannot know what I've gone through since the day Lord Porter came to see me. It was torture."

No wonder Northrup had acted so strangely the night before their planned wedding. "And it's taken you all this time to come forward?" Northrup dipped his head. "I was horrified by it all. My parents wanted to keep what Suzy had done a secret for as long as possible. All her friends believe she is visiting our aunt in Brighton. My father forbade me to tell anyone until we were certain the wedding had taken place. He went after them, but it was too late. It's destroyed him, our entire family. I still cannot believe Suzy would be so foolish. I know you must hate me and I know I have no right to ask your forgiveness."

"But you are here to ask it anyway, aren't you?" Alice said, her tone softer.

He lifted his head and looked at her beseechingly. "I have only the smallest of hopes that you will forgive me. Dear Alice, I have missed you."

"I don't hate you," Alice said, gazing at their still-entwined hands.

"Then dare I hope that you can forgive me? That perhaps we can start anew?"

Alice looked at the man she'd planned to marry and felt nothing. Not even that small admiration and affection she'd once held for him. But her father was correct. Lord Northrup's story was terrible and believable and she sincerely trusted that he regretted what had happened. It had only been three weeks since she'd stood at the church in her wedding gown, her stomach all aflutter, looking forward to a life with this man. Could she throw away the only future she had?

Unbidden, thoughts of Henderson, his kiss, made Alice even more uncertain. But Henderson hadn't pledged his love or devotion. He really hadn't done anything other than kiss her and make her feel things she'd never felt before in her life. Certainly, he hadn't asked to marry her or requested an audience with her father. And he'd said more than once that kissing her was a mistake. A very stupid and silly mistake, Alice thought, hating that even now, even at this moment when Harvey was kneeling before her with tears falling down his cheeks, all she could think about was Henderson.

Alice forced a small smile. "Perhaps we can."

"Perhaps you can *what?*" Henderson stood at the entrance to the library, looking very much like a man on the verge of violence.

* * *

Henderson had been on his way back to Tregrennar when he'd seen a carriage drive past him, a liver-spotted springer spaniel, tongue lolling happily, hanging out the small window. It could only be Cleo, Richard Hubbard's constant companion, which meant Lord Hubbard was on his way home.

Henderson stopped dead, watching until the carriage was out of sight. This was his chance to speak with Lord Hubbard about marrying Alice, but he hadn't had time to formulate his thoughts. While he knew Lord Hubbard liked him well enough, that didn't mean he wanted a bastard for a son-in-law. What father would? The Hubbards' pedigree was immaculate. Richard was the son of a duke, Elda was the daughter of a marquess. From his experience, sons of dukes and daughters of marquesses did not want their children marrying low-born bastards.

Henderson's sire could be anyone, but was almost certainly not a member of the peerage. His grandparents and mother refused to discuss the matter, and the only thing he did know, from an overheard conversation when he was ten years old, was that the man was a laborer. Henderson still remembered the distaste in his grandmother's voice when she mentioned his father. No one loved him more than his grandmother, so to hear her speak ill of whomever had sired him had made Henderson slightly sick to his stomach. Tainted.

His mother, Sylvia, wanted to get rid of him after she pushed him out into the world. She'd made arrangements with a woman who promised to find a good home for the baby. Like a puppy, he was to be given away and never thought of again. To Sylvia, he represented nothing more than a foolish decision that she wished would go away. It was his grandmother, with her soft heart, who had taken one look at his wrinkled little face and vowed to keep him in their home. His grandmamma simply could not bring herself to take him to the woman or to a foundling home, which was where most bastard children ended up. Henderson had learned much about his early years from loyal servants who adored his grandmother and had a less than favorable view of his mother.

Sylvia had refused to look at him, hold him, touch him. If she ever had, Henderson had no memory of it. When he was a boy, he was not allowed to eat with the family and was instead fed in either the kitchens or his small room on the third floor, as far away from his mother as possible. If she did refer to him, which was infrequent, she called him "that thing."

"That thing trampled on my flowers this morning." He'd been ten, old enough to realize who he was, who she was. Other mothers were kind. They laid their hands atop their children's heads and ruffled their hair. They embraced them when they were hurt. They did not call their children things.

"I'm not a thing," he'd said, his cheeks burning hotly. "I'm your son." She'd wheeled around, her face filled with rage, and slapped him. "You are not my son."

After she'd stormed off, his grandmother had drawn him into a warm hug and held him, reassuring him that he was not a thing, that he was a fine little boy whom she loved with all her heart. Henderson had been comforted by her words, but the terrible hurt that his mother didn't love him, and indeed loathed him, never truly went away.

* * *

As he walked slowly toward Tregrennar, rehearsing in his head what he would say to Lord Hubbard, the circumstances of his birth loomed large. The Hubbards did not put on airs, but how would they feel about a son-in-law who didn't have an ounce of blue blood running through his veins? Not only that, but a man who was born from sin? Giving his head a hard shake, Henderson tried to put such doubts from his mind. The Hubbards thought of him as a son. Hadn't Mrs. Hubbard said just yesterday that everyone in the family loved him? Surely they would welcome him as a true member of their family.

The house was silent when he entered, and a light shining in the parlor told him the ladies of the house and perhaps Lord Hubbard were likely there spending a quiet evening. The door to the parlor was ajar, and he walked in without a thought. Certainly without a thought of what he might find on the other side: A man on bended knee, Alice looking at the gentleman, her eyes soft. And the words she spoke that felt like a shot to his heart: *Perhaps we can.*

"Perhaps we can *what*?" The two separated guiltily, and that's when Henderson recognized the chap who'd been holding his future wife's hand in his. Lord Northrup. "What the bloody hell is he doing here?"

"Henderson, please."

Lord Northrup stood, stepping slightly in front of Alice as if he were protecting her, which only caused Henderson's blood to run hotter. "Who is this man?" Northrup asked, looking him over as if he were in laborer's garb and not wearing a finely cut suit.

"This is Henderson Southwell," Alice said. "I believe I've mentioned him. Joseph's friend."

"Ah, yes. The charity case," Northrup drawled.

"I never implied such a thing and you know it," Alice said, glaring at the viscount.

"Very well," Northrup said easily. "My apologies. I thought I was being kind in my description, given he stands before us looking as if he would like to commit murder." Northrup raised one eyebrow, all charm, as if he hadn't a care that Henderson itched to pummel the man within an inch of his life. Something dark and primitive had uncoiled inside Henderson when he saw the other man touching Alice.

Henderson looked from one to the other, hating that he suddenly felt like an outsider. It seemed obvious that Alice had told Northrup more about him than he cared for the man to know; it put him at a severe disadvantage. "I asked a question," he said, directing his attention to Alice, his voice softening only slightly. "What is he doing here?"

Alice opened her mouth to answer, but Northrup spoke. "Not that it's any of your business, Mr. Southwell, but I am here making amends with my fiancée."

"She's not your bloody fiancée."

Northrup breathed in sharply through his nose. "You should address your betters in a more civilized manner, Southwell. If it's possible," Northrup said, and Henderson had to use all his self-control not to launch himself at the pompous ass.

"For goodness sake, will you two stop?" Alice said, though she directed her question to Northrup, which felt like a minor victory to Henderson.

"Alice, what is the meaning of this?" Henderson asked, choosing to ignore the foppish fool standing in front of Alice. "This man left you standing in the church. He has no right to touch you, to even be in the same room as you. Is your father aware of this?"

"Lord Hubbard brought me here, fully knowing my intent," Northrup said with annoying smugness.

Henderson felt the blood drain away from his head, and for a terrible moment, he thought he might sway on his feet. "Is this true, Alice?" he asked, knowing his voice sounded odd and raspy.

"Yes, Mr. Southwell, it is." Of course, calling him Mr. Southwell was only proper, but hearing her say it, her tone so damned cold, made Henderson's chest ache.

"But surely you have not forgiven what he did." Alice stood, and Henderson watched in disbelief as she slowly brought her hand up to rest on Lord Northrup's arm. He swallowed heavily. "I don't believe it. You cannot be serious. You cannot be so foolish as to forgive this man—"

"There were circumstances," Alice said.

"Circumstances?" he shouted. "*Circumstances*?"

"My dear, I fail to understand why you are even engaging in conversation with his man. In fact, what is he even doing in your home?" Northrup looked at him as if he were a mangy dog that had somehow found its way into Tregrennar.

"What is all this ruckus?" Lord Hubbard came through the door looking more than annoyed.

"This man insulted me," Lord Northrup said. "And is upsetting your daughter."

Richard looked at Henderson, his brows furrowed. "What *are* you doing here, Mr. Southwell? I understood you had no plans to come to St. Ives." His tone was biting, all aristocrat, and even though Henderson had known Richard Hubbard for years, he had never heard that tone directed at him.

For the first time in his life, Henderson felt like an outsider in the one of the few places in England where he had always felt welcome.

"Mama insisted that he stay here while he was in St. Ives, Papa. Lord Northrup was unaware of this and has been quite unkind," Alice said, giving Northrup a pointed look. Her defense of him somehow made things worse. He felt as if he were exactly what Northrup had called him—a charity case. To think he had walked to Tregrennar thinking he would ask Lord Hubbard for his daughter's hand. My God, what a bloody idiot he was.

"I see. Well. Perhaps now that I am home, his presence is no longer needed."

"Here here," Northrup said, and Henderson didn't miss the glare of anger Alice gave her former fiancé.

"I shall depart in the morning, sir," Henderson said stiffly.

"Oh, Papa, is that really necessary?" Alice asked. "It's *Henderson*."

"It's for the best," Henderson said, looking briefly from Lord Northrup to Alice. "Please do tell your mother thank you for the hospitality. I will leave at first light."

* * *

Alice watched in disbelief as Henderson left the room, fighting the urge to follow him. She whirled on Lord Northrup, angrier than she could ever recall being.

"You were insufferable," she said, and was made angrier still when her father chastised her with a click of his tongue. "Papa, Mr. Southwell is a particular friend of this family and should not be made, ever, to feel unwelcome. He was upset that Lord Northrup was here because he cares for my feelings. Perhaps more than any of you do." Alice could feel hot tears threaten. "You owe him an apology, my lord. And if you cannot bring yourself to do so, I believe any suggestion of reconciliation shall not be considered."

To her surprise, Lord Northrup bowed and said, "Of course, you are correct. I'm afraid I allowed my temper to get the best of me. I say, I didn't like the proprietary way he was looking at you and I fear I let my dander up."

Alice was slightly mollified, but still angry.

"Alice," her father said, using his lesson-teaching tone. "You must realize that most families would not welcome Mr. Southwell into their homes as we have. If it wasn't for Joseph, no one in this house would associate with someone of his class."

Despite the truth of her father's words, Alice was shocked that her father had said them.

"Your family was generous, indeed, to do so," Northrup said.

"It wasn't charity." She looked to her father. "Was it?"

Richard shifted uncomfortably. "Northrup, would you mind allowing me to speak to my daughter in private?"

"Of course. Good evening, sir." He turned to Alice, his brown eyes soft and beseeching. "Please do consider what we discussed, Alice. I will do anything in my power to make you forgive me."

Alice nodded. "I will think about it, my lord, but I cannot make you any promises."

He smiled brilliantly, then gave her father a look that Alice couldn't interpret. "That is all I can ask for. Good evening."

After Northrup left, Alice made her way back to her original seat and lowered herself into it, feeling drained and exhausted. "I'm so confused, Papa."

"Understandable, my dear. It isn't every day an errant fiancé turns up at one's door begging forgiveness."

After a brief and probably unconvincing smile, Alice said, "Yes, but that's not what I meant. I was referring to what you said about Henderson. How you acted. As if he wasn't welcome in our home anymore. I'm certain he was terribly hurt."

Richard let out a heavy sigh before dragging another chair closer to her. "You know I like Henderson, and you are correct, he has always been welcome in our home. But you must understand that if it wasn't for Joseph, someone like Henderson would never have rubbed elbows with our ilk. Think, Alice. We have no idea who his father is. Yes, his grandparents are fine people with a large estate, but they are commoners. Without Joseph's insistence, Mr. Southwell is certainly not the type of man I would associate with. Nor would I want my children to."

"Then why did you allow it?"

"Joseph begged your mother and she finally relented. You know she could never say no to him. We have never regretted the decision. Henderson proved to be a fine young man with impeccable manners."

"But not impeccable bloodlines," Alice said softly.

"It does matter. Blood will tell, you know," Richard said, his tone gentle. "It always did and it always will."

Alice closed her eyes briefly, seeing again the look on Henderson's face when he'd left the room. "I don't believe that," she said finally. "Henderson is one of the finest men I know. I don't give a fig who his father is, and, frankly, Father, I cannot believe you do."

Richard winked at her. "You always call me 'Father' when you are particularly angry."

"Do not patronize me." The tears burned even hotter in her eyes.

"Oh, Alice, you are so young. Someday you'll realize, as Lord Northrup and I do, that nothing good ever comes from mingling with the lower classes. Joseph found out the hard way."

Alice could not stop the horrified gasp that erupted from her. "You cannot possibly believe that Henderson had anything to do with Joseph's death. He wasn't even there that night."

"No, he wasn't. But Henderson was the risk-taker. The clown. The one who would egg Joseph to do things your brother never would have done. He may have acted the gentleman when he was with all of us, but when Joseph and he were alone, they were always up to mischief."

"You're wrong," Alice said, no longer able to stop the tears from falling.

"His first summer here, I caught Mr. Southwell trying to teach Joseph to stand upon a horse and ride it. Apparently, he'd read something about American cowboys doing such a thing and wanted Joseph to try it. My son could have broken his neck. Do you really think Joseph would have taken it in his head to do such a thing if Henderson hadn't come up with the idea?"

Alice had no answer. Her father was probably right—Henderson and Joseph had gotten into all kinds of mischief when they were together. But one could hardly blame Henderson for Joseph's death. It was absurd.

"You seemed so glad to see him in London."

"And I was. Truly. But now…perhaps he's overstayed his welcome."

* * *

That night, Alice lay in bed staring at her canopy and feeling horrid about the evening's events. Frowning, she recalled with a certain amount of dismay how her mother had agreed with her father, that Henderson should go now that Lord Northrup was here, as if Henny might taint his lordship with his presence. Would her father have sent him away if Lord Northrup hadn't accompanied him home? She thought not. It was obvious to Alice that her parents still hoped she would marry Lord Northrup, and she wasn't certain how she felt about that.

"Your father explained things to me, Alice," her mother had said earlier that evening, "and I think it's a blessing, really. He's a very good match, I always thought so. You couldn't hope to do better."

"I suppose not," Alice had said. Lord Northrup, despite his flaws, was a good man. He was a bit of a snob, but what member of the aristocracy was not? From his perspective, Alice had to admit Henderson had seemed a bit overbearing and out of line. Yes, Lord Northrup seemed to be a good match if one was not part of that match. Alice's heart did not speed up when he entered the room, and the thought of kissing him the way Henderson had kissed her made her slightly queasy. While Henderson's kiss… It was magical.

Her chest hurt to know her father would no longer welcome him into their home. Nothing made any sense, not her father welcoming Lord Northrup so easily back into their lives nor pushing Henderson out.

"I might never see him again," she said aloud, and suddenly her eyes filled with tears and spilled over to leave wet spots on either side of her pillow. When Henderson had left before, Alice had always assumed he would return. Someday. Even after years had gone by, she would think of him, think about how lovely it would be when he returned.

Now, though, he would not come to their home in London and he would never set foot in Tregrennar again.

She would never kiss him. Never hold him. Never speak to him.

It was impossible. *Wrong.*

Alice sat up, her breathing harsh, and swiped the tears from her eyes. She had to say good-bye, had to kiss him and hold him and remember how that felt. If she had thought that kiss in the library would be their last, well, she would have taken care to remember every moment, every touch, every sound he made.

She tiptoed to her vanity and held her small clock to the moonlight so she might see the time, smiling when she realized at this late hour of two o'clock, everyone would be abed. She knew where Henderson was, of course, for her mother had put him in the same room where he always stayed.

Alice put on her wrap and opened her door silently, her heart in her throat. *This is wrong.* Ignoring the strident voice in her head that sounded remarkably like her grandmother, the duchess, she moved silently down the hall until she reached Henderson's room. *Sorry, Grandmama, but I have to say good-bye.*

Alice stood outside his door, her bare toes curling into the carpet that lined the hall, her arms down straight and stiff, her fingers waggling in her uncertainty. She would just say good-bye. Perhaps kiss his cheek. A hug might be permissible. After all, this was Henderson, her friend. Her friend who could kiss her and make her knees weak. Oh God. *If you knock, you know what could happen. What you want to happen.*

Alice lifted her hand suddenly, then hesitated, her knuckle just inches from the wood of the door. Then she knocked softly and held her breath.

Chapter 10

Henderson lay in bed, hands tucked beneath his head, and stared at the ceiling, trying to come up with a reason he was still under Tregrennar's roof. A soft breeze, carrying with it the familiar scent of the sea, drifted over his naked torso. This room, so familiar to him, would no longer be his. The cruel thing was that perhaps it had all been an illusion, wishful thinking for the little bastard who had been lucky enough to befriend the grandson of a duke.

He should have left immediately after Lord Hubbard told him to go, but something had stopped him. He was curious.

How was it the man who'd treated him as a son for so many years prior to Joseph's death, who had greeted him so happily not a few weeks prior, had become the cold man he'd seen that evening? It didn't sit well with him at all. Had he done something so terribly wrong by demanding why Lord Northrup was holding Alice's hand on bended knee? How was he to have known Lord Northrup had somehow, miraculously, gotten back into the good graces of the very man who'd wanted to sue him following the jilting?

Unless Henderson always *had* been a charity case.

Henderson remembered a boy from Eton who'd had few friends. Joseph, with his soft heart, had welcomed Paul into their small group, and Henderson had taken his lead and been especially kind to the boy, even though, simply put, Paul was obnoxious. The lad didn't know how to act, was always making awkward jokes that no one thought were funny, or repeating someone else's lines when they'd received a laugh. After a time, Henderson had deeply regretted his kindness, for Paul clung to him, taking his small kindnesses and turning them into something far different in his head. Paul called Henderson his best chum, invited him to his home for Easter break. Henderson was never unkind to Paul, but his friendship was restrained, awkward. *Unwanted.*

Was that how Lord Hubbard felt about him? Had he been tolerated for Joseph's sake and was now the unwanted one?

A small tap on his door shook him away from his thoughts, and he wondered if perhaps Lord Hubbard had come to offer some explanation or an apology. He hastily donned his robe, but instead of finding Lord Hubbard at his door, there stood Alice, dressed in her bloody nightgown and wrap, looking so beautiful his first instinct was to shut the door in her smiling face. His second instinct, though, was far different.

He stepped back, his entire body tense, with one terrible thought: *See what you have done, Lord Hubbard? You have driven your innocent daughter into the arms of a bastard.*

"You shouldn't be here," he said, forcing himself to step deeper into the room. This was a pivotal moment. Should he act the gentleman? Or should he act like the man who lurked inside him, the man with his father's blood coursing through his veins, a man who would take an innocent and walk away forever?

"My father and his lordship were horrid to you this evening and I wanted to apologize," Alice said.

"You could have written me a letter."

"Which, given my past, I would not have sent." She gave him a small smile. "You are right, though. That is not the only reason or even the biggest reason I am here."

Alice moved into the room and walked across to the window, and his chest hurt to see her lovely hair catch the breeze and fly out. He wanted to go up behind her, lay his lips on her neck, wrap his arms around her, let his hands touch her breasts and feel their fullness. He wanted to press his cock against her pretty derrière, let her feel how much he wanted her, let his hand drift between her legs and press and press and move until she was too weak to stand.

"Why are you here, then?" He smiled grimly, hearing how coarse his voice sounded.

She trailed a finger on the window, leaving behind the smallest smudge. "It occurred to me that when you leave tomorrow, it is very likely I shall never see you again." Henderson nodded, even though she was facing away from him. "And never..." She turned, clutching her hands in front of her and looking so very young and innocent, Henderson nearly told her to leave.

But he didn't. He couldn't. My God, he had loved this girl for as long as forever, and she was in his room and he knew what she was saying. Perhaps she didn't realize entirely how dangerous this situation was, but he knew. He knew that when an innocent woman went into a man's room late at night wearing nothing but a gown and wrap, she was not going to leave innocent.

"Never what?" he asked, his voice harsh.

She dipped her head and worried her hands together. "I shall most likely marry Lord Northrup."

He hadn't been expecting that, and whatever ardor he had been feeling, which was quite a lot, was doused, or very nearly so. "Why?"

She blinked, and he realized he'd nearly shouted at her. "Because I was engaged to marry him and my parents are very pleased that he is here, hat in hand. I was supposed to have married him and nothing really has changed. Not his affection for me nor my affection for him."

God, something was squeezing his chest and it hurt like the very devil. "Do you love him?"

Her response was immediate and satisfying. "No, I do not. But I do like and admire him and I daresay I'm not going to have too many more chances at finding a suitable husband." The word suitable seemed to Henderson to hang in the air, a thick, ugly word. She looked at him almost as if she were beseeching him to understand. "I want my own household and a family. I've wanted that for as long as I can remember."

"With whichever titled gentleman offers such a life to you," Henderson said, unwilling to stop the cynicism he felt.

"Yes, I suppose so."

"Then why in hell are you here, with me, wearing nothing but your gown? You do realize it is wrong for you to be here, that if someone were to discover you, the consequences would be more than dire. You do try me, Alice. And I believe you know it."

She had the good grace to blush. "Yes, I know."

Henderson placed his hands on his hips and shook his head. "I believe you should go back to your own bed, Alice. Because if you insist on staying, you'll soon be lying in mine."

* * *

Alice knew what he meant; she was not a total innocent. "I…I just wanted to say good-bye," she said in a small voice, and he dipped his head and let out a long sigh.

"No. You are not a naïve sixteen-year-old anymore, Alice. That is not why you came to my room tonight." Then he furrowed his brow, as uncertainty seemed to strike him. "Is it?"

"No. You're right. I wanted... I should go." Alice, her gaze fixed on the carpet beneath her feet, hurried to his door, giving Henderson a wide berth as she walked by him. With her hand on the doorknob, she hesitated. "I'm so sorry, Henderson. I thought one more kiss. I didn't think past that, truly." She started to heave the door open, but a strong, tanned hand appeared by her face, preventing her from leaving.

She stood still, waiting, feeling the heat of him behind her even though he did not touch her. That hand, splayed wide, his forearm corded with muscle, was not in the least menacing. It was thrilling. For several long moments they stood there like that, silent, and Alice thought she might moan aloud if he did not touch her. She could hear his breaths, almost sense the internal fight within him. She heard him mutter something, deep and low.

With his left hand, he moved her hair, brushing his fingertips gently across her neck, so her blond locks hung down her left side, exposing her neck to the air, to his touch. She shivered and brought in a sharp breath, not daring to say a word lest he stop. Her entire body felt as if it were shimmering on the edge of something wonderful and unknown. When he placed his lips at the crease of her neck, she couldn't help but let out a soft sound. Nothing had prepared her for what the simple touch of a man's mouth on the sensitive skin of her neck could do to her entire body. She sang with it.

Hesitantly, Alice brought up the hand that still clutched the doorknob and wrapped it around his wrist, pulling his arm to her so she could press her cheek against his cool flesh. She wasn't bold enough to turn to face him, so it was the only way she knew to silently tell him, *yes.* A shudder wracked his body, and he drew in a breath, his mouth so close to her ear, the sound seemed unnaturally loud. Every sense was magnified, every touch was new and beautiful and overwhelming.

Henderson move his left hand to her waist, a warm presence and somehow completely familiar. He had never touched her this way, with such deliberate intent. Dragging his hand down, he explored the shape of her derrière, slipped his hand briefly, enticingly, between her legs before bringing his hand back up to rest against her stomach, just below her breasts.

"Tell me to stop," he said harshly in her ear.

She swallowed thickly. "I don't want you to." So soft was her whisper, she wondered at first if he had heard her. Then, he moved his hand up to cup one breast, to drag his thumb over her excruciatingly aching nipple, and she knew he had.

"Ah, Alice, this is so wrong." She let out a small sound of protest. "You know it is. But I can't seem to stop myself. Do you know how much I want you?" She shook her head, unable to speak. Her skin felt heated, strange, as if it craved Henderson's touch the way a flower craves the sunlight. It was too much, somehow, and yet not enough. His hand on her breast; she could not have imagined what that would feel like, how that touch would send spikes of pleasure between her legs, making her move her hips restlessly. He pulled her flush against him, letting out a deep sound that sent a vibration through her body. Even with her limited experience, she knew that he wanted her.

Another ragged breath puffed against her cheek before he took her arms and slowly turned her around to face him. It was almost impossible to look up at him, and her cheeks were aflame.

"I'm not taking your virginity."

She lifted her gaze and looked into those eyes, the color of sea holly, slightly stunned that he would say such a thing. Was that what he thought she wanted? And then another thought: is that why I truly came here? Suddenly, she felt completely out of her element, a little girl pretending to be a woman. Perhaps in the back of her mind that dangerous thought had skittered past her consciousness, that she would give herself to him. But what she truly had wanted was to kiss Henderson, to hold him, and, yes, for him to touch her and make her feel those drugged and thrilling sensations when they kissed.

"I hadn't thought you would," she said, letting out a nervous laugh. "Truly, Henderson, I didn't think at all. You're leaving in the morning and I might never again have a chance to…"

"A chance to what?" he prompted, impatience tinging his words when she remained silent.

"To feel what you make me feel." It was nearly impossible to put into words what she wanted to say, for her experience, even with three fiancés, was limited to a few stolen kisses. No man had come close to making her feel the pleasure Henderson had, and she was fairly certain no one ever would.

He closed his eyes briefly and dropped his hands, stepping back. "I'm no more skilled than most men, Alice. Go to bed."

"Hender—"

"Bloody hell, Alice, you're to marry another man. I'm flattered that you want to experiment with me, the family's charity case, but I would appreciate it if my last night in Tregrennar could be spent in peace."

Tears instantly filled Alice's eyes. "You know that's not what you are, Henny," she said fiercely.

"Do I? I'm not so sure. And here you are, with your fiancé not a few doors away, begging me to kiss you. I'll be damned if I do, Alice."

Alice blinked at his angry words. "That's not how this is at all. It's not. And Lord Northrup is not my fiancé." Tears coursed down her face. "You know I would never..." Her words ended on a sob and she stood there helplessly, feeling cold now that Henderson was no longer touching her.

Henderson shook his head, a helpless gesture, before drawing her into his arms where she promptly wet his robe with her tears.

"It's all right, Alice. It's been a trying day for you."

She nodded and hiccupped. "It has. Most brutally awful. And now you're leaving and I shall never see you again. You're going to In-India and I'll be here..." Her voice trailed off as she realized she would not be in St. Ives. She would be in Manchester with Lord Northrup—if she decided to marry him. Henderson's arms were warm and strong and comforting. There was nothing at all carnal in their embrace as he whispered soothing words and moved his hand up and down her back the way a man soothes a frightened horse. With her hands still clutching the lapel of his robe, Alice stood there and slowly gathered herself together, wishing this moment could last forever.

"Feeling better?" he asked after a time.

She nodded but didn't move away, and he continued to stroke his hand up and down her back, dipping slightly lower each time. She became aware of his manhood growing hard as his hand stroked down to cup her derrière, and her breath quickened slightly. What had been an innocent caress turned slowly more erotic, and Alice closed her eyes to revel in the feelings he was evoking. She became dimly aware that Henderson was slowly lifting the back of her robe and gown, cool air on naked flesh, until her skirts were gathered around her waist. His bare hand, gentle and warm on her bum, was perhaps the most delicious sensation she had ever experienced.

Alice separated the material of Henderson's robe, exposing his chest, and pressed her lips against him, smiling when she heard a harsh intake of breath. He pulled her against him and let out a groan before dipping his head so that he could kiss her. He was not gentle, but Alice didn't care. This was what she'd wanted, this wonderful thrilling feeling. His tongue was hot and insistent, sweeping into her mouth, demanding that she kiss him with the same ardor. Alice was more than happy to comply. With a sound of relief and need, she threw herself into the kiss, reveling in the taste of him, the way his body seemed to enfold her in his embrace. Between her legs, that aching place was wet with need, and she pressed against him, trying to lessen the feeling but only increasing it. Henderson trailed kisses from her mouth to her chin and neck, consuming her, as his hands drifted up her back, beneath her gown, skimming smoothly over her, until she was, except for the gown now gathered above her breasts, completely naked. Cupping one breast, he took her nipple into his mouth, suckling, licking, and Alice let out a sound she hadn't realized she could make. "Oh, yes. Yes."

He moved to the other nipple and did the same, while his other hand teased the abandoned breast.

"Henderson."

He lifted his head, and she prayed she would never forget how he looked at her; it was as if something glowed from within. "Yes, love." She shook her head. She didn't know how to ask for what she needed, wanted. "You want me to stop." It was not a question.

"No. I want…more."

His features relaxed and he smiled. Without breaking eye contact, he moved one hand down her belly, nearer and nearer to where every delicious sensation was centered. Her eyes drifted closed when he reached the apex of her thighs. Suddenly, she was in his arms and in seconds deposited onto his bed with Henderson beside her, his robe fully open now, his manhood clearly visible. Alice dared to look, and was frankly shocked by how large and stiff it was. All the statues she'd ever seen hardly resembled that jutting appendage.

"I'm not taking your virginity, Alice. Though there is nothing more I would like than to be inside you, I cannot."

"I know."

"But I can give you pleasure."

Alice smiled. "You already have."

He shook his head mysteriously. "I have not. But I will."

He lay down beside her and kissed her, deepening the kiss as his hand once again found the place between her legs. Alice had thought she understood what pleasure was until he began to stroke her. "Oh. Oh, goodness." He dipped his head and took one nipple into his mouth, and Alice thought she might shatter. Nothing could have prepared her for the feelings his simple caresses were creating. All she knew was that she wanted more and more and for him to never, ever stop.

"Take me in your hand," Henderson said, his voice low and grating, as if saying those words took the greatest effort. His large hand wrapped around her smaller one and he guided her to his manhood, showing her how to touch him. "Oh, God, Alice." It was quite amazing, she thought, steel covered with a fine silk. When she shyly moved her hand, it seemed to grow harder, and Henderson moaned. "Yes, love."

Again, his hand was between her legs, rubbing that nub she'd had no idea could create such glory. She matched his rhythm, moving her hand in time to his caresses, until she was mindless, until she worked on instinct, unaware of anything but the sensations flowing through her body. And then, the glory, the release, it came and she cried out, her body shaking uncontrollably as wave after wave of pure bliss shot through her. As she slowly returned to normal, Henderson's head nestled next to hers, and a terrible sadness enveloped her.

They would never share this again. This truly was good-bye.

Sadness mingled with shame and guilt. Shame, because she knew what they had done was wrong, perhaps even a sin, although she would be a virgin on her wedding night. Guilt, because her almost-fiancé lay abed in this same wing and here she was, naked, sated, lying next to a man who was not her husband and not her fiancé. And perhaps not even her friend anymore. Her lover? God, that word seemed so sordid.

"I should not have come tonight," she said softly.

"No, you should not have." Even as he said the words, his embrace tightened slightly, and she smiled.

"I should go." She stirred and was slightly disappointed when he turned onto his back, releasing her. In the lamplight, his hair looked almost black, not the rich chocolate she knew it was. A curl fell over his forehead and she fought the urge to sweep it back. Feeling self-conscious, she crossed her arms and hurried to where her nightgown and robe lay on the floor, like discarded virtue. Stepping into a dark corner, and with her back to him, she donned her nightgown and then drew on her robe before turning, only to find Henderson staring at the ceiling, not her.

She stood uncertainly, not knowing what to say or do. If this were truly good-bye, it was a terrible one and not at all what she'd wanted. What had she wanted? Keeping her eyes on him, Alice walked to the edge of the bed furthest from where he lay.

"Good-bye, Henny. That was...was jolly good." She wished the floor would swallow her whole.

"I'm glad I could be of service." Alice's entire body heated at his callous words, and she stepped back when he suddenly turned toward her. "I apologize. That was ill done of me. It has been a trying evening and this...unexpected visit was, well, unexpected."

"I understand."

"I don't think you do, but I'll let it go at that, shall I? Good-bye, little bug. It *was* jolly good."

Alice could feel tears pricking at her eyes. When Henderson had first stayed with them that summer so long ago, she had trailed behind Joseph and him endlessly, until Henderson had turned to her brother and said, "There's a little bug following us, you know." He'd started affectionately calling her "little bug" whenever they were alone, but it was the first time since his return that he'd done so. She smiled, then spun around, fearing she would start crying again—and just look where that had brought her the last time.

* * *

Henderson watched her go, and as the door closed softly behind her, he squeezed his eyes shut and pressed the heels of his hands over them. What the hell had he allowed? Being older, and supposedly a gentleman, Henderson had no business allowing Alice into his room. And yet, when he'd seen her standing there, looking so damned lovely, he let her in. He'd held her, knowing what could come of it. If there was one single thing he could give himself some credit for it was not taking her virginity, though God above knew he'd been tempted.

Alice had been so responsive, so lovely, so everything that he'd dreamt she would be. Would he ever get the sound she made when she found her release out of his head? He thought not. He prayed not. In one quick motion, he sat up and left the bed, grimacing when he saw the proof of his own release on the bed covers. Let the maids think what they wanted; he was quite certain it would not be the first time they'd found such a present in the morning. What they would not find, no matter how early they came to his room, was him. He'd already finished packing the night before. Used to dressing without the help of a valet, though he had to admit it was rather nice when one was available, Henderson dressed quickly, gathered up his satchel, and headed out the door. The rest of his luggage would be sent to the inn later, he knew. The Hubbards' staff was efficient and he had no doubt that by luncheon, he would have all his things delivered.

Henderson made his way down the wooden stairs, his footsteps quiet on the thick carpet runner that ran their length. Slipping out the door, he looked back once, knowing he would never set foot in this grand old house again. For the first time since he'd been brought home with Joseph, he felt unwanted.

* * *

The White Hart Inn was just down the street from a church, and not wanting to disturb the innkeepers at that late—or early—hour, Henderson decided to sit on a bench outside the large stone building. The wide street, divided by a small square, was completely deserted and the village was almost unearthly quiet. Not even the birds had begun their racket of welcoming the dawn. Henderson, his satchel clutched in his hands, leaned his head back against the hard surface of the bench and closed his eyes, trying to shut out the events of the night.

It was a futile exercise. If not for Lord Berkley and his promise to help in the famine efforts, Henderson would have gone directly to the new rail station and waited there for the next available train, and his luggage be damned.

"So, Joseph, what now?"

Henderson let out a humorless laugh, a sharp puff of air that created a plume of vapor in front of him. For a mid-July morning, it was decidedly chilly, though St. Ives never did get very warm. He'd thought, after enduring the oppressive heat of India, that he would never have complained about a chill in the air. This morning, in his foul mood, he felt like complaining about everything.

It was unlikely he would ever see Alice again. Certainly he would never hold her, kiss her, make love to her again. Why had he ever thought he could? He'd known, even as a lad at Eton, when Joseph had invited him to St. Ives for the summer, he'd known even then it was a bad idea. Yet the lure of St. Ives, of being the best friend of a boy whose grandfather was a duke, who promised the best fishing in all of England, had proved too much. He wanted to go back in time, to the room they'd shared at Eton, and tell that boy to go home alone.

* * *

A baker opening up his shop across the street drew Henderson from his memories of the past, and he realized he was famished. Pushing himself off the bench, he made his way across the street just as the eastern sky was beginning to turn a lovely shade of yellow-red and the birds were starting to greet the new day.

A young woman, probably no more than twenty years old, fresh-faced with cheeks rosy from her work, greeted him shyly as he made his way to the counter to peruse the shop's offerings. She wore a white cap on her head and a white apron over a sky blue dress, and it struck Henderson at that moment that this was the type of girl he should set his cap for, a shop girl with lively blue eyes and a neat little braid.

"How can I help you, sir?" she asked, her Cornish accent thick and rather charming.

"A scone, please."

"With marmalade? We make the best, you know."

Henderson gave her a brief smile. "Of course."

"Are you here for the festival?" She tilted her head at him and Henderson had the distinct feeling she was flirting with him. "Oh, no, you're an artist." Yes, flirting, which only made him feel even more depressed, for he was fairly certain had Lord Berkley walked in, she would not have flirted with him. Was it the cut of his clothes? His accent that wasn't purely aristocratic? His manner? What marked him as a commoner, someone this girl felt free to flirt with?

"I'm here on business," he said, his tone more curt than he'd meant it, but bloody hell, it was annoying to him to realize even a simple Cornish girl would recognize his ilk.

And if she did, how had Lord and Lady Hubbard felt when he'd first come to Tregrennar?

Henderson paid for the scone and left, catching himself in the reflection of a nearby shop, still dark and empty at this early hour. Turning away, he went directly to the inn and hoped the proprietors were up and about, for he was in no mood to hang about the street like some sort of vagabond. Even though, considering he had no home and no position, despite his accumulated wealth, that was nearly what he was.

And he'd thought to offer for Alice's hand. A red hot flash of humiliation washed over him, and continued to visit him throughout the day. Restless and bored, he wandered the Island that afternoon, exploring the wild strip of land that had once been separated from the mainland but was now connected by a long, curving spit of earth. Thick walls, remnants of a time when the Cornish Britons had fortified it, seemed to lead to a small building of stone, locked in time, that had once been a lookout used by the coast guard to seek smuggling ships trying to sneak toward shore. The wind tore at his jacket, and it fluttered behind him, audibly snapping in the wind. The sea was rough, sending spray ashore as it crashed into the rocky beach, and he reveled in the icy chill of it. At the far end of the island was a group of artists, tripods set up and fortified with rocks against the wind, who were trying to capture on canvas the violence of the sea and the charming village of St. Ives in the distance.

Seeing them only made him think of Alice, who was an accomplished painter—at least he had always thought so. He wandered to the end, near a great pile of rocks called the Carncrows, trudging along a narrow path, curious to see how well the painters were capturing the tumultuous sea, the way the sun streamed through thickening clouds.

He wasn't paying much attention to the artists themselves, the small group of men and women who had gathered at the very tip of the land, until he heard a distinctive laugh and stiffened. Henderson had never thought himself a lucky man; indeed, many occurrences in his life would make anyone think the opposite. Standing there, amidst the group, was Alice. She was wearing a light blue gown that the wind was plastering against her, revealing her form in such a distinct way, Henderson couldn't help but remember her long, smooth limbs, muscles taut as he pleasured her. Tendrils of hair fought with the wind, whipping around her head, drawing him like the snakes of Medusa. Would he ever be able to look at her without his heart wanting to explode from his chest?

And then he saw Lord Northrup and his step markedly slowed. He recognized two other women, as well, friends of Alice's whom he'd last seen at Joseph's funeral—Harriet and Eliza.

Stopping short, he debated simply turning about and praying no one in the party would recognize him. Luck was not on his side and why should it be?

"Mr. Southwell? Is that you?"

This was a fine kettle of fish. He could hardly pretend not to hear Miss Anderson nor pretend she was mistaken, so he resisted the urge to close his eyes in frustration and instead plastered a wholly unconvincing smile on his face. Though he focused his attention on Harriet, who had ducked her head as if horrified to have called out to him, he could see Alice stiffen and turn slightly away. What must she be thinking? That he'd followed her out here? He was thankful for only one thing, that the red on his cheeks could be blamed on the bracing wind and not his complete humiliation.

"I thought you'd left." This from Lord Northrup, looking just so *excited* to see him.

"I have not concluded my business here," Henderson said.

"What sort of business is that?" Northrup seemed amused that he would have business in St. Ives.

"He's seeking support for famine relief from Lord Berkley," Alice said.

Lord Northrup's brows rose in surprise. "Are you really? How interesting. I hadn't realized Lord Berkley had an interest."

"He hadn't until I visited him," Henderson said with a tight smile.

"Famine is such a dreary topic," interjected the fifth person in their little crowd, a gentleman with a pencil thin mustache who was impeccably clothed despite the wind that tore around them. "Allow me to introduce myself. Frederick St. Claire."

"Henderson Southwell. It is a pleasure meeting you, Mr. St. Claire."

St. Claire looked at him as if mentally determining whether Henderson was worthy of his time, and Henderson could almost picture his surname swirling about the man's head as he searched his memory for a Southwell worth conversing with.

"He was a dear friend of my late brother, Joseph. They went to Eton and Oxford together and Henderson often spent the summers here in St. Ives."

St. Claire shot a quick look to Northrup, and Henderson had the distinct feeling the two had discussed him. "Ah." Such meaning in that small syllable.

To Henderson's surprise, Northrup turned to him and said, "I'd like to know more about your efforts, if you wouldn't mind, Southwell. I've read of the atrocities in the *Times*, of course, but I would like to know what your plans are." And turning to Alice, he said, "You didn't tell me why Mr. Southwell was here, my dear." He shrugged in a self-effacing way. "I suppose you hadn't known about my interest in the famine relief effort."

"No, I hadn't," Alice said, studying Northrup as if she'd never seen him before. And Henderson, rather cynically, wondered if the viscount was simply trying to get into Alice's good graces.

"I do. I've petitioned Lord Lytton myself, not that it did any good. I'm afraid my influence in political matters is quite meager. Berkley's father, on the other hand, had a great deal of clout; his name alone may lend some influence."

Despite himself, Henderson was impressed that Northrup actually knew what he was speaking of, and if he had petitioned Lord Lytton, he was an ally, indeed. "That is my hope, my lord. I would welcome any assistance you can offer. Lord Berkley and I are meeting this evening and I shall let him know we have found another interested party, if you don't mind."

"Of course not. It will be my pleasure."

Henderson was keenly aware of Alice's interest in their conversation, and he hated that she was looking at Northrup with admiration, hated that she was looking at the other man at all, to be honest. He wanted to loathe Northrup, to put him in the category of enemy, but how could he do that now when the fellow had so generously offered to help him when so many men had not?

"Would you two stop talking politics," St. Claire said impatiently. "I need to complete my masterpiece." He held a hand out to a painting, anchored to a sturdy tripod with two iron clamps, that was decidedly not a masterpiece, and the three women giggled, Eliza the loudest of all. "You wound me, ladies. I thought it was a fair rendering."

"Your seagull is rather lovely," Eliza said softly, her cheeks blushing.

"Is that what that thing is in the sky. I thought perhaps it was an oddly shaped cloud," Northrup said, and they all laughed easily.

Henderson began to distinctly feel unwanted, and while the others turned their attention to St. Claire's awful painting, he took the time to look over at what Alice had been working on and was pleased to see hers was quite good.

"What do you think?" she asked quietly, seeing where he was looking. "I'm not nearly as proficient with oils as I am with watercolor."

"I didn't know you were here," Henderson said, his voice low so the others could not hear. "I was walking to forget last night." He searched her face, his eyes drifting down to her plush mouth, and wished they were alone, for the desire to kiss her was nearly overwhelming. The last he'd seen her, she'd been naked, running across the room to gather her night clothes. It had been a glorious sight and one he never wanted to forget, despite his words to the contrary.

A small crease formed between her eyes. "You want to forget when all day I've been praying that I always remember."

With that, she turned away and joined the others, leaving Henderson standing alone. "I'll bid you good day," he said to no one in particular, and only Harriet turned toward him, a distinct look of disappointment on her face. Harriet's family owned a lucrative tin mine, and though her family was wealthy, she was as common as he. A thought occurred to him, a terrible one indeed, that if he were to court Harriet, he would be able to see Alice far more often.

"Good-bye, Mr. Southwell," Harriet said in a rush, her hands twisting nervously. She always had been awkwardly shy, if he recalled. That hopeful look in her eyes made him feel like a complete cad for even thinking of using her to get close to Alice. When she'd been younger, she'd had a terrible crush on him, one he had always been careful not to encourage. "W-will you be attending the festival?"

"Festival?"

Harriet seemed to go mute, so Eliza answered for her. "John Knill. It's this year, you know. And of course my family is holding the traditional ball." She hesitated and looked quickly to Harriet, who stared intently at the ground. "You are invited, of course."

"Yes, do come," Northrup said, smiling easily.

"If you think your mother wouldn't mind," Henderson said, darting a quick glance at Alice to see her reaction, but she'd turned away to work on her painting.

"She would love to have you, I'm sure. Please do."

Henderson smiled. "It would be my pleasure. Thank you. I think now I'll leave you to your paintings," he said, giving St. Claire's a dubious look, which earned him some laughter.

"You must stay," St. Claire said, apparently surprising everyone in the group. "We've an odd number, you see."

If anything, Harriet's stare at the grass below her feet became even more intense, and Alice froze briefly, mid-stroke. That told him two things: She had been listening even though she was pretending to ignore them all, and the thought of him staying affected her. That alone fed the devil inside him.

"Of course, if you'd like." Henderson looked at St. Claire, using all his acting ability not to chuckle at the man's ridiculous mustache. He was reed thin, dressed impeccably from his straw hat (Henderson wondered how the thing was staying on his head in this wind) to his well-shined shoes. Groomed to perfection, the result, Henderson thought, of a well-trained valet who understood his employer's tastes. Northrup was dressed much the same, though he held his hat in his hand in concession to the wind. Henderson, on the other than, had worn an old pair of boots, a pair of trousers that needed a good pressing, and a jacket that had seen better days, the type of ensemble a man throws on when he's going for a bracing walk along the shore alone. And he'd had the practical sense not to struggle with a hat at all. Perhaps impracticality was all that separated the classes, he mused.

St. Claire went back to his painting, and the group stood behind him, giving him friendly advice. Henderson wandered over to watch Alice. It was difficult to see her face, for she wore a wide-brimmed hat tied beneath her chin with a satin ribbon, which still allowed her hair to fly free in the breeze. Her painting was quite good and not at all feminine. Using broad strokes and thickly applied paint, she had created the sort of work that got more beautiful the farther back one stood. Once in a while, she would take a step or two back to see what she had done, and Henderson moved forward, smiling and knowing that the next time she stepped back, she would knock into him. Which she did, letting out a small sound of surprise. She did not step immediately forward, which he had expected her to do, and so he leaned forward, just slightly, and whispered, "I want to taste you."

* * *

Alice stiffened and quickly stepped forward, but when he moved to stand beside her, she tried her best not to let him know she was trying to keep from smiling. She was a bit vexed with him. After her shameful, wonderful, heart-searing good-bye, here he was, flirting outrageously with her. She'd truly thought when she'd walked from his room in the wee hours of the morning—not more than ten hours ago!—that she would never see him again. It had been a grand good-bye, tragic and romantic, and all day she'd been a bit weepy thinking about how she would never again in her life experience such bliss. Here he was, though, standing next to her, looking sinfully handsome and windblown, while the man she might marry was just a few feet away. Good Lord, have mercy.

"Will you please go away?" she asked conversationally.

"Never."

What a thrilling, awful thing for him to say. She couldn't imagine what had gotten into him. Or her, for that matter. Even now, hours after he'd touched her so intimately, she could feel that wonderful sensation between her thighs.

"I thought you'd left St. Ives. That it would be another four years at least until I saw you again."

"Really, Mr. Southwell, must you—" Her sentence was interrupted by a scream, the bloodcurdling type that meant something horrible had happened. Alice half expected to turn and find that one of her friends had fallen into the sea-drenched rocks below them. Instead she turned to see Harriet, her face deathly pale, pointing below her as the others ran toward her.

"My God, it's a body," Northrup said, looking down at the large rocks at the base of the bluff. "A man."

Northrup immediately began a descent, and Henderson followed behind as the three women and St. Claire looked on in shock. Alice had never seen a dead person other than one carefully arranged in a casket, and seeing the pale, unmoving corpse was horrifying. It appeared to be a man, floating face down and nudging up against the rocks with each incoming wave. He was fully dressed, as far as she could tell.

"I do hope it's no one we know," Alice said.

The two men each grabbed an arm and heaved him up onto a large flat rock that sat above the surging sea.

"You might want to look away," Henderson called up to the group standing on the bluff. Harriet and Eliza turned away, but Alice could not, her gaze fixed on the man. He was missing one shoe, his pale foot visible beneath his trousers, and Alice inexplicably felt tears push at her eyes. It was that missing shoe; she couldn't help thinking that the poor man would be sad to know it had been swept away into the sea, and even though she knew it was not possible, she couldn't stop herself from thinking that foot was likely cold.

"I know him," Henderson said, looking sharply up at Alice. "It's Sebastian Turner. I saw him just two nights ago in the village."

"Oh, no. Are you certain?" Alice asked, staring down at the pale and slightly bloated face. It didn't look like Sebastian at all to her.

Henderson hunkered down and studied the man. "Yes. It doesn't appear he has been in the water long. He had a scar on the chin from cricket. A lad was swinging the bat and hit him by mistake. I was there when it happened. It's Sebastian, I'm sure. These are the clothes he was wearing last night. It doesn't make sense. How would he have gotten here?"

Alice put one hand against her mouth as if she could hold in the pain. Sebastian Turner had been one of Joseph's friends, part of a group of young men who were often in their house. It seemed impossible that the lifeless body on the rock was he. He'd had the most infectious laugh.

"Let's get him up, shall we, Mr. Southwell? Then we can fetch the coroner."

The group was silent as they watched Henderson and Northrup struggle to haul the body to the grassy area where they stood. As they grew near, Harriet and Eliza stepped back, and St. Claire moved with them and shielded them from seeing the body. Alice, though, stood there still, watching as Sebastian's hand banged against a rock. "Careful," she said, though she knew it didn't make any difference to the poor man anymore. When the two men settled the body on the grass, Henderson straightened, his eyes still on Sebastian's body. "I don't understand it. How can another one of us have died? Just two days ago, he was telling me he was getting married. I just..." He swallowed heavily, and Alice took a step toward him, thinking to give him comfort, just as Northrup took up her hand.

"Come on now, Alice, this is nothing for a young lady to see," he said kindly as he drew her toward the other women huddled together.

"I knew him too," she said. "He was Joseph's friend. This is horrid. How could it have happened? He was an excellent swimmer. All of them were. They used to go out and ride the surf like seals and swim and swim. I don't understand."

"He may have struck his head and fallen in. I'm sure he didn't suffer, my dear."

Alice took a deep and shaking breath. "I do hope not."

When Alice reached her friends, Harriet drew her in for a welcome embrace. "It's a terrible thing on such a lovely day. Death is always difficult but to have it be someone we know... Who shall tell his parents?"

"I expect the coroner will," Alice said softly. She knew Sebastian's parents vaguely, and wondered if they were already worried about their son.

"Do you think it might have been foul play?" Harriet asked, and immediately snapped her mouth shut as if realizing this was not the time nor place for her love of the macabre. Alice gave her friend a look of exasperation tinged with no small amount of annoyance, and Harriet, in turn, managed to look slightly repentant.

"I'll stay here with him while you go into the village and fetch the coroner," Henderson called.

"Good man," Northrup said, and the oddest expression touched Henderson's face. Alice gave him a long look, and he gazed at her, his eyes bleak, his jaw set. She nodded a good-bye and he dropped his eyes. Alice got the feeling he was sick and tired of good-byes.

* * *

Before returning to the village, the much-subdued group gathered their art supplies. St. Claire grabbed up his painting, and for a moment Alice thought he might fling it into the sea. The fun they'd been having, just feet away from where a man lay dead, seemed somehow obscene.

Alice suppressed a shiver and tried to get the image of Sebastian bobbing in the water from her mind, but it was impossible. Why had she stood there watching? Now she would never get the sight of him out of her head: his pale skin, the blond hair plastered to his head. Sebastian had been a handsome man, jaunty and lively, the one who would laugh at inappropriate moments, the one of them all who seemed to have the most *life* in him. And now he was dead.

"I wish we hadn't come today," she said softly.

Eliza put a hand on her arm. "If we hadn't, he'd still be there. Perhaps he'd never have been discovered and his parents would always wonder. That would have been much worse, don't you think?"

Alice nodded and gave her friend a small smile of thanks. "You're right. I am glad we found him. He wouldn't have liked to have worried his parents." The tears that had been pressing against her eyes threatened to spill over, and Alice lifted her head toward the wind so they would dry before falling.

The group was silent for a long while until Northrup, who had maneuvered to walk beside her, said, "I would like to apologize to you. And I shall also apologize to Mr. Southwell when I see him next. I was unfair to him last night and judged him badly."

Alice smiled up at him. "He is a good man, my lord. I am glad you are able to see that. And it was very kind of you to lend assistance to the famine relief effort. I could tell Mr. Southwell was appreciative."

He smiled, seemingly satisfied with her response, but Alice felt slightly bothered that Northrup was befriending Henderson. Perhaps she was cynical—no doubt she was—but she couldn't help wonder if Northrup was simply saying things he knew would please her so she would forgive him.

"If it pleased you, my dear, I would sail to India myself and feed all the starving."

Alice laughed. "No need for that, sir."

"I want you to know I am sincere in trying to win back your heart," he said low, but Harriet tilted her head slightly and must have heard, for she smiled.

Alice turned away, suddenly uncomfortable with the conversation. He'd never really had her heart, so how could he win it back? She was very nearly tempted to say that, but could not, not when he'd been looking at her with such hope in his eyes.

Chapter 11

"Three of you dead. That is odd."

Henderson sat with Lord Berkley in the White Hart Inn's small dining room, partaking of some of the best brandy Henderson had had the pleasure of drinking in years. Berkley had brought it himself. They had planned to meet to discuss their strategy for gaining influence for famine relief, but the talk all around the small village was of Sebastian's death.

"Young men don't just die like that," Henderson said, not bothering to hide his very real concern. "Not in my experience."

Berkley looked at him over his snifter. "You suspect foul play?"

He shook his head. "I'm not certain, but don't you find it odd that three of my chums from Oxford are dead?"

"Who's left? If you're not the killer, some other chap is," Berkley said blandly. "But please do not accuse some poor man of murder unless you are completely certain. It is rather unpleasant living with that sort of rumor."

Henderson gave Berkley a puzzled look.

"Ah, that's right. You've been out of the country and didn't hear that I threw my wife from the highest tower of Costille." He chuckled and swirled the brandy in his glass.

"I take it you did not."

Studying his drink he said, "I wanted to, but no. I did not."

Henderson let out a gust of amusement. "I'm probably mad for thinking such a thing. They all died in very different ways. All accidents. Still…"

"You need to find the answer to this question: why. If you have that, then you have a reason and the murderer. What did the three men know or see or do that could have incited someone to murder?"

Henderson thought back on their friendship and found nothing in his memory that could have caused someone to want to murder any of his friends. And really, Gerald had been there the night Joseph fell from the roof. Certainly if he had witnessed a murder, he would have told someone. It had been a foolish thought but one he could not put from his mind. Of all their group, Gerald, who was slight and bookish, was the least likely to be capable of murder. If not Gerald, then who? Henderson couldn't fathom why anyone would want them dead.

"I'm being foolish," Henderson said. "Three dead men in the course of four years. Not a very efficient killer, is he?"

"Perhaps not efficient, but if there *is* a murderer about, he's very clever. It's hard enough to get away with one murder, never mind three." Berkley winked, and for a moment Henderson thought the man was being serious and was actually confessing to murdering his wife. But when the older man started laughing, Henderson felt a bit ridiculous.

"Here's a sobering thought. If there is a murderer out there targeting our small group of friends, I could be next."

Berkley seemed amused by the thought, which was strangely reassuring. "You cannot die before you produce an heir. How unseemly."

"That hardly matters in my case. I'm not tied down by a title. If I died, it would create only the merest ripple. Perhaps that's why I'm still alive." Those words were still in his head, when he felt his heart pick up a beat. Each of the men who had died was the eldest in his family and most had titles.

Berkley seemed to pick up on his thoughts. "What is it?"

Henderson shook his head. "There was a student at Oxford, a second son. I remember only because he caused such a scene the day he was informed that his older brother had died." He furrowed his brow. "One of us congratulated him. I cannot remember who it was or if it was even someone from our group. I just remember him going a bit mad and thinking what an insensitive thing for one of us to say. I was rather ashamed for the chap who'd said it, even though I didn't know who it was."

Berkley chuckled. "So you think he's trying to kill off all the first-born sons to enact some sort of vengeance?"

Henderson shrugged. "Foolish thought."

"Are you a first-born son?"

Now that made him laugh. "I'm the only son."

"Perhaps the killer is like me," Berkley said. "My time in America changed my perspective. I have little use for titles and fortunes and far more interest in a man's character."

Henderson chuckled. "I wish every member of the aristocracy would spend some time in America." Henderson hadn't realized he'd allowed such a bitter tone his words, but apparently he had.

"I take it one member of the aristocracy in particular?" he asked, raising a black brow. Henderson could feel his cheeks flush, and he cursed his fair skin. It seemed he was always blushing lately, not a very manly reaction.

Berkley let out a sharp bark of laughter. "Only a woman could cause that sort of blush," he said.

Henderson looked down at his drink, wishing the conversation had not turned in this direction. His feelings for Alice Hubbard would seem ridiculous to a man like Berkley. "It matters not. She's engaged. Or nearly so."

"Nearly so?"

Henderson swore and forced a stiff smile. "I'd prefer not to discuss this. I'd rather put my bollocks in boiling oil."

Berkley let out another of his sharp laughs. It burst from him, starting and ending abruptly. "Perhaps I can help you on this matter. Likely more than I can help you with the famine relief."

Shaking his head, Henderson said, "No thank you."

Berkley leaned back and looked like he was enjoying Henderson's discomfort. "A St. Ives girl?"

"I'm not discussing this." His tone brooked no argument, which Berkley seemed to find amusing.

"We are already discussing this," Berkley pointed out, sounding infuriatingly logical.

"Yes. A St. Ives girl with a very high-placed father who would not take kindly to a bastard courting his daughter."

"I wouldn't characterize you as such, sir. You seem a decent enough fellow."

Henderson wondered whether the man was pretending to be obtuse. "Perhaps I should be completely honest with you if you are going to help me. My family is hardly esteemed. My grandparents are landed gentry, yes, and used all of their limited influence and quite a lot of their money to get me into Eton. But my mother had me without the benefit of marriage and I have no idea who my father is. I am, literally, a bastard."

Berkley studied him for a long moment, so long Henderson began to feel rather uncomfortable. For many men, his birth would make a difference as to whether they associated themselves with him, and he wondered if Lord Berkley were one of them. How ironic that he'd spent much of his youth completely unashamed of his birth, when now it had become such a stumbling block. He had little doubt that if he'd had a "lord" in front of his name, he'd still be staying at Tregrennar and vying for the hand of the woman he loved.

"You think that makes a difference to me." It was a statement.

"It would to many men."

"Perhaps if I hadn't spent so much time in America, it would have. But living in such a raw and wild place gives a man perspective. Some of the greatest men I knew were of low birth. And they didn't give a damn whether I was the King of England or a beggar's son. At first, it shocked me. Bothered me quite a lot. By the end, though, as I said, nothing mattered but the character of a man. Whether I could count on him to be honest and fair. I can tell you one thing, my father was horrified by my democratic views."

"Thank you, my lord."

"So, you see, I am in a rare position to help you. I have a lofty title and a deep understanding of the common man. Who is this paragon who has interested you so?"

"Miss Hubbard," Henderson said with some reluctance, but it was strangely comforting to say her name aloud.

Berkley let out a whistle. "Hubbard. He has a daughter who is of marrying age? Good Lord, I'm getting old. Allison or Alicia…"

"Alice," Henderson muttered.

"Done," Berkley said.

Henderson gave the man a sharp look. "What's done?"

"Whatever it is that you want done, my good man." He gave Henderson a smile that would have seemed oily on any other man. "My father taught me one thing: Information is power. And it just so happens I have some information that Lord Hubbard would not appreciate being made public. My father also took meticulous notes on all his transactions and I'm a curious fellow. I read them all."

"No," Henderson said. "I admire Lord Hubbard and will do nothing to harm him."

Berkley widened his eyes. "Who is saying anything about harming him? I daresay we won't even have to resort to that sort of blackmail. At least I hope not. That sort of thing doesn't always sit well with me. Besides, I need something to take me out of my monstrosity of a house."

* * *

"Now, this is strange." Elda was holding an expensive piece of stationery in her hand.

"What is strange, Mama?" Christina asked after swallowing a rather large bit of boiled potato, winning a smile from her older sister.

"Lord Berkley wishes to pay us a call." Elda gave Alice a thoughtful look, then shook her head slightly. "Have you thought about Lord Northrup's proposal, my dear?"

"Oh, Mama, for goodness sake. Get that calculating look out of your eyes," Alice said, pointing her spoon at her mother.

Christina looked from one woman to the other, clearly confused.

"She's thinking of Lord Berkley for me," Alice said, exasperated. "I already have one almost-fiancé under the roof and she wants to add another."

Christina giggled into her napkin.

"He's an earl, Alice. Lord Northrup is only a viscount," Elda pointed out, before turning to Christina and studying her younger daughter thoughtfully.

"Mother!"

Elda had the good grace to look slightly chagrined.

"Don't tell me you were thinking about me," Christina said, shocked. It only took about ten seconds for her to embrace the idea. "What does he look like?" Alice could tell she was trying to sound nonchalant and was failing miserably.

"He's more than double your age," Alice said, wrinkling her nose.

"True, true," Elda said with some reluctance. "But why on earth is he asking to call? Of course we shall welcome him. His father was quite esteemed."

"Welcome whom?" Richard asked, walking into the room the way he did everything—quickly and with little concern for what was happening around him.

"Lord Berkley."

"The son?"

And to Alice's horror, her father immediately looked at her. *Really*.

"Yes. I thought it was odd. It's not as if we know him. I haven't seen him since he was a young boy."

"What does the note say?" Richard asked, already losing patience with the conversation.

Elda opened the note. "I would like to call on you and your family tomorrow afternoon so that I may reacquaint myself with you. Truly yours, Augustus Lawton, Earl of Berkley."

Richard stole a piece of sausage from his younger daughter's plate and she slapped at his hand playfully. "Short and sweet. Do we have any prior engagements tomorrow?"

"Not until evening. The Airsdales have invited us for a small showing. Apparently, they are hosting some French artist for the summer. Gagin or Gaugan. I've never heard of him, which isn't shocking given my complete lack of interest in the world of art, but Mrs. Airsdale believes him to be quite accomplished."

Richard stifled a groan but smiled at his wife. "Then of course we should accept Berkley's request."

"Perhaps I can invite my friends for luncheon to even out the numbers," Alice said, knowing her mother would object.

"The numbers are even, my dear," she said with calm steel. As a girl who had not yet come out, Christina could hardly be considered when "evening out the numbers" but Alice didn't argue. To be honest, after yesterday's events, talking about anything else was a relief.

The Hubbards, in silent agreement, had decided not to discuss the gruesome discovery made yesterday on the beach. The entire day had been upsetting in so many ways, least of which was Henderson's appearance on the Island. She wasn't quite certain she believed his meeting them had been complete happenstance, though he had appeared to be surprised. Happily surprised.

And if she had to admit it, she had been happily surprised as well. She'd imagined he would have returned immediately to London, not stayed in St Ives where he could haunt her. It had always seemed to her that cutting things off cleanly was the best course, and one she would hardly have been able to accomplish with Northrup under her roof and Henderson wandering about St. Ives looking for her. And being invited to balls where he would no doubt ask for a dance.

I want to taste you.

Those words, just thinking of them, made her body burn. It seemed so un-Henderson like, and made Alice wonder if their stolen time together was preoccupying him as much as it was her. If she had known what would happen and, more importantly, how it would make her *feel*, she never would have gone to his room. Henderson had called her naïve that night, and she hadn't realized just how naïve until now. At the Island yesterday, he hadn't touched her, but those words—oh Lord, just those words made her feel as if he were touching her. Worst of all, it was thrilling.

Alice let out a sigh, which earned her a look of concern from her mother. "Yesterday's events," she said by way of explanation, telling the truth even though she knew her mother would misinterpret what she said. Elda immediately let it go, which Alice had known she would; her mother often refused to discuss or acknowledge upsetting events and was always visibly relieved to learn she would not have to dwell on them. It wasn't that Elda did not care—she cared rather too deeply and wished it would all go away. That was why she was so relieved that Northrup was back and wooing Alice. It meant the end of an unpleasant chapter.

"Papa, do you think there is any truth to the rumors that Lord Berkley's wife died of anything more than an accident? It would be so exciting to think we are entertaining an actual murderer," Christina said, unable to hide her fascination with the man.

Richard placed his fork slowly and purposefully on the table and turned toward his younger daughter. "There will be no more such talk, young lady. Do I make myself clear?"

Christina lowered her head, though Alice had a feeling she was not feeling even a bit of shame. "Yes, sir." She was quiet for a few moments, and Alice could almost see the words she was trying not to say pushing against her sister's tongue. "But it would be exciting, even to just pretend."

Richard cast his wife a look of frustration, and her mother pressed her lips together in an effort to keep from smiling.

"Pretend all you want, but if you so much as make even a hint about murder or dead wives, I will lock you in your room for a year," Richard said, but an emptier threat had never been uttered by her father. Christina had her father wrapped around her little finger and everyone in the house, including Richard, knew it.

"Yes, Papa," Christina said. "But what if he brings up the subject of his dead wife?"

Richard scowled at Christina, and she begrudgingly agreed that nothing should be said.

* * *

The next day was blustery and unusually cold, and the sea turned violent, with large waves smashing against the shore and sending spray up onto the cobblestone streets of St. Ives. A steady wind-blown rain fell, and Henderson couldn't be certain when the drops fell against the window, sounding like small pebbles being thrown against the glass, whether it was the rain or the spray from the sea.

As soon as Berkley's carriage pulled up to his hotel, Henderson hastened out, not waiting for the footman to lower the stairs, instead doing the deed himself and pushing quickly into the interior where Berkley sat, looking elegant and every inch the earl he was. A large black umbrella was propped in the corner next to him, and Berkley gave it a pointed look before taking in Henderson's half-drenched state. Henderson gave himself the mental reminder to make use of a valet, at least when he was in England. A valet would most certainly have provided him an umbrella. Though his clothes were expensive, his hair neatly trimmed, and his face freshly shaven, he still did not have the polished look of Berkley, nor of Northrup. If he wanted to somehow win Alice's hand in marriage, he must at least look the part and not remind Lord Hubbard at every turn that he was nothing more than a commoner.

Berkley gave him an assessing look, as if he were thinking the same thing. He was silent for a few minutes before asking, "How is it that you know the Hubbards?"

"I met their late son, Joseph, at Eton. We became best friends and I often spent summers at Tregrennar. The Hubbards were always kind and treated me like a member of the family."

Moving his thumb slowly over his chin, Berkley seemed to absorb this information before shaking his head. "And so you fell in love with the daughter, couldn't allow your feelings to be known, because, well, you were a guest in the house and Alice was Joseph's younger sister, and so, de facto, *your* little sister."

"That's about the gist of it. When Joseph died, it crushed us all. I was supposed to have been with him that night, but I made other plans."

"Ah. You feel partly responsible."

"Wholly responsible. I left for India directly after the funeral. I didn't say good-bye, I just left, believing in my heart it was for the best. I was only twenty-one and Alice was just seventeen, not even out yet. She got engaged a year after I left."

Berkley appeared taken aback. "I thought you said she was *nearly* engaged. If she's engaged, that quite changes things, Southwell."

"You misunderstand. Her first fiancé died just prior to the wedding. In the church, as a matter of fact. This latest fiancé jilted her at the altar but arrived not two days ago to beg her forgiveness. As far as I know, she hasn't forgiven it fully yet, though her parents seem more than willing to forgive him. There's been no announcement, and the actual engagement was nullified when Northrup failed to show up at the church."

"Harvey Heddingford? That Lord Northrup?"

"The same. Why, do you know him?"

Berkley smiled. "No," he said calmly. "But my father did."

Henderson recognized the look on Berkley's face. Even though he hadn't known the man long, he could tell when something devious was brewing inside him. "I do not want to win the lady through extortion, my lord."

Berkley held up his hand, a wholly unconvincing look of innocence on his face. "I would never stoop to such levels. I would, however, enlighten Lord Hubbard of any interesting financial predicament that would harm his own purse." Berkley sighed. "The information I have is old and may not even be pertinent to the current situation, so I will tread carefully."

"Northrup is in financial straits?"

"He was two years ago. Gambling debts to a few gentlemen who were, let us say, less than happy with the situation. My father's reach never fails to surprise me."

Henderson thought on this as the rain slashed against the carriage, a noise that periodically lessened as they went under trees along the way to Tregrennar. If Northrup was still heavily in debt, he had no right to marry Alice. Perhaps Henderson was not the wealthiest man in England, but he had amassed a nice nest egg whilst in India and knew he could build a comfortable life with Alice, one that very closely matched the life she was accustomed to.

"The Hubbards are aware I am coming, are they not?"

Berkley smiled blandly. "Now what would be the fun in that?"

Chapter 12

"Two men are getting out of the carriage," Christina called to Alice and her mother, who were waiting in the parlor pretending not to be sitting on the edge of their seats in anticipation of the earl's arrival. "I cannot see them at all through the rain. They have an umbrella hiding them. Were you expecting two gentlemen, Mama?"

"I was not," Elda said, and it was clear to Alice that she was slightly alarmed. Rising, she opened the door and caught the attention of a footman, instructing him to tell Mrs. Godfrey there would be an additional person for luncheon. "There, that's settled. I do hope Mrs. Godfrey isn't too upset. It is only one addition."

"I'm certain she will handle the news with aplomb, Mama," Alice said. "I do wonder who he has brought."

"The more the merrier," Northrup said, in the exaggerated cheerfulness he'd adopted since his arrival. He was being extremely solicitous to Alice, and was so agreeable it was difficult to remain angry with him. Still, Alice found herself resisting him and could only blame her new feelings for Henderson. Northrup had kissed her a few times, and had very nearly gotten carried away on one occasion (for which he'd profusely apologized), but his kisses did not nearly elicit the passion that Henderson's had. Just thinking about it—which she did more than she should—would cause her entire body to heat. It made her want to find that wonderful release she'd found with Henderson, and longing, a subtle pressure between her legs, had her pressing her limbs together far too often. And that left her aching for more.

The butler entered and announced their visitors with solemn dignity. "His Lordship the Earl of Berkley and Mr. Southwell, madam."

Alice, who had been trying to look pointedly uninterested, for she didn't want to encourage her mother at all in trying to push her toward the earl, snapped her head up. Henderson, the rascal, smiled broadly, first at her mother and then at her. With narrowed eyes, Alice tried in vain to stop her heart from picking up a beat and her lips from tilting up at the corners. Henderson would know, of course, that despite her mock anger, she was entirely too pleased to see him at Tregrennar again.

"A pleasure, Lord Berkley, Mr. Southwell," Elda said, giving a slight disapproving emphasis to Henderson's name. "I would like to offer my condolences on the loss of your father."

Berkley nodded. "Thank you, my lady."

"I hadn't realized you were acquainted with Mr. Southwell, my lord."

"I met Mr. Southwell only recently when he approached me regarding the famine relief." Alice tore her gaze away from Henderson to look at Lord Berkley, who epitomized elegance and wealth. Berkley was tall and lean, with thick dark hair pushed back from a strong forehead, lined by worry or time, Alice wasn't certain which. He was handsome, true, but Alice did not care for the arrogant way he looked at those in the room, nor for his lazy smile, which exuded confidence and privilege. It was almost as if he were playing some secret joke on everyone and he was the only one who knew.

"Oh, yes. Of course. I recall now you were on Mr. Southwell's list."

"I rather think it was my father who was on that list, but I shall do what I can for the relief. Mr. Southwell is quite passionate and has convinced me to join his efforts."

"As have I," Lord Northrup said, and for some reason, he sounded overloud, like a child who wants to be noticed.

Elda turned a startled gaze his way, as if she'd quite forgotten Northrup was in the room. That did not bode well for her efforts to deter her mother's efforts toward Lord Berkley, Alice thought morosely. Lord Berkley was precisely the sort of man her mother would love for her to marry—wealthy and with a prestigious title that any mother would adore for her daughter.

"Of course. It is so good to see you again, Mr. Southwell."

"It has been ages, my lady," Henderson said on a laugh. Alice watched, delighted, as her mother couldn't stop her smile. No matter that her father had rudely asked him to leave, Alice knew her mother was pleased to have Henderson beneath her roof again despite her effort to appear otherwise.

"Mr. Southwell is a particular friend of the family," Elda said. "Did you know this, my lord?"

"Indeed I did," he said, and Alice could swear he darted her a quick look. For some reason, that look made her blush. "Mr. Southwell has mentioned how he spent many happy summers here as a youth. I am glad I was able to convince him to come today."

"And did he need convincing?" Alice asked, unable to stop herself.

"As a matter of fact, he did. I fear I am not a social creature, and having Mr. Southwell along makes it much easier to walk into a home of virtual strangers. I know I visited here as a youth, but it is so long ago, I feared you might have forgotten me." He smiled easily at her mother, and Alice could see she was falling under Berkley's spell. Berkley hardly seemed the sort of man who would be anxious about paying a local family a visit, and she wondered why he would say such a thing? Had Henderson somehow begged an invitation?

The women sat together on a long settee and the men followed and found seats as well, Henderson and Berkley choosing two wingbacked chairs that faced them and Northrup pulling another chair into the group. Alice couldn't help but notice that Henderson, for all his easy grins, seemed slightly nervous; he kept darting looks to the door as if he expected someone to come remove him from the room. Likely her father, Alice thought darkly. Her father was expected to join them for luncheon, and Alice did wonder at the reaction he would have when he saw Henderson at the table. No doubt he would be as displeased as she was pleased.

"You father was a frequent guest at Tregrennar," Elda said. "And of course I recall you, as well. You entertained us by playing the piano, if I remember."

Berkley's smile grew tight, as if it were not a pleasant memory. "Ah, yes. I played with great determination and little talent, as I recall."

Elda let out a small, uncertain, laugh. Alice felt sorry for her mother, for it was difficult to know when Lord Berkley was joking or being ironic or simply contrary. He turned to Henderson and asked, "Do you play the piano?"

Henderson shook his head. "The violin."

"What?" Alice could not stop that exclamation from erupting, unladylike, from her mouth. "How do we not know this?"

He shrugged. "I suppose you never asked. And I did not bring my violin out when I was here."

"Why ever not?" Elda asked. "You and Joseph could have played together." She turned to Lord Berkley. "My late son was an enthusiastic piano player."

"I have never played in front of an audience, much to my teacher's dismay. I tried to once and froze, still as a statue, then burst into humiliating tears. It was the Von Hausen competition and my teacher gave up on me, then and there. I was twelve and far too old for such an emotional display, according to him."

"The Von Hausen competition?" Alice looked at this man whom she thought she knew better than any other and could not believe he had kept such a secret from them all. If he had been selected to perform at that competition at such a young age, he must be a master at the instrument.

"I suppose I didn't want any of you to treat me differently. If you knew, you might have insisted I play for you and I don't know if I could have."

Henderson fairly squirmed beneath everyone's astonished stares, until Lord Berkley turned to Lord Northrup, and asked, "Do you play an instrument, Northrup?"

"I sing."

Badly, Alice thought, but gave him an encouraging smile. He was her almost-fiancé, after all.

"We'll have to hear you some time," Berkley said, sounding completely uninterested. "And what brings you to St. Ives, Northrup? This hardly seems the place for such a cosmopolitan fellow as yourself."

Northrup's cheeks turned ruddy. "I am a guest of the Hubbards."

"How very charitable of them," he said blandly, and Henderson gave him a look that could only be described as a warning.

"It is hardly charity to have the man who plans to marry your daughter as a guest," Northrup said with a small sniff.

"My felicitations," Berkley said, turning his dark gaze toward her. Alice could not tell if his eyes were brown or a very dark blue, but either way, having them pinned on her was disconcerting.

"Lord Northrup misspoke." Elda looked nervously from Northrup to Berkley. "They are not officially engaged." Knowing her mother was vying for Berkley did not lessen Alice's gratitude for her mother saying those words aloud. She'd feared her parents had come to the forgone conclusion that she and Northrup would marry.

"We _were_ engaged," Alice said feeling a bit of a devil for saying that aloud.

"But Northrup failed to appear at the church." Henderson, who had seemed nervous not ten minutes before, now seemed to be having a bit too much fun. "He's here to win his lady back."

"Indeed?" Berkley asked, giving Northrup an assessing look.

"This is a private affair," Northrup said, clearly annoyed by this turn of the conversation.

"Actually, it was in the newspaper." Biting her lip to stop from laughing at Christina's comment, Alice gave her sister a look that begged her to stop. She might have known Christina would ignore her. "The newspapers, well, one newspaper, called Alice the bad—"

"Chris-*tina*," Elda said.

"The newspaper called me the bad luck bride. You see, I've been engaged to three different fellows and, as you can see, I remain unmarried."

"Do we need to discuss this?" Northrup asked tightly. "There are much more pleasant topics we can explore."

"Like murder."

Alice froze at her sister's words. She had promised not to bring up murder in front of Lord Berkley, but had done so anyway. One look at her mother, and Alice knew Christina might not see the outside of her room for a month.

"Murder?" Berkley asked silkily.

Christina looked at her mother in confusion; then her face paled—no doubt as she remembered that she was sitting in the room with a man who had once been accused of murder and she had promised her father not to discuss it. "Yes, poor Mr. Turner. Some are saying he was murdered because it appears he'd been stabbed. In the back."

"Oh. Mr. Turner," Elda said, nearly sagging with relief. "So sad. Are they really saying it could be murder? Where did you hear such a thing?"

"Martha's second cousin's brother works in the mortuary."

"Martha shouldn't go around telling such tales. And you, young lady, should not repeat them."

"Yes, ma'am." Christina dipped her head, pretending shame. "But I heard the same from Patricia Ellsberry." Christina turned toward the men. "Her father is a physician."

"That would be a horrible thing, indeed," Elda said. "I cannot imagine anyone who would want to kill Mr. Turner. He was such a pleasant young man."

Alice happened to look at Henderson at that moment and saw something flicker in his eyes, as he no doubt recalled their meeting just prior to his death.

"Mr. Southwell was one of the last people to see Mr. Turner alive."

Alice looked at Northrup with disbelief, not so much at what he'd said but rather how he'd said it, as if Henderson could somehow be the murderer.

"Indeed I was, my lord," Henderson said. "He was a good friend and I'm glad I was able to spend some time with him before this happened." "I'm certain you were," Northrup said apologetically, as if realizing how awful he sounded. He cast a look toward Alice and she had a feeling he was trying to gauge whether she was angry with him or not. He brightened markedly when her father entered the room. "Lord Hubbard."

The men rose, and her father immediately started toward Lord Berkley, hesitating only briefly when he realized Henderson was standing next to him. "I do apologize for not being here when you arrived," he said, shaking the other man's hand before turning to Henderson and nodding. "Mr. Southwell, a pleasure."

"Indeed," Henderson said.

"I insisted Mr. Southwell accompany me," Lord Berkley said. "I do hope you do not mind my bringing along a guest."

"Of course not," Richard said warmly. "Mr. Southwell is always welcome here."

Moments later, their butler announced luncheon was served, and as the group headed to the dining room, Alice trailed slightly behind. She wasn't certain what was going on, why Henderson was here or why Lord Berkley seemed to have taken an immediate dislike to Northrup. For his part, Northrup appeared to be out of sorts, as if the world had tilted a bit on its axis, leaving him out of balance.

During luncheon, Berkley regaled them with stories of America, much to Christina's delight, and Alice noticed how many times the earl brought Henderson into the conversation whilst completely ignoring Lord Northrup. Her father appeared almost smitten with Berkley and her mother was looking at the earl as if she'd never seen such a paragon of manhood in her life. This all would have boded ill, thought Alice, if it hadn't been so very apparent—at least to her—why Berkley was here and why he'd brought Henderson along with him. It appeared to her that Henderson had gained himself a powerful and charming ally.

After they'd finished dining, Lord Northrup, who was seated next to her, leaned over and quietly asked Alice if she might like to take a turn in the garden.

"Why don't we all go?" Lord Berkley said, and Alice nearly laughed aloud, for it was clear to her that Northrup had lowered his voice so that no one else could hear the request. What fine hearing the man had. "It's a lovely day and I have heard your grounds are well-maintained. I'm going to be making some changes at Costille, and I would like to hear your thoughts, my lady."

With that, Alice's mother was completely won over and Alice had to stop herself from rolling her eyes. If Berkley had heard a single syllable about their garden, she would be fully shocked. Northrup, on the other hand, was having a difficult time hiding his annoyance, and Alice gave him a look of understanding. "Another time," she whispered.

* * *

As the group headed en masse to the garden, Alice on Northrup's arm, she was intensely aware of Henderson following just behind them. Lord Berkley was completely engaging her parents, and Alice could see Northrup was nearly in fits trying to hear what they were talking about. Every time either of her parents laughed, he would stiffen and let out a small puff of air.

"I fear I cannot have Lord Berkley monopolize your parents so thoroughly, my dear. If you'll forgive me." And with that, he dropped her hand and picked up his pace so that he was part of the group containing her parents. Berkley welcomed him with such enthusiasm, Alice's suspicions were only confirmed. She was left standing alone for approximately three seconds before she found herself next to Henderson, her face red from embarrassment. Or pleasure. Just, she was certain, as Berkley had intended.

"What are you doing here?" she whispered. "And do not tell me it was to have luncheon or I shall strangle you."

"I came to win your heart," he said lightly.

"You already have my heart," she said grumpily.

"Then I am here to win your mother and father's hearts."

Alice stopped abruptly, her eyes on the small group in front of them being so entertained by Lord Berkley, they were unaware the two of them were lagging behind. "What are you saying?"

"I'm saying I want to court you. I don't want you to marry Lord Northrup. I want you to marry me, instead."

The way he said it, as if he were telling her he was planning to order beef for supper, was quite maddening. "Do you."

"Indeed I do. And someday I will be able to tell you precisely why marrying anyone other than me would be a colossal mistake."

She snorted. "Then it's a good thing you told me now, after three failed weddings. Goodness sakes, Henny, are you mad? When did this grand revelation occur to you? After..." She couldn't finish the sentence;

it was too mortifying. "My God, is *that* what this about? You feel *guilty* about the other evening?"

He looked affronted, which made Alice even angrier. What else was she to think? In all their lives he'd never looked at her with anything but brotherly affection. All those hours in the library, when she was dreaming about him falling in love, he'd remained the perfect gentleman. Never had she had one inkling that he saw her as anything but a little girl. Yes, they had gotten carried away the other night, and yes, Henderson had seemed to enjoy the moment, but she had practically thrown herself at him. She had gone into his room half naked. What healthy man would have turned away a woman who acted like such a wanton?

He took a few steps away, then jerked his head for her to follow him. The party in front of them laughed at something Lord Berkley said, and Alice ground her teeth together. It was clear to her that Henderson had somehow recruited his lordship into helping his cause and she prayed Berkley didn't know the entire sordid story.

"I want to court you because I love you. I have loved you, as a matter of fact, for years."

Alice narrowed her eyes, but her heart gave a painful twist. "I don't believe you. You left."

His eyes flickered briefly, darkly. "I know. I shouldn't have. I have so much to explain to you." He darted a look to the others. "I fear I shall never have the opportunity. But I want you to know that I am not giving up." He grinned and her heart sang. "Fair warning."

Alice wanted nothing more than to kiss that grin off his face. She looked over to where Lord Berkley was still entertaining his audience. "He is your partner in crime, isn't he?"

"I haven't a clue what you mean," he said, but it was obvious that he did. "Shall we join the others? Your father has already given me two scathing looks and I am treading in dangerous waters as it is after being thrown out of your house."

"You were not thrown out." He lifted a brow. "It was strongly hinted that you should leave only because it was clear Lord Northrup was upset. But I daresay, with Lord Berkley suddenly expressing interest in me, poor Northrup will soon fall out of favor. He's not *really* interested, is he?"

"No." And then he said the sweetest thing. "That...doesn't bother you, does it?"

"Would you step aside if I was interested in him?"

"Not in a million years." And just before they reached the other group, he said, "I really did come to stop the wedding, you know." Then he turned and jogged ahead, leaving her to stare in disbelief at his retreating back.

* * *

Now that Henderson had made his declaration, the sense of panic he felt at the thought of losing Alice forever only grew, until it felt like a living thing inside his gut. Every time she looked at Lord Northrup, laughed at something he said, or gave him a look of understanding, Henderson wanted to carry her away like some primitive man. Instead, he had to suffer their looks, Northrup's proprietary manner, as if it were a forgone conclusion that they were to be married.

It did not escape his attention that the Hubbards were assessing Berkley as a possible son-in-law. They never looked at *him* in that light, never gave him the assessing look Lord Hubbard was now giving the earl as Berkley commented on a particularly good example of Lady Hubbard's prized roses. Alice's hand was now firmly tucked in the crook of Northrup's arm and Henderson had a feeling he would not be able to drag her away from the determined man. What made it almost worse was that Northrup had dismissed him as a rival and was completely centering his attention on Berkley, who had absolutely no interest in Alice. Thank God. For if he had, Henderson was quite certain he would never have Alice for himself. The Hubbards were just that smitten. Berkley had an ease about him, a confidence that he was likely born with.

For her part, Alice was pointedly ignoring him, and Henderson did not know if this was a good thing or bad.

"Mr. Southwell." Henderson looked down to see Christina standing next to him and wondered how long she'd been there and if she'd noticed how intensely he'd been staring at her sister. "Is it true you saw Mr. Turner just before he died?" She'd lowered her voice so no one but he could hear her question.

"I don't know that it was directly prior, but I saw him that night, yes."

Christina chewed her lip a bit. "When I was very little, before you were Joseph's friend, my brother had a group of friends. We would all go to the beach and they would ride the waves in. I used to wish I were a boy and older so I could play with them. Boys seemed to have so much more fun than girls." She looked over to where her parents were, still engaged in conversation with Lord Berkley. "They're all dead."

Henderson looked sharply at Christina. "What do you mean?"

"All of them. Joseph, Tristan Cummings, and now Sebastian. And Peter before that. He was the first."

"Peter?"

"Peter Jeffreys. He died before you met Joseph, I believe. Don't you think that's odd? That all of them who were friends are dead? I was thinking about that last night, and it occurred to me that it seems an unlikely coincidence."

"Indeed," Henderson said, his brow furrowed.

Christina gave him a small smile, as if glad he was taking her seriously. "Once I realized that, I started wondering why. Why would someone kill them all, if indeed they were all murdered? Joseph's death was an accident so perhaps I'm just being silly. Still…"

"You are not being silly," Henderson said, his voice low. "I came to very much the same conclusion not long ago, but I couldn't make sense of it either. And Joseph's death doesn't seem to fit. He did fall from the roof." Henderson turned away from the group, and dipped his head. "Was Mr. Grant part of that group of boys, Christina?"

"Gerald Grant? No, not that I recall. Why do you ask?"

Henderson shrugged. "No reason. Only that he was one of the lads there the night Joseph died. He's the one who told me what happened. And everyone else who was there that night is dead."

Christina's eyes grew wide. "Do you think he's the murderer?" she whispered, clearly excited by the prospect.

Henderson chuckled, but felt a twinge of unease.

"That means he could have killed four people. Four." Her eyes were wide with the excitement of it all.

"Highly unlikely. And what possible reason would he have for killing even one of them? I think it's important not to start spreading such rumors, my girl. Every single one of those men died in an accident. Only Mr. Turner, if what you say is true about his being stabbed, appears to have met his demise through foul means."

"True," Christina said reluctantly, and Henderson let out a small chuckle at her disappointment. Alice's younger sister was quite bloodthirsty. Suddenly she grasped his arm. "You're the only one left," she said. "Oh, Mr. Southwell, what if you are in danger?"

That very thought had crossed Henderson's mind, but he had no intention of sharing it with this young woman. "If what you say is true, and Peter Jeffreys was the first victim of our murderer, then I would not be part of that group."

"But you became part of it," she pointed out.

That thought had crossed Henderson's mind as well. Perhaps, he thought, he should visit Gerald Grant and see if he could sense any madness in the man. For only a madman could systematically kill four men.

"Mr. Southwell." It was Lord Berkley calling him over to join their group. Was that a look of annoyance in Lord Hubbard's eye? Such slights, small as they were, hurt. He'd always thought of Richard as a sort of surrogate father, and when he'd been younger, he'd actually daydreamed about what it would be like to be part of Joseph's family. To think all those years Richard had only been indulging his elder son was like a punch to his gut—that painful and that nauseating.

Henderson had no idea what Berkley's plan was, but it was becoming more obvious by the moment. He was making certain Lord Hubbard was aware they were friends (which they were) and that Berkley thought of him as an equal (which they were most decidedly not). Henderson didn't have the first idea why Berkley was taking him under his aristocratic wing. Joseph had always said Henderson had a way about him that put others at ease, and Henderson had accumulated quite a few highly placed friends over the years. When he'd sailed from India, he'd left behind a large group of men who were as passionate as he about famine relief. The fact they'd elected him to return to England to garner support for their efforts had been as humbling as it had been precipitous, given the timing of Alice's ill-fated wedding.

Alice laughed at something Northrup said, and Henderson again felt that sense of panic, that he was too late, mingling with the growing realization that he was not enough. Her former fiancés had all been titled (or at least the family had believed this to be the case), all from well-respected and prestigious families. He was the bastard of a country girl, a man who'd been lucky enough to have kind and well-to-do grandparents. Many others like him had ended up in orphanages or worse.

Henderson stepped into the circle, wishing he felt more that he belonged. Glancing briefly at the proprietary grasp Northrup had on Alice's gloved hand, Henderson forced himself to smile as if he hadn't a care in the world, as if he hadn't just proclaimed his love for a woman who was standing with another man.

"You beckoned," Henderson said, giving Berkley an easy and mocking bow.

"I did. I've been telling the Hubbards about my adventures in America and the opportunity there. I would be remiss if I didn't include you in the conversation, given your superior negotiating skills." Henderson suppressed the temptation to roll his eyes at what he deemed an obvious attempt to build him up in the eyes of the Hubbards. Berkley knew nothing of his negotiating skills, nor any other skill, truth be told. "Mine are woefully inadequate and it occurred to me that you and Lord Hubbard could assist me in gaining more investors. Rails, you know. Steel. The very things titled gentlemen like ourselves are not allowed to discuss but are allowed to benefit from."

Northrup, who must have noticed his name had been omitted, perked up and darted a look at the Hubbards before saying, "As gauche as it is, I have some experience in investing."

Berkley gave him what could only be described as an indulgent smile, the type a parent gives a child who has just boasted about some unfounded talent. "I'm happy to hear your thoughts as well, Northrup. Of course." Then he turned back to Henderson and proceeded to pepper him with questions, which thankfully Henderson, who actually did have a talent for investing, easily answered. It didn't escape Henderson, as the three men, with Northrup hovering in the periphery, got deep into the discussion, that Lord Hubbard began to give him a series of thoughtful looks.

"I hadn't realized you were so well-schooled in investment," Lord Hubbard said finally. "I suppose I assumed you were in India working solely on the famine relief."

"While I have become involved in relief, my lord, I fear business is what initially sent me to India. It was those very investments that have made me so concerned about the famine. India is an excellent education, I assure you, in both the good and the ills that come from progress."

"Enough about business," Lord Northrup announced. "I fear the ladies are growing bored with all our talk of numbers and such." The ladies in question were not even within range of hearing, and Henderson guessed it was actually Northrup who was bored.

"I would expect, Northrup, that you would be particularly interested in such a discussion, given your financial state," Lord Berkley said without inflection. It was an unforgivable thing to say in public, particularly in front of the father of the woman a man hoped to marry, but Berkley held his bland smile even when Lord Hubbard gave him an outraged look. My God, Henderson hadn't known he'd had such a brilliant ally in Berkley until that very moment. Why he'd decided to help him, Henderson couldn't say. He only knew he planned to make certain Lord Berkley was aware of his gratitude.

"I say, Berkley, that was not well done," Lord Hubbard said.

Lord Berkley looked slightly shocked to be called out on his rudeness. "I do apologize, Northrup. I had no idea it wasn't common knowledge. I fear I've spent far too much time in America. Such discussions of financial failures are quite common over there. Why, men brag about how much money they've lost gambling. It's almost a badge of honor."

"Sir!" Hubbard said, clearly appalled.

To which Berkley gave another confused look. "I was apologizing," he said, sounding contrite and slightly perplexed at Lord Hubbard's continued censure.

"I can assure you, my lord," Northrup hastened to say, "I have incurred no debt."

"Not recently," Lord Berkley said silkily, and Northrup's cheeks turned ruddy.

And that was when Lord Hubbard seemed to realize that Berkley wasn't being uncouth, but rather crafty in his revelation of Northrup's financial state. Henderson saw the moment irritation became begrudging respect for Berkley's behavior, as Lord Hubbard narrowed his eyes and gave Berkley an assessing look. Henderson could almost see Lord Hubbard's thoughts forming, that Lord Berkley was actually helping to save his daughter from a man who was in financial difficulty, that he should be grateful for the information even if it had been delivered a bit discourteously.

Northrup turned to Lord Hubbard, his expression slightly panicked. "Lord Hubbard, I can assure you—"

"No need," Hubbard said, holding up his hand to stop Northrup's entreaty. "There's not a man among us who hasn't incurred some sort of debt." He smiled at the younger man, but Henderson noted the smile could only be described as grim, and for the first time, Henderson believed he might actually have a shot at marrying Alice.

* * *

After Henderson and Lord Berkley left, her father and Northrup were unusually quiet at dinner, and Alice couldn't help but notice there seemed to be a tension between the two men. Where before the two would exchange droll stories about this or that acquaintance, on this night they were strangely silent.

"What did you think of Lord Berkley?" Elda asked to no one in particular.

"I didn't care for the man." This from Northrup at the very same moment Richard said, "I found him enlightening."

Elda laughed. "Now those are two very different assessments."

"I think he was hiding a deep intelligence behind his charm." The look on Alice's father's face was priceless after Christina made this pronouncement. It was almost as if he had never realized how very perceptive his younger daughter was.

"Indeed?"

Christina looked slightly embarrassed to be the focus of Richard's attention. "I sensed that behind everything he said there was some deeper meaning, something we were not privy to. Not disingenuousness," she said thoughtfully, trying to come up with an explanation for her assessment. "Rather as if he were trying to hide just how intelligent he is. Though I cannot imagine why."

"Perhaps he simply isn't intelligent," Northrup said on a laugh, and Alice felt a twinge of pity for him. It had been clear throughout the afternoon that her parents were enthralled with Lord Berkley. It would be a difficult task for any man to be noticed when Berkley was in the room. Which made it even more perplexing why Alice's attention throughout the day had been on Henderson.

Every time he laughed, each time he moved near her, her face grew warm and she felt a thrill go through her. With all of Berkley's charms, it was Henderson who seemed to have some sort of hold over her. It was almost as if sharing that incredibly intimate night with him had somehow created a bond between them. Even now, even with Henderson back at his hotel, she could feel the pull. Had some sort of spell been cast on her that night, turning her into the wanton creature that sat with her family and almost-fiancé at the dinner table but could only think about what it felt like when Henderson had kissed her breast? Could only fantasize about a way it would be possible for that to happen again?

"What did you think of Lord Berkley, Alice?" Elda asked pointedly, ignoring the small intake of breath from Northrup. In that moment Elda had declared her preference, and Northrup was keenly aware of it.

"I thought him quite charming and very handsome and not in the least someone whom I would like to know better," Alice said with what she thought would put a final period on the story her mother was creating in her mind, a story that ended with her marrying Lord Berkley.

Northrup gave her a small smile of gratitude—or was it smugness?—and Alice took a large bite of roasted pork, ignoring her mother's frown.

Elda sighed and returned her attention to her meal. The five of them ate in silence for a time before Christina nearly had her choking on her meal.

"I like Mr. Southwell much better than Lord Berkley. I'd forgotten how nice and kind he is. A shame he doesn't have a title."

"Or a father," Northrup said under his breath but loud enough for all at the table to hear.

"Of course he has a father," Christina said. "Everyone has a father."

"Can we not discuss this at the dinner table," Richard said.

Christina looked around the table, unaware that she had stirred up a conversation that innocent ears should never hear. "Why is Henderson's father not a proper subject of discussion? Oh, was he a bad man?"

"I don't believe Henderson knows who his father is," Northrup said, jumping slightly when Richard slammed down his fork. "I apologize, it's just that I don't understand why he is allowed in our company, nor why Lord Berkley has apparently taken such a liking to the man."

Alice could tell Christina was about to launch into a staunch defense of Henderson, so she spoke up to end the conversation. "I will explain to Christina later, if you will allow it, Mother."

"Please be circumspect, Alice."

"Of course." Then turning to Northrup, Alice said, trying to keep the emotion she felt out of her voice, "Henderson has been part of this family for years. I know it is difficult for you to understand, but please respect our choice of whom we associate with." Her tone was calm and gentle, but inside she was fighting a terrible urge to lose her temper. She understood Northrup's concerns and his prejudice. Very few families, if they knew of his birth, would allow someone like Henderson into their home as a guest, and she had always been so proud of her family for ignoring social mores and treating Henderson as an equal. In her mind, he was not only equal, he was superior to them all. Henderson was all that was kind and good and she would breathe her last making certain everyone knew it.

Chapter 13

When Alice was a girl, she remembered feeling terribly jealous of Harriet, whose father owned one of the local tin mines. Harriet, because her father "worked" in the tin mines, was allowed to participate in the procession from Guild Hall to Knill's Steeple on Worvas Hill while she, the daughter of an aristocrat, was not. Ten girls under age ten, all daughters of fishermen or tin miners, a widow, and the mayor, a mix determined by John Knill more than seventy years prior. Alice had been six, Harriet five, and she watched with fierce envy as her younger friend marched along, not truly understanding why she had not been chosen.

At eleven, John Knill day was the most exciting day of her life. At sixteen, it seemed rather silly to her. Why were they still performing this ceremony for a man who was long dead, and whom many now believed was a bit touched in the head?

Fifteen years after her first John Knill day, the ceremony was identical except for the little girls and perhaps the style of dress, and Alice looked at the celebration with fondness and nostalgia and was glad her little village protected its traditions—even if they were a bit odd. Seeing the excitement on the faces of the ten girls who had been chosen made her remember how happy Harriet had been that day, one of the few happy days her friend had ever had as a child.

Everyone in St. Ives and many from the surrounding villages watched the procession of ten girls, all in their pretty white dresses, as they made their way through town in memory of John Knill, who invented the celebration in his own honor. Every five years, the townspeople would gather and they'd all head to the pyramid obelisk on Worvas Hill. Alice waved to Harriet, who was standing across the lane looking rather miserable. It was obvious from the stern look on her mother's face that

Harriet must have done something objectionable. Harriet, in her mother's eyes, was always doing something objectionable. Alice gave her a smile and a wink, and her friend's face brightened a bit. Of all her friends, Alice prayed Harriet would find a husband who could take her away from her mother.

Everywhere she looked she saw familiar faces, but not the one face she'd hoped to see—Henderson's. He'd been there when she was sixteen, hanging about with Joseph and a few other lads. Funny how so many memories of her youth included him. The people of St. Ives loved their traditions, and this one was one of their favorites and for Alice, this would be the first time she'd be old enough to attend the John Knill ball.

She remembered with fondness when she was sixteen and had snuck out of the house and, along with her friends, spied on those dancing at the ball hosted for years by Eliza's family.

"I'm going to meet my husband at the John Knill ball," Harriet had announced as the four of them had sighed in unison to see one young couple gazing adoringly into one another's eyes.

"If you wait that long, you'll be an old maid," Rebecca had stated.

"I'll only be twenty-two."

"Twenty-two is well on the shelf. That's what my mother says, at any rate." Rebecca always held a wealth of information, most of which came from either her mother or older siblings.

Five years later, all four women were unmarried with only Alice having a prospective husband. Since Berkley's visit, Lord Northrup had only increased his campaign to win her hand, much to her mother's clear annoyance. As they were getting ready for the ball, Alice's mother had come into her room and wondered out loud if Lord Northrup was overstaying his welcome.

"Mama, you would not be saying that if Lord Berkley had not made an appearance."

Her mother didn't even try to deny it. "Lord Berkley would be an excellent match for you, Alice."

Alice, whose maid was finishing up her intricate coiffure, stared at her mother through the mirror's reflection. "What if I were to say to you that I didn't want to marry either Lord Northrup or Lord Berkley?"

"I would say you were being silly. Both are good men. It's just that Lord Berkley is the slightly better man."

Alice laughed and her mother joined her. "You have to admit, darling, when the two men are side by side there really is no comparison."

"I do not have to admit any such thing." She paused to thank her maid before dismissing her. "You are correct, Mama, but it's not about a title or his stature. I truly don't care for how Lord Northrup treats Henderson."

Elda waved a dismissive hand. "Oh, that. He's a snob. Most people are."

"Lord Berkley isn't."

Elda smiled. "That's why he's the better man for you, my dear."

It was on the tip of Alice's tongue to tell her mother that she thought Henderson the best man of all, but she knew that would only cause her mother distress. It was one thing to welcome a man into your home, it was quite another to allow that man to marry your daughter. Henderson's declaration had been in the forefront of her thoughts during the three days since Lord Berkley had visited that first time. The earl had returned one other time, but Henderson had not accompanied him. Knowing he was still in St. Ives was driving her a bit mad. On the few outings she had made with Christina or her friends she had been tense, as if at any moment Henderson would leap out and publicly announce his intentions. Worse, she wanted him to. In the days since his visit, she couldn't stop wondering where he was, what he was doing, if he had been serious when he'd said he loved her.

What bosh. He couldn't love her.

But his parting words to her when they'd been alone haunted her: *I really did come to stop the wedding, you know.*

Was it possible? Had he actually hurried from India to stop her wedding? She thought back on that morning and tried to recall how Henderson had looked, how he had looked at her. No, she thought, he hadn't acted like a man relieved, like a man who'd nearly lost the woman he loved to another. Oh, why was he fueling her doubts this way? A man who loved a woman did not leave for four years then return on the day of her third planned wedding and suddenly announce he was in love. But a man who was ashamed of his actions, who felt guilt and obligation after ruining a girl, would make such a declaration.

Alice pressed her cool fingertips to her temples, drawing a worried look from her mother. "I'm fine," she said. "I have to admit these recent events have been quite wearing. I came to St. Ives to escape excitement and intrigue and it seems it has followed me home."

Her mother gave her a quick hug. "Someday you may crave this sort of excitement, my dear. I do admit having Lord Northrup show up to beg forgiveness and having Lord Berkley show interest in you is rather more excitement than I expected this summer as well."

Alice stared in the mirror at her reflection for a long moment, seeing only the girl she always saw. "Would it be so terrible if I never married, Mama?"

Elda sighed and put two gentle hands on her shoulders. "No," she said, giving Alice a small squeeze. "It would mean I would never lose you. But it would also mean I would never get to hold your children and watch them grow. And neither would you. I cannot imagine how very dreary my life would have been if I didn't have you children. We'll figure this all out, shall we?"

"Yes. I just hope you support my decision."

"I'm sure I will."

* * *

The night of the John Knill ball was with thick with fog. Light from the Godrevy Lighthouse hardly made it to shore as it sliced through the night. The air was moist and by the time Henderson walked up the steps of the Lowell Hall, his hair was covered with a fine mist that created annoying curls even though he had applied a thin layer of pomade to keep it in place.

It had been more years than he could count since he had taken part in an English ball. Joseph had gained him entry into a few, but he never had been comfortable in his formal wear. Lord Berkley, horrified that he didn't employ a valet, had let him borrow his for the evening. The poor man was put in a state when he saw what Henderson had been planning to wear, and quickly engaged a tailor to "create a proper fit, sir." Henderson had to admit the suit fit him far better than it had, and he felt rather polished in his pristine clothes, highly polished boots, and intricately tied cravat. Perhaps when he returned to England for good and set up a house, he would make use of a valet.

As he entered the home, brightly lit with glittering gaslight chandeliers, he was struck by how many people were already inside. The house buzzed with conversation, punctuated with laughter, and Henderson took a fortifying breath. Although he had spent many summers in St. Ives, he didn't know many people outside their small circle of friends, and now Henderson found himself amongst a crowd of strangers. He searched for a familiar face, and went still when he recognized Gerald Grant. Four years hadn't changed him all that much. He'd been a bit younger than the rest of them, and he still looked like a schoolboy. One look at him and Henderson almost laughed aloud at the thought that Gerald, who at best reached his chest and was as slight as a bean pole, could have been responsible for the deaths of four robust men. He'd forgotten how diminutive he was, a wiry, ginger-haired man with pale blue eyes who seemed about as threatening as a puppy.

Still, it did not hurt to speak to him, for old time's sake.

"Hello, Mr. Grant. It's been a long time and I see the years have been good to you."

"My word, Henderson, is that you? As I live and breathe, I cannot believe my eyes. How long has it been?"

"Four years, give or take."

"What are you doing here?" It was a simple enough question, but given his mood, he thought he heard just the slightest emphasis on the word "you."

"I was invited by the hostess's daughter, Miss Eliza Lowell."

Gerald grinned. "Get that chip off your shoulder, Southie, I meant what are you doing here in St. Ives?"

Henderson remembered that old irritation he had felt whenever the lot of them had included Gerald in their plans. No one had called him Southie but Joseph, and the fact that the other man did so now was profoundly annoying. "No one calls me Southie anymore. And I'm here on business with Lord Berkley."

"Business. Ah. Have you heard about Sebastian? Tragedy that. Thought it might be murder, but I hear the coroner just today called it an accident."

"I saw him the night before he died. In fact, I was there when his body was found."

Gerald's eyes widened. "You don't say. The night before? I suppose in a way that's a good thing. You got to see him, say good-bye. Get caught up, all that."

They stood together in awkward silence, Gerald rocking from heel to toe as he looked over the crowd. "He didn't mention a Mr. Stewart?"

Now, that was odd. Sebastian had asked him the very same question. *Joseph ever mention a chap named Stewart?*

Schooling his features, Henderson tried to act bored, as if that question didn't leave him reeling. "Stewart? No, why?"

Gerald shook his head. "No reason. Just an old school chum." He turned fully to Henderson and smiled, putting out his hand. "It was good seeing you again, Henderson. Perhaps before you return to wherever you came from—ha ha—we can get together and catch up."

"Of course. It was good to see you, Gerald."

Henderson watched the smaller man walk away, his curiosity more than piqued. Who the hell was Mr. Stewart?

His thoughts were interrupted when he saw Lord Berkley coming toward him, looking none the worse for having loaned his valet out.

"I see Mr. Carter made himself useful," Berkley said, referring to his valet.

"I think I'm finally seeing the value of having a valet," Henderson said on a laugh. The two men hadn't seen each other since their visit with the Hubbards, after which he'd expressed his gratitude to his new friend. Berkley had waved his thanks away, saying the entire campaign was a welcome distraction.

"The Hubbards are here already with Northrup trailing behind them like a puppy, and Lady Hubbard has been trying to catch my eye for about an hour. I do believe she has completely misunderstood my interest in them, so I will endeavor to do a better job of pushing their interests toward you."

Henderson saw Alice with Northrup on the opposite side of the room and felt a sick twist of nausea at the thought of failing in his quest to win her hand. She wore a light blue gown that exposed her back and shoulders, and the thought that the other man might actually touch her, lay his hand upon that impossibly soft skin, made him a little mad. Berkley's low chuckle pulled him from his thoughts, and he felt his cheeks blush to be caught staring so intently at Alice.

"I think you should learn better to school your features, Mr. Southwell. If her father saw you looking at Alice just now, I fear he would have thrown you from the room. My God, you really do have it bad. She's completely ruined you."

Dragging his eyes away from Alice, Henderson took a deep breath. "I love her with all my heart."

"Then it's very good you found me."

"I am grateful, but I still don't understand why you are going to such lengths to help a stranger."

Berkley shrugged and wiped a bit of lint from his jacket. "If I wasn't here, I'd be in that horror of a house I own."

"You cannot renovate?"

"My lovely late wife destroyed all records pertaining to the home. My father loved Costille, one of the few things we shared. After a small fire ruined one of the rooms, he commissioned an artist to make a catalogue of all the rooms to record every last detail. He was obsessed with maintaining the history of the old girl, and now it's all ruined." Berkley shook his head. "I do not care to discuss this, if you don't mind, Southwell. The reason I came to this ball was to forget about what was destroyed and lost, not to brood upon it. I do enough brooding when I am home." Berkley's voice faded away as if something, or someone, across the room had gained his attention.

Henderson couldn't help the fleeting—and disloyal—thought that the rage Berkley must have felt when he saw his ruined home would have driven some men to murder.

Harriet Anderson passed by at that moment, her head down as she hurried along. "Hello, Miss Anderson," Henderson called, and the woman stopped abruptly, as if slamming into a wall. Henderson had always thought Harriet pretty, if a little awkward, and because he had been painfully aware of her crush when she'd been younger, he'd always endeavored to be kind to her.

"Oh! Mr. Southwell. I didn't see you there. I'm so glad you decided to come." She glanced quickly up at Berkley, who was now fully distracted.

"Miss Anderson, please allow me to introduce you to Augustus Lawton, Earl of Berkley. Lord Berkley, one of Miss Hubbard's dearest friends, Miss Harriet Anderson."

"Yes, a pleasure," he said, without looking down at Harriet, who stood looking up at him expectantly, her expression falling slightly as he walked quickly away.

Harriet let out a small laugh. "I do believe I have never made a smaller impression on someone."

Watching Berkley walk away, Henderson shrugged. "I daresay he didn't realize how rude he just was. Clearly he was distracted."

And then, as they both watched, they realized just what had distracted Lord Berkley to the point of rudeness—Harriet's sister, Clara.

"It looks as though Clara has gained yet another admirer," Harriet said, her voice tinged with amusement.

Turning, Henderson looked at Harriet, trying to gauge whether she'd been insulted by Berkley's behavior, but he saw nothing in her expression that would indicate anything other than amusement. Clara Anderson was a stunning girl. Even when he'd been in St. Ives four years earlier he remembered admiring her, along with every other man in St. Ives, and he was frankly perplexed that she was still unmarried. It must be difficult, he thought, to be the younger sister of such a beauty. Harriet was pretty and clever, but unfortunately paled in comparison to her older sister.

A dance card hung from Harriet's wrist, and Henderson was suddenly inspired to ask for a dance. "Miss Anderson, do you have any dances open?"

In all his life, he'd never seen a woman's cheeks blush so quickly and so red. She glanced down at her wrist as if surprised to see the card dangling there; then she looked up at him and, impossibly, her cheeks grew even more scarlet. "I—I'm sorry. No."

It was the oddest thing. Henderson was quite certain she was *lying*.

Now, why would she lie? Henderson should have let it go, a gentleman would have, but curiosity won out over politeness. Here was a girl who had had a crush on him in her youth, who, frankly, still seemed to have a bit of a crush, and she was refusing to dance with him. The same woman who had seemed so relaxed a minute before, now looked as if her bloomers were on fire and she was impatient to find a bucket of water to douse the flames.

"I'm sorry, Miss Anderson, but I don't believe you." He said the words softly, and she immediately dipped her head.

"I feel horrid, Mr. Southwell. I do." She took a deep breath. "It's my parents. Do you recall the Christmas ball? I had just come out and you were there with Joseph. My parents. I, oh, this is mortifying."

"You were forbidden to dance with me."

She nodded, little jerking movements.

"I hadn't realized," he said.

"I'm sorry. I would love to dance with you, I would. But my mother would see and I'd never hear the end of it. You must understand, my mother—"

Henderson held up a hand. "Please, there is no need to explain. I completely understand."

"Do you?" she asked rather fiercely for such a shy girl. "Because I don't understand."

He smiled at her and the crease between her eyes smoothed. It was odd to him, this prejudice, and he'd only just recently experienced it. He supposed one could tolerate a bastard child and pretend to be welcoming, but when that child becomes a man and begins to look at a high-born lady, things change entirely. He'd been gone from England for far too long. Or perhaps not long enough. "Please, do not distress yourself over this. I shall have my dance another time, when your mama is not in the room."

Harriet smiled. "I'd better go. Thank you for being so understanding, Mr. Southwell."

Henderson watched her walk away, feeling a deep uneasiness. All these years, people had been whispering behind his back, keeping their daughters away, and he *hadn't known*. Though looking back, it had been a bit odd the number of full dance cards he'd encountered. A few girls had danced with him, but now he wondered if it was only because they hadn't known. Part of him wished his grandfather had never made that push to send him to Eton, to make him believe he was equal to anyone. To find out the truth now was rather devastating.

Of course he knew that bastards were not something parents looked for in a son-in-law. He wasn't *that* naïve. He supposed he hadn't realized the extent of it all. Joseph and the Hubbards must have shielded him from comments when he was younger. Their protection, their acceptance, had allowed him to move among the elite, particularly in the country, much more easily than if Joseph had not been his champion. But Joseph was long gone and he was left to experience such bigotry without his friend's protection. It was damned unmanning.

Particularly since the woman he loved now seemed further from reach than ever.

* * *

"I do not think I can bear to see him touch you any longer."

Those words, low and harsh, nearly made her swoon with desire. Alice was standing at the refreshment table, about to pour herself some lemonade, when Henderson came up behind her and whispered in her ear, causing her entire body to heat. She paused, then continued to pour, aware her hands were now shaking just slightly.

Turning, schooling her features so no one would see the desire in her gaze, she mentally prepared herself to greet him coolly. But when she saw him, Alice had to use every ounce of will to hide her feelings. He was just that stunning.

"Good evening, Miss Hubbard," he said. Henderson was a handsome man, tall and lean, but she couldn't recall seeing him in formal wear. Freshly shaved, hair trimmed, clothes tailored to precision, he looked like a member of the aristocracy. Only his grin ruined, or rather improved, the effect.

She was suddenly, fiercely glad that Henderson had been invited to the ball, even though his presence caused her all kinds of anxiety.

"You are looking rather dapper this evening, Mr. Southwell," she said, just a tad more breathy than usual.

Henderson looked down at himself as if he were unaware what a striking figure he cut. "I have Lord Berkley's valet to thank. The man turned a sow's ear into a silk purse. Or in this case, a silk cravat."

"Quite dashing."

"And you, Miss Hubbard, are lovely as well." His warm gaze looked her up and down, making Alice feel more beautiful than she had ever felt. "Where is my nemesis? The last I saw him, he was hovering around you like a bee to a flower."

Alice pressed her lips together to stop from laughing. "He is dancing with Eliza," she said, nodding toward the dance floor. "He really is such a charming man." An odd sound erupted from Henderson and Alice this time could not suppress her laughter. "Did you *growl*?"

"I don't believe you understand the state I am in, Alice. I need to touch you. Now."

Her eyes widened slightly and she could feel her body react shamefully to his pronouncement. She didn't know what had come over her ever since that one foolish, wonderful night. It was supposed to have been one night, a good-bye, a way to live the rest of her life without regrets. Henderson was not supposed to still be here, tunneling into her heart relentlessly, saying outrageous things that made her entire body heat. "Henny, that is hardly a proper thing to say." She desperately wanted to seek equilibrium and trying for some sort of decorum was the only way she knew to do it.

"And I am hardly proper." He looked about, making certain they could not be overheard. "I should have thrown you from my room. If I had, I wouldn't know what lies beneath that gown. I would not spend every night aching for you, every minute of the day wanting you. I swear by all that's holy, you will be mine, Alice. I cannot allow something as inconsequential as my birth to keep you from me."

She swallowed and looked away, unable to witness the anguish in his face. The impact of what he was saying swirled around her; it was heady stuff but it also filled her with trepidation. This was no game to Henderson; he meant every word he said and Alice was suddenly uncertain what to do with such knowledge. He stood before her, declaring his love for her. There was no glint of humor in his gaze as there had been on their walk in the garden. Instead, she saw pain and desperation. And love. Biting her lip, she scanned the ballroom for her mother and father, and was shocked to see them both looking at the two of them, concern in their eyes.

"My parents have been watching us, Henderson."

"I hardly care."

"But I do, and I know you do too. You cannot come up to me in the middle of a ball, with my fiancé"—at his sharp intake of breath, she held up a supplicating hand—"the man I *was* planning to marry, in the very same room. Henderson, you cannot." She rubbed her forehead wearily. Between Lord Northrup, her parents pushing her toward Lord Berkley, who had absolutely no interest in her, and Henderson, who was standing in front of her declaring himself to her, she had never been so entirely confused in her life.

"I cannot? But I have. I love you and I intend to marry you and I intend to prove to your father that I am worthy of you." His expression suddenly changed, growing hard and almost unrecognizable. "Unless you do not want me to. My God," he said, letting out a humorless laugh. "It never occurred to me that you were simply humoring me. That you, like everyone else, only pitied me."

"My dear, our dance." Lord Northrup turned toward Henderson and extended his hand, and Alice wrenched her gaze away from him. "So good you could come, Mr. Southwell. Formal wear suits you."

To Alice's burning ears, Lord Northrup sounded incredibly patronizing, even though she suspected he was simply being kind.

"Of course, my lord," Alice said, extending her hand and acutely aware Henderson likely wanted to wrench her away from Northrup. "And Henderson. You could not be more wrong, and I intend to prove that to you." She smiled at him, praying he understood completely what she meant. By the sudden light in his beautiful eyes, she realized he did and the relief she felt, that she hadn't hurt him, was profound.

As she whirled around the dance floor with the man everyone in the room assumed she would marry, Alice could only think of Henderson. Her heart, so heavy not long ago, felt as if it would lift her to the ceiling. *I love him. I really do.*

"My darling, you're not listening to me at all."

Alice looked up to see that indulgent smile on Northrup's face that she'd seen so many times, as if he were looking at a silly child who believed in fairies. "I was not, my lord. I do apologize."

"I noticed Lord Berkley has not visited with your parents this evening. I do hope that means he has turned his attention away from you. It was rather disconcerting, you know, to think your parents could be swayed in favor of another suitor. After all, we are practically engaged."

Alice found herself shaking her head. "No, my lord, we are not."

Dancing at the John Knill ball was not the place to formally end things with Lord Northrup, so Alice gave him a small smile meant to lessen the blow of her words. Northrup tightened his lips slightly, but other than that did not react to her words. She imagined he still thought he needed to grovel for missing their wedding.

"Of course. I understand. I only hoped that we could have come to a resolution by now, given my perfectly reasonable explanation for having missed the ceremony." What started off as a gentle discourse ended with clipped words that clearly showed he was losing his patience.

"I'm glad we are in accordance then," Alice said, choosing to misunderstand his tone. "If you don't mind, I would like to end our dance a bit early. These shoes." She grimaced to show she was in pain, and he led her to her parents, who still stood together at the edge of the dancing. Instead of glaring at Henderson, they were now glaring at Lord Berkley, who seemed to be enthralled with Harriet's sister Clara.

After Northrup left her side, her mother leaned toward her. "Lord Northrup seems out of sorts. Is everything well between you two?" her mother asked, and Alice nearly laughed aloud at how transparent her mother was. Lord Berkley could be out of the race, it seemed, and now they were happy to bet on the other horse once again.

"Nothing that cannot be resolved," Alice said, trying to be as truthful as possible. She could hardly announce that she was in love with Henderson and he had all but proposed to her. This would require some patience and time, for she knew as much as her parents admired Henderson, they did not see him as potential husband material. As the granddaughter of a duke and an earl, she would be expected to marry a titled man or at least one from a titled family. Not only was Henderson a bastard, he was the bastard of two commoners, so far below her own station it was nearly unthinkable that she consider such a marriage. But she was more than considering it.

She was looking forward to it.

Hugging the joy that threatened to burst forth, Alice couldn't help but allow something of what she was feeling to show on her face as she watched Henderson on the other side of the room. He was looking at her, his gaze intense, and she smiled at him just to let him know all was well. Then he motioned his head to the right. The doors that led to the terrace were to his right.

As she watched, he slowly strolled to the French doors, pulled one open, and stepped out into the darkness. Alice thought her heart might jump right out of her chest. How on earth could she casually make her way to the terrace with her parents seemingly watching her like two hawks?

"Aren't you two going to dance?" she asked, trying to think of some way she could rid herself of her parents without seeming obvious.

Elda gave Richard a look and her father let out a sigh. "Very well. My lady, would you do me the honor of joining me on the dance floor?" he asked formally, and Elda let out a laugh.

"It would be my pleasure. But unfortunately, my dance card is quite full," Elda said, pointing to her imaginary dance card, which her father pretended to take from her and rip into tiny pieces.

With that, he brought his wife onto the dance floor with a wink for Alice, which only made her feel guilty for her subterfuge.

Are you really going to do this?

She knew what would happen if she met Henderson outside. They would kiss and he would declare his love for her again and Alice knew this time she would do the same. When she'd gone to his room all those nights ago, she truly hadn't realized just what might happen. She knew it was wrong and risqué, but this was Henderson and they'd hardly shared more than a kiss. Yes, she'd gone to say good-bye, and yes, she realized they might kiss—and perhaps a bit more. But in all her imaginings she had not thought the evening would end as it had, with them naked in bed and with her nearly losing her virginity.

This time, she knew precisely what she was doing. Certainly, they would not make love, not at the John Knill ball, but this was much more calculated on Alice's part. She knew she was going out to the terrace to declare herself, and she knew they would kiss and plan and scheme and try to come up with a way to make her parents agree to their match.

Giving her parents a fond look, Alice made her way to the French doors where Henderson had just disappeared. She stood there with her back to the door, her hand on the latch, and watched the dancers twirling by, her heart beating hard in her chest. Trying to look as nonchalant as possible, she pushed down the latch and slipped outside, keeping her eyes on her parents who were on the farthest part of the dance floor. Thankfully, they seemed absorbed in conversation and were not looking around, but rather at each other, so Alice felt confident she had made her escape without being seen. The cool air washed over her as she stepped into the darkness.

The terrace was narrow and stretched the length of the large home. Looking left then right, Alice took only one tentative step before a large, warm hand grasped her upper arm and pulled her swiftly and surely away from the light of the ballroom. She followed Henderson willingly, trying not to laugh aloud. Had she ever felt this happy in her life?

Henderson spun her about and they came to a stop, well hidden from anyone who might casually step out onto the terrace by a small alcove formed by another set of doors. He immediately dipped his head to kiss her, but she slapped a gloved hand over her mouth, preventing him. Letting out a small sound of protest, Henderson jerked his head back and stared down at her, his eyes glittering in the light of the bright moon.

"I need to tell you something," Alice said in a rush.

"Go on." His words were stiff, his entire body taut and waiting.

"I love you. I don't want there to be any confusion on your part. I love you with all my heart and I always have. When you left, you took my heart with you and now you've brought it back. I never loved any of the men I was planning to marry, but you left and you never wrote and I didn't know what to do."

He laid a hand against one cheek, and Alice pressed against it, as if she could somehow absorb him into her. Then, letting out a long, heavy breath, he said, "That's all I needed to know, Alice. I realize your parents will resist a match between us, but I will not give up until your father gives his consent."

"We could elope," Alice said with some reluctance and just as much hope, and was mostly glad when Henderson immediately rejected that idea.

"Your father would never forgive me. I think your parents will come around, love."

Alice smiled. "I like that. Love. Oh, Henderson," she said, throwing her arms around him. "Why can this not be as easy as telling my parents we are in love?"

She felt his arms wrap around her and for that moment had never felt more safe in her life. "Perhaps it will be as simple as that. Your parents don't hate me, they're just being good parents I suppose. Not wanting to taint the bloodline with God knows what. My father could be a criminal for all I know."

"Or he could be a duke."

Henderson chuckled. "Or a king."

"Yes, I like that. A king. You do have rather a princely air about you this evening."

"A good valet does wonders." He let out a low sound. "God, it's good to have you in my arms again. I feared it would never happen."

Henderson pulled back just enough so that he could dip his head and kiss her, his lips warm and firm and wonderful against hers. On a sigh, Alice opened her mouth, welcoming his greedy tongue, feeling the desire that had been on the edge of her consciousness for days surge through her body. What was it about Henderson that spoke to her body this way, that made her wish they were naked and that they were joined? Such thoughts should embarrass or shame her, but all Alice could think about was how beautiful it would be when they finally consummated their love.

His manhood pressed against her center, and Alice let out a soft moan. It felt too good, too much. As if her body wanted to burst out of her skin, and she knew what the ending was to this feeling, that blissful completion. To feel that again, now, was so very, very tempting. "We should stop, Henderson. I feel... I feel too much."

"I know. I know. But just another kiss and ..." He brought one hand to skim the flesh above her gown before cupping one breast as he let out another guttural, primitive sound that made Alice's blood grow even hotter. The night air was cool, but Alice had long ceased to feel anything but Henderson's touch, hear anything but the low masculine sounds he made whenever they kissed. Her nipple grew erect beneath his palm and he moved his hand over her, teasing her, making the feeling between her legs intensify to the point that she began to move her hips in an effort to ease the ache.

"Please, Henderson. We have to stop," she said, her voice tense with need.

He chuckled low. "One more kiss," he said, and dipped his head so he could mouth her nipple over her gown.

Alice let out a small screech, the sensations too much. She was close to grabbing his hand and dragging him off the terrace and into the garden. Never in her life had she felt this way, as if she had no control over her body. It was very nearly frightening, the need that was coursing through her, making her contemplate such a thing.

"Henderson, stop. Oh, God, don't..." *I can't take any more.*

He did stop, abruptly so, and it took Alice a second to understand what had happened, that her father, with a feral sound she'd never heard in her life, had ripped Henderson from her arms.

"Get your filthy hands off my daughter, you low-born cur," he said, his voice terrible and harsh in the quiet of the night.

"My lord, I—" But Henderson's words were stopped when Richard backhanded Henderson across the face, the sound of the impact sharp and awful.

Henderson looked as stunned as Alice felt. Never had she seen her father act in violence. It was so far from his gentle nature, Alice could only stand frozen in shock at what was happening. What had they been thinking; they both knew how dangerous such a clandestine meeting could be.

"I assure you, sir, I mean no disrespect to—"

"Say another word and I shall murder you where you stand."

"Father, no. You don't understand." He continued to stare at Henderson, his expression cold. "Father, please. Nothing untoward happened, we...Papa?"

Her father stumbled backward, one hand clutching at his chest, the other reaching out blindly behind him for the terrace rail, but missing. Before he could fall heavily to the hard marble beneath their feet, Henderson lunged forward and caught him and Alice let out a small scream.

Henderson, holding her father awkwardly in his arms, looked up at her. "Tell your mother to call a physician."

Chapter 14

"Killing Lord Hubbard was not part of the plan."

Henderson gave Lord Berkley a withering look, unamused by the man's comment, and Berkley mumbled an apology.

"Thank God he did not die. At least not yet. I do not believe Lady Hubbard would ever forgive me if he does." After the physician had been called, Berkley urged Henderson to leave once it became clear that Lord Hubbard's death wasn't imminent. He could not get the way Alice's face looked out of his mind, grief etched with guilt and remorse. When it came to Alice, it seemed Henderson was unable to use common sense or even attempt decorum. Berkley very nearly had to drag him from the terrace, where a small crowd had gathered. The only saving grace was that no one knew what had precipitated the attack. At least he could be grateful that Alice had not been ruined.

Henderson took a sip of the very fine brandy Berkley always seemed to have on hand, no matter where they were. Proprietors didn't seem to mind, especially when he gave them a generous tip. This evening, they sat morosely in a small tavern just outside of St. Ives. It was an ancient place with low ceilings and wide plank floors that had likely seen a century of spilt ale. The old gentleman behind the bar might have been there since the beginning, so bent and wrinkled was he. Even his clothes seemed to be from another century, as if he'd found something that fit him when he was a lad and continued to wear it to this day.

"The course of true love never did run smooth," Berkley said.

"This is a rutted and muddy road, indeed," Henderson said. "What of you? You looked rather taken with Clara Anderson."

"She is one of the most beautiful women I have ever seen, but I am not in the market for another wife. I still have a rotten taste in my mouth from the last beautiful wife."

While Henderson thought it would have been far more convenient to meet in Berkley's home, the earl truly did seem to loathe being there, using the large estate only as a place to work and sleep. Henderson had come to value the other man's friendship for far more reasons than that he was attempting to help him gain Alice as his bride. He supposed it might be that Berkley seemed to take nothing seriously, and Henderson took everything seriously.

"I am running out of time," Henderson said. "Parliament is back in session in just more than a month and we are not prepared. I have a feeling Northrup's enthusiasm for famine relief will wane as soon as Miss Hubbard formally breaks it off with him and I shall have to rely on you alone. And this," he said, pointing to an article in the *Times* about riots in India, "only makes matters more urgent. I cannot forget famine relief is the reason I returned to England, that there are people counting on my efforts to make change."

Berkley drummed his fingers on the table and looked thoughtful. "I mean no insult, but why send you, a man with no influence and few connections, on such a daunting errand?"

Henderson gave Berkley a sheepish grin. "For one, I volunteered. I'd received a letter just that morning from my grandmother, who mentioned Miss Southwell had just announced her third engagement. She knew, of course, that I was friendly with the family and I supposed she thought I might be interested in hearing the news. And of course I was more than interested. For another, I am a passionate speaker and am not without influential friends. At least I thought so. Perhaps I overstated my influence or had grand ideas about just how far loyalty would go. It has been four years since I left, and it's been an eye opening few weeks since I returned."

"Oh?"

"It seems the influential friends I thought I had were actually influential friends of Joseph's. I've written to nearly everyone I can recall from our days at Oxford but have received not a single response. I was a bit of tagalong. I had no idea, you see."

"Ah. It can be difficult to see oneself as others do. I learned that lesson myself, which is why I headed to America, where no one knew me." He laughed softly and took a deep drink. "Now, with my father's death, there are certain people who expect me to step into his role and I'm afraid I have little interest and fewer skills."

Henderson was slightly taken aback. "Are you withdrawing your support for the relief?"

"Absolutely not. But once I have exerted myself on that effort, I think I shall retire from politics. That was my father's forte, not mine. Though I must admit my antipathy toward my father's work has turned, of late, toward admiration. To keep all that information, stored away, to be used later takes an enormous amount of foresight and I can see how it could be amusing to wield such information against one's enemies. I have a feeling, though, that he also wielded it against those who thought him an ally."

Henderson had to admit he was curious about what Berkley had found out about Lord Hubbard. The knowledge that he held something that could be used to sway the man toward Henderson's goal of marrying Alice lived in the corner of his mind, like some sort of small animal scurrying about begging for notice. "I know I said I would not use the information, and I will not, but what *did* you find out about Lord Hubbard?"

Berkley smiled as if pleased he'd come around, and Henderson couldn't help but feel slightly disappointed in himself for asking.

"I have a letter from him that indicates his interest in investing in a Portuguese slave ship."

"My God."

"Yes. My father has a letter in which Lord Hubbard expresses his unhappiness with the situation but in which he promises his funds at any rate despite his reservations and the fact the slave trade has been banned here since early in this century." Berkley shrugged, then shook his head. "A second letter indicates he never did send the money, that his conscience would not allow him to support the transportation of Africans to Brazil, I believe it was. The fact my father kept the letters is astonishing. Both are very nearly forty years old, and there they were, carefully catalogued, just waiting for the day when such information could be useful. It was my understanding from Lady Hubbard that Alice's parents were friends of my father. Yet he kept those letters. The first one could gain someone a powerful favor if one was inclined to use it."

Henderson felt slightly sick about the idea of confronting Lord Hubbard now, as he lay recovering from a heart attack, with such information. Indeed, it was difficult to believe Lord Hubbard would have considered tying himself to such a scheme and Henderson found himself vastly relieved to know the young Hubbard had changed his mind. "I'll never use it. Please destroy them both."

Berkley smiled again. "I already have."

* * *

Guilt felt like a live thing inside her, gnawing away at her stomach, making her physically ill. She had very nearly killed her father. It was impossible to contemplate that he could have died, that he still might die. She would never forget the look on her mother's face when she'd rushed out onto the terrace and had seen Richard in Henderson's arms. It had taken perhaps one second before her expression changed subtly, her countenance filled with worry and then a terrible coldness when she looked at Alice. Later, Alice realized that her mother had been waiting just inside the French doors, that somehow Alice had been seen making her escape to the terrace, and that her father had gone to fetch her.

Sitting on the edge of her bed, Alice stared at her toes peeking out beneath her nightgown and prayed with all her might that her father would live. It was four in the morning and her eyes burned from tears and lack of sleep. Yet even with the guilt, the fear, her thoughts often went to Henderson, his face pale but for the livid red mark on one cheek from her own father's hand.

Her mother hadn't said a word, not one word, to her all evening. Not, "Go to bed, you must be tired" not, "I'm sure he'll be fine." The silence was awful because Alice felt in her heart that she deserved it. If she had simply accepted Northrup back when he'd come to beg forgiveness, none of this would have happened. Alice wouldn't have fallen in love with Henderson, she would not have gone to his room on the pretense of saying good-bye, her father would not be lying pale and still on his bed. Her mother would still love her.

Tears fell once again down her cheeks. A small knock on her door gave Alice some hope that her mother was coming to talk to her. Perhaps when Alice told her how much she loved Henderson, how it had all been a terrible mistake, she would understand. But when she called the visitor to enter, it was Christina who came silently into her room, her eyes red-rimmed from crying. She ran to Alice and threw herself against her, letting out body-racking sobs that Alice tried to pull into herself.

When Christina's tears subsided, she pulled back and wiped her cheeks with her sleeves. "What happened tonight? Mama isn't saying anything and they're speaking so quietly in Papa's room I cannot hear a word."

Alice gave her sister a fond smile. "Even with a glass?"

"Even with a glass," her sister said without an ounce of shame at having been found out eavesdropping.

Alice wasn't certain she should tell Christina what had happened, but after some thought decided it would be a good way to teach Christina the dangers of veering from propriety. One should always be proper, even when one was tempted not to be. She had not been herself, not since Henderson had come back to St. Ives, and had been acting in ways she never would have dreamed.

"It's my fault," Alice said, and shook her head when Christina made to protest. "It is. I was out on the terrace with Mr. Southwell. Alone. And we were kissing. Papa found us together and was so angry. I've never seen him that angry. He actually struck Henderson, Mr. Southwell, in the face. It was terrible."

To Alice's surprise, Christina smiled. "I knew you loved him. And it was obvious he loved you. I'm so sorry, Alice."

"I shouldn't have been out there with him. I knew it was wrong and I knew he would kiss me but I went anyway. I…" She swallowed past a throat gone suddenly thick. "I tricked Mama and Papa into dancing so that I could go out and meet him. What a horrible daughter I am and now I've nearly killed our papa."

Alice sat beside Christina, twisting the material of her gown between her hands until it resembled a cloth dust devil. "Mama is so angry with me, Christina. I think that's the worst of it. She couldn't even look at me, she was so ashamed." She let out a small laugh. "And to think I believed I'd be able to convince them that Mr. Southwell would be a good match for me. Do you know what Papa said, Christina? He told Mr. Southwell to get his dirty hands off me and called him a low-born cur. Papa! He was so very angry."

Christina's brows furrowed. "That doesn't sound like something Papa would say," she said thoughtfully. "Do you think it's possible that Papa misinterpreted what he saw? That he thought perhaps Mr. Southwell was making unwanted advances? I know Papa can be a bit of a snob, but I find it difficult to believe he would say such a thing to Mr. Southwell. We all like him."

Pressing the heels of her hands against her tear-swollen eyes, Alice said, "It doesn't matter. Either way, Papa will never contemplate a match between us. A true gentleman would never have kissed me that way."

To her surprise, Christina burst out laughing. "Really, Alice, for someone who's been engaged three times, you can be so naïve."

"What are you saying?"

"You know Aunt Agatha adores genealogy."

Alice gave Christina a confused look at her abrupt change in topic. "Of course. She's the keeper of the family tree."

Christina got an impish look on her face. "It just so happens that I was helping Aunt Agatha two summers ago. You remember when I went to visit her? It was dreadfully boring, but I discovered the most shocking and interesting information." She paused. "About Mama and Papa."

"What?" Alice asked, not truly believing her sister would say anything of interest.

"Perhaps the next time you visit Aunt Agatha's library, you should pay close attention to Mama and Papa's wedding date. And Joseph's birth date."

Alice's mouth opened in disbelief at what her sister was implying. "No. Really?"

"Unless Joseph was born a full three months early."

Nothing could have surprised Alice more. Her mother and father, who had always schooled her to be proper at all times, had done *that* before they were even married? It was unthinkable.

"Are you absolutely certain?"

Christina gave a sharp nod. "Aunt Agatha swore me to secrecy, but I do believe this is a special circumstance. Aunt Agatha felt as the keeper of family information, she could not lie. Three months, Alice. Three."

Alice gave her sister a scowl. "You're too young to be thinking about such things."

"Aunt had no such qualms and that was two years ago. I think she was rather relieved that she wasn't the only one holding on to such a secret. I do believe Mama would be livid if she knew the true dates were listed in that book. Can you imagine? I think Mama would have a heart attack too."

Shaking her head, Alice said, "I cannot imagine why Aunt Agatha felt it was so important not to fib a little, but I have to say I am glad. Not that I could bring that up to Mama and Papa. Not now. Nothing has truly changed."

Christina wrapped one arm around her shoulders and gave her a tight squeeze. "When Papa is feeling better, perhaps you can speak to him about Mr. Southwell. It would be a tragedy to keep you apart."

Alice swallowed heavily. "Yes, it would."

Chapter 15

Three days later, the family physician pronounced that Lord Hubbard would not die, then ordered him to remain in bed for two weeks. It was gratifying for everyone in the family to hear Richard complaining loudly about the bed rest.

Elda had summoned Oliver from London, and he arrived to find his robust father pale and abed. Though he'd put on a brave front when visiting his father, he broke down upon leaving Richard's room, only adding to the heavy weight of guilt already on Alice's shoulders. Her mother still had not spoken a word to her, and it was, frankly, driving her mad.

Three days of silence. Three days of wondering if she would ever be forgiven, if she would ever see Henderson again. It was only when Richard began complaining that the shroud of uncertainty was lifted from Tregrennar. For now, Papa would live.

Alice spent most of those three days in her room. She had not visited her father. The one time she'd ventured to his door, Papa's valet, Mr. Tisdale, had quietly told her that her father was not up to seeing her. The fact that Christina and Oliver had visited with him earlier that day only made Alice's heart ache all the more. If she could turn back time, she would, but she couldn't. The first two days, all Alice could think of was that she would not be able to tell her father she loved him and that she was sorry before he died. By the third day, Alice had stopped her self-flagellation and was able to view what had happened with slightly less emotion. She concluded two things. One: Yes, she had been wrong to go out onto the terrace with Henderson. Two: Her actions had not caused her father's heart attack. She could accept some blame, but not all of it, and the fact that her mother refused to speak to her, that her father would not even see her, fueled a growing anger. Of course, the knowledge that her mother and father had actually had relations prior to their marriage and that a pregnancy no doubt accelerated the wedding only added to that fuel.

One might think she'd been caught on the terrace with a married man. Naked.

A few hours after the physician departed, Alice was in her room reading when her mother entered quietly. She seemed subdued and so unlike the woman she'd been not four days prior. Alice longed to go to her, but sensed her embrace would not be welcome.

"Your father told me what happened, Alice. Once he is fully recovered, we will commence with your wedding arrangements to Lord Northrup, who thankfully is still willing to marry you."

Alice could feel a blush bloom on her cheeks. "Lord Northrup knows what happened?"

"Of course not. No one knows but your father and me."

"Then why must I marry Northrup?" She literally bit her tongue to stop herself from saying, *It's not as if I were foolish enough to lose my virginity.* Oh, but it was a temptation that was difficult to resist.

"Because he has asked for your hand. Again. And your father agreed."

Anger replaced concern so swiftly, Alice could feel her body heat with it. "Lord Northrup has seen Papa yet I was not allowed?"

Elda waved her hand as if that was inconsequential. "Lord Northrup wanted to be certain to do the correct thing, the proper thing, and be sure that he had consent in case your father did not get well."

Alice opened her mouth to protest, but her mother's steely look stopped her.

"You must make me a promise. You will never see Henderson Southwell again."

This was her punishment for kissing a man? Marriage to a man she did not love and a promise to never see the man she did love? Everything inside Alice rebelled at the thought of how unfair it was.

"I'm sorry, Mama, but I cannot make such a promise. I love Henderson and he loves me."

Elda's eyes widened slightly and her mouth turned downward; then her face softened and Alice finally saw the mother she'd known all her life. She'd hardly recognized the one who'd walked through her door. "I'm certain you believe you do, but I must say that cannot be possible. He's been gone for four years and you've hardly seen him since he's returned. Yes, he is handsome and I understand there may be some allure to the forbidden, but you cannot be foolish."

Elda sat down on the small vanity stool, her skirts rustling in such a familiar way, Alice's heart ached. She wanted her lively smiling mother back, not this sad and stern and determined woman. "There are times in a mother's life when she must make decisions for her children that are not popular, that may seem harsh. But I have no doubt that marriage to Mr. Southwell would not suit you. It matters not that he was once welcomed into our home. That welcome is no longer forthcoming. Do you understand me?"

Alice could feel the now-familiar ache in her throat. "No. I do not. It is unfair to punish us for doing nothing more than kissing. Are you blaming us for what happened to Father?" What had seemed a logical conclusion in her own mind, suddenly seemed outrageously unjust when her mother came to that same conclusion.

Elda smiled gently. "Not entirely. But he would not have gotten so gravely ill had he not seen the two of you together. Mr. Southwell was not acting like a gentleman."

"And I was not acting like a lady. Mama, I love him and I was there of my own free will. If Father had not come along, I might have acted even more foolishly. Haven't you ever done something you knew you should not?"

Her brow furrowed slightly. "He was not forcing himself on you?"

Letting out a small laugh, Alice said, "My God, no. No. Was that why Father was so upset—he thought Henderson's advances were unwelcome? I can assure you, Mama, they were not. I'm not proud of that, but I would never want anyone to think ill of Henderson."

"That changes nothing. Oh, Alice, can you not see how very inappropriate such a match would be? I like Mr. Southwell enough, but we've never met his family. We know nothing of them. Do you not see how this could be just as uncomfortable for them as it would be for us?"

"They are not indigents living on a poor farm. They are well-respected landowners who were able to send their grandson to Eton and Oxford. Goodness sakes, Mama, you have never been a snob."

"My daughter has never wanted to marry so far beneath her."

Her mother's words stunned her. "How can you speak so of him? He was Joseph's best friend."

"Yes, he was. Against our better judgement, I would like to add. Alice, you are the grand—"

"—daughter of a duke and an earl. Yes, Mother, I know. It is not Henderson's fault that he is who he is. He is a good man and I love him."

Elda rubbed her eyes with her fingertips. "Doors would be closed to you, do you understand? People who have been friends with you your entire life, will no longer want you in their home. Is that what you want?"

"That wouldn't happen—"

"I've seen it happen," Elda said harshly. Taking a deep, calming breath, she said, "My cousin Beatrice married a grocer. I haven't seen her in years. They're living in some tiny house in Kent, scraping by, with a brood of children they cannot afford. Everything she had is gone, her friends, her family, her station in life. I will not see you throw away your life like that."

"So this is about money? I'm sorry, Mother, because Lord Northrup doesn't appear to be all that well-heeled. Lord Berkley hinted at a gambling problem."

Elda stood suddenly. "I am not going to continue to argue with you, Alice. You cannot marry Mr. Southwell and that is that."

Alice blinked at the anger her mother was displaying, but remained silent as Elda left the room.

"I am going to marry him, Mama," she whispered after her mother had rather forcefully shut the door. She gave a small shrug, but one that held a world of defiance. "And I'm afraid there is nothing you can do about it."

* * *

Sebastian's fiancée, Cecelia Whitemore, lived in a modest home on the outskirts of St. Ives village but with a view of the Atlantic that took one's breath away. The charm of the house, situated on a bluff and surrounded by cabbage trees and roses in full bloom, was ruined by the large black wreath adorning the door, a tribute to the man their daughter would never marry. Henderson stopped at the stone arbor, where a riot of roses obliterated the stone, and paused when he saw the obvious sign of mourning, the second such wreath he'd encountered in recent weeks. And as before, Henderson decided it was vital that he ignore it and continue with his interview. Perhaps it was insensitive of him, visiting Sebastian's fiancée so soon after his death, but Henderson could not wait.

Henderson stepped onto the ancient stone step and turned the bell, a clever little design in the shape of a limpet shell, the sound overly cheerful given the black wreath. A man with diminutive spectacles and impressive muttonchops, speckled with a fair amount of gray, opened the door and looked at him curiously before turning and saying, "I have this, Mrs. Spratt."

Henderson waited for the shadow of the woman to disappear before introducing himself. "Hello, sir. My name is Henderson Southwell and I was a friend of Sebastian Turner. I was wondering if I might speak with your daughter. I do realize this is a terrible time for her and your family, and I would not have disturbed her for anything had I not deemed this extremely important."

"I am her father," he said in a distinct Cornish accent, though Henderson had already guessed as much. "You are correct, Mr. Southwell, this is a terrible time for us. Do you mind telling me why you need to speak with my daughter?"

"I wanted to know if Sebastian had ever told her about a Mr. Stewart."

Suddenly, the door opened wider, and Cecelia was there, her eyes wide. She was a pretty girl, with dark brown hair parted severely down the middle, but the style somehow suited her even features and pale, smooth skin. She looked to her father and back to Henderson, one hand still clutching the door as if she might fall if she let go. "We need to talk to him, Father," she said.

Mr. Whitemore led him to a small, sunlit parlor with comfortable furniture and a fireplace of golden stone that dominated one wall. After indicating he should take a seat, Cecelia left to fetch her mother and Mr. Whitemore sat, silently, as they waited for the women to return. It was a damned uncomfortable minute, one in which Henderson looked about the room as if finding everything about it fascinating, while Mr. Whitemore stared at the carpet at his feet. When the women entered, Henderson sprang to his feet, nearly knocking his hat, which he'd placed beside him, to the floor.

After introducing him to her mother, Cecelia sat down serenely and stared at him with her calm, brown eyes. "Why did you ask about a Mr. Stewart?"

"This may seem a strange call, but Sebastian mentioned this Mr. Stewart when I saw him last, the night before he passed. He asked me if Joseph Hubbard had ever mentioned a Mr. Stewart to me. It struck me as odd because he said if Joseph had, I would certainly remember it. I didn't think anything of it at the time. I don't know who Mr. Stewart is and I told him so, and that was the end of the conversation. And then, three days ago, at the John Knill ball, I ran into Gerald Grant. He was one of the lads who was sometimes part of our group. When I saw Gerald, he asked me if Sebastian had spoken of a Mr. Stewart that last night before he passed."

Cecelia looked impossibly pale. "You truly don't know who Mr. Stewart is?"

Henderson looked at each person in the room, completely baffled why they were, to a one, looking at him as if they were seeing a ghost.

"Mr. Stewart died years ago," Mr. Whitemore said, his deep voice sounding overly loud in the small room. "A tree limb fell on him as he was riding beneath it." Mr. Whitemore looked at his daughter and nodded.

"Everyone knew the story," she said, her voice trembling slightly. "Mr. Stewart owned a shop in the village and was well-liked by everyone. I even recall going to his funeral. Everyone went. No one knew what really happened. But I know because Sebastian told me."

* * *

Five boys were in the forest that day, building a fort in an oak tree. Joseph, Peter Jeffreys, Tristan Cummings, Sebastian Turner and Gerald Grant. Gerald was the youngest, only twelve years old and trying to prove to the older boys that he was worthy of their company. It had been Joseph's idea to build the fort, something that didn't surprise Henderson, for he was always coming up with some adventure, even when they were older and in university. Henderson could almost picture them, boys on the cusp of being men, likely competing to see who was the strongest of the bunch, heaving up thick limbs high into the tree to build their fortress in the sky.

And then there was Gerald, too young to be with boys who had already started growing peach fuzz on their faces, who already were beginning to develop the muscles required to handle such heavy branches. He'd just been a kid who was trying to prove himself. The older boys teased him as older boys will; he was such an easy target and his face would get so red when they made him angry. He grabbed the largest of the limbs, told the other boys he needed no help, and so they sat back and watched, likely shouting encouragement or needling him or doing what boys will do when they're all together having a grand time.

Gerald had almost gotten that branch up to the fort, gaining the grudging admiration of his friends, when they heard the soft sound of hooves on the dirt road below them. Peter, who wasn't even supposed to be out of the house, begged the other boys to remain quiet as Gerald hung on to that branch with all his might. Sebastian was watching Gerald, ready to give assistance if it looked like the younger boy needed help, and he swore to Cecelia that Gerald simply let go, just as Mr. Stewart was beneath him.

"He watched Gerald's hands open up," Cecelia said, demonstrating with her own hands. "But Sebastian could never be completely certain, not certain enough to ever say anything. That branch fell on Mr. Stewart and killed him on the spot. The boys all swore they would never tell and they never did. But it ate at Sebastian and he just couldn't take the guilt anymore, so he told me. And now..."

"They're all dead," Henderson said, and Mrs. Whitemore pushed a handkerchief against her mouth to stifle a sob. "Have you told anyone what you know?"

Cecelia shook her head quickly. "I'm afraid he'll kill me. That no one will believe me and he'll kill me."

"Don't tell a soul, Miss Whitemore. I'll make certain you are not harmed, but the authorities must be told."

"No, please don't," Cecelia said. "We're the only ones who know. If you were able to determine that I might know, then surely Gerald will too."

Henderson smiled gently. "He can't kill everyone in St. Ives. I swear to you, no one will ever know where I got my information."

Miss Whitemore did not look convinced, but Henderson did not know what else he could say to her to relieve her mind. What was clear to him was that Gerald very likely had knowingly killed four men to protect his terrible secret. Henderson wanted to be sure he didn't kill again.

Once he departed the Whitemores', Henderson went directly to Costille House to ask Lord Berkley for this advice, for he wasn't familiar with St. Ives' constabulary, or even if they had one. Having been the subject of a murder investigation, Lord Berkley would at the very least know with whom he should speak. He arrived at Costille in the late afternoon as the mellowing sun was hitting the large building's façade, softening it and almost making it look welcoming. The sprawling estate held little appeal to Henderson, who preferred more modern design, and he didn't fully understand Lord Berkley's obsession with the place. Likely it had something to do with tradition and heritage, two concepts Henderson had little experience with.

Berkley's butler, looking more harried than usual, ushered him in hastily. Somewhere deep in the house was a terrible racket, and this was where the butler led him, practically pushing him inside the door of what appeared to be a music room. The instruments, a harp, a piano, and a row of—my God, the most beautiful violins Henderson had ever seen in one location—were untouched. But Berkley was ripping ornate paneling from the room, along with thick, floral wallpaper, swearing like a seaman.

"He doesn't care for the décor," the butler whispered before backing out of the room and leaving Henderson with what appeared to be a madman. Berkley was in his shirtsleeves, his hair a wild mass about his head, his shirt clinging to him from sweat. He wrenched an entire section of paneling from the wall, letting it fall with a violent bang, then stood back, his head hung low.

"Bitch!" He yelled so loudly, Henderson actually jerked back in surprise.

Henderson contemplated slowly backing from the room and pretending he'd never entered, but decided to simply let his presence be known. "My lord," he said into the silence that followed.

Berkley started laughing, then turned, shaking his head. "I think, having seen me at my worst, we are now on a first name basis. You may call me Augustus, or Gus as my friends in America used to do."

Henderson raised a brow. "Gus. I fear I cannot be quite that informal with you, sir. And you may call me Henderson, of course. If you don't mind my asking, what has made you so angry?"

"There was a mural here from the fifteenth century and now it is gone. My God, she hated me." He let out another laugh, but this one was filled with bitterness and anger. He clapped his hands loudly, as if doing so ended whatever dark mood he was in. "To what do I owe the pleasure of your company, Henderson?"

He smiled. "I have solved a murder, actually four murders, and I need your help."

Chapter 16

Four days after the John Knill ball, Alice was tiptoeing past her father's door on her way out to visit with Harriet, when she stopped just outside his room. She could hear voices within, likely her father and his valet, and she slipped inside the door without knocking, for the thought that she would be turned away again was unbearable.

Indeed, it was Richard's valet in the room, and he turned, a look of surprise on his face when he saw her standing there. Mr. Tisdale moved quickly toward her, making little shooing gestures with his hands, much to Alice's annoyance, but was interrupted by her father. "Let her in, Mr. Tisdale," he said, sounding weary.

The valet let out a small puff of air, so small Alice doubted her father even heard that tiny gesture of defiance, before nodding his head. "Good morning, Miss Hubbard," he said before exiting the room.

Alice, her throat closing at the sight of her papa in bed even though he looked well and had good color, stepped to the edge of the bed and grabbed at the hand her father offered.

"I don't want to speak of the ball, not yet. But I had to come and see you and tell you how very sorry I am that you are ill. And that I love you. And that no one should ever bar me from seeing you, no matter what I have done." Richard opened his mouth to speak, his dear eyes full of forgiveness for his elder daughter, but she interrupted whatever it was he was going to say. "That is all I'm going to say, Papa. We'll talk more another time and at much greater length, I assure you." She smiled down at him impishly. "I fear what I have to say will not be what you want to hear, and I want to be certain you are much better." Bending down to kiss his cheek, Alice saw her father's eyes narrow in displeasure.

"I'm off, Papa. We'll talk later." She nearly ran from his room, not even stopping when he called her name, but simply waving a hand as if she could wave away whatever it was he wanted to say. Closing the door firmly behind her, Alice breathed a sigh of relief and smiled.

* * *

It was Harriet's turn to host their small gathering, a weekly meeting during which the girls pretended to knit but often simply talked. The Anderson house was Alice's least favorite of the three homes she visited as part of their little knitting group. Harriet's home was even more formal than hers, an oppressive place where the sound of laughter was infrequent, the staff dour, and the overall mood oppressive. At all the other homes, the four girls could gather informally and chat and laugh and gossip. But Mrs. Anderson would frequently step into the room on one excuse or another to check up on them, stifling whatever fun they could have. She was an omnipresent specter of unease, and behind Harriet's back, for the other girls didn't want to hurt Harriet's feelings, they called her the Termagant.

Which was why Alice was surprised when Harriet herself opened the door when she rang. "My family is not here," she said, full of lightness and air. Alice was taken aback, but laughed at her friend's obvious happiness. "Eliza and Rebecca are already here. How is your father?"

They began walking toward the parlor at a more subdued pace, for the housekeeper appeared, coming from the opposite direction, and Harriet had always believed she was a spy for her mother. With a cold look at the woman as they passed her, Alice gave Harriet a small encouraging nudge. They'd been best friends for as long as Alice could remember and she could read her well. "That is why I was a bit late. I stopped into his room to see how he was faring, and he is doing well," she said as they entered the parlor.

"I'm so relieved to hear he is doing better."

"Much better, thank you. It was quite the fright, but the physician says with bed rest and fewer rich foods, Papa will be with us for a long time," Alice said.

They all sat, their knitting by their sides, and it was clear very little actual knitting was going to be done that day. So much had happened since they'd met, and Alice's stomach felt a bit jumbled by it all.

"Had your father been ill prior to the attack? I'm always lecturing my father to take better care of himself but he hardly listens to me. Perhaps your father's scare will knock some sense into my own father," Rebecca said.

Alice thought back and couldn't find anything in her memory that would hint of any illness except for some minor heartburn he'd complained of a few times at breakfast, hardly anything to be concerned about. "Nothing." She looked at each of her friends, knowing she could trust them with her deepest secrets. After all, she knew all of their secrets.

Still, she pressed her lips together, uncertain whether this was the time to tell her friends about Henderson. Darting a look at Harriet, Alice said, "I have something to tell you all and it must go no further than this room." She gave them all a level look, and nearly smiled at the rabid anticipation she saw in their eyes. Nothing piqued her friends' interest more than gossip, even if it was gossip about one of them. On her walk over, Alice had debated with herself whether she should divulge her secret love of Henderson, particularly given Harriet's girlhood crush. If she'd thought Harriet was truly in love with Henderson, she would have told her separately, but she knew Harriet would have confided in her if her feelings were deep.

"I am to blame for my father's attack."

After a rush of protest from her friends, Alice raised a hand to silence them. "I am. And this is why. Please don't think ill of me, I beg you." She bit her lip, and her friends, who had been rather gleeful to hear a bit of gossip, now looked concerned.

"What is it, Alice? No matter what it is, we are your friends and you can tell us," Harriet said.

Closing her eyes, for that made it somehow easier to say aloud, Alice said, "I was with a man on the terrace, kissing, and my father caught us." At the collective gasp she heard, Alice's eyes flew open. "And that's not the worst of it."

"It's worse?" Eliza asked, her expression one of pure shock.

Alice nodded and couldn't stop the grin from blooming on her face, much to her friends' collective dismay. "It was Henderson."

The silence that followed was, to say the least, complete.

"I love him," she said, looking at Harriet, who suddenly found the floor fascinating. "And he loves me and we hope to marry."

"Of course your parents are opposed." This from Eliza, and Alice had to suppress a small amount of anger at the certainty in her words.

"Yes, they are. But I shall change their minds."

The other three girls looked at each other, as if trying to gauge how to feel about this announcement.

"How long have you felt this way?" Harriet ask softly, still unable to look at Alice, and she realized she *had* hurt Harriet more than she could have guessed.

"When I was young, I felt foolish for liking my brother's best friend."

"And I was making such a cake of myself over him," Harriet said, a small smile on her face.

"I didn't want to discourage you or compete with you, so I didn't say a word even though I fancied myself in love with him when I was younger. I thought it was a silly girlhood crush, but since his return, my love has only grown. It seems almost impossible to believe, but Henderson felt the same way, all this time. Neither of us knew how the other felt." From the expressions on her friends' faces, she might have told them all she was gravely ill. The silence told her more than words: they were not only shocked, but, worse, opposed.

"Will someone please say something?"

"Why do you have to have all the men in St. Ives? In all of England?" This from Harriet, who was laughing aloud, but Alice thought she sensed a small bit of bitterness behind her words. "Can't you leave any for us?" Harriet, she realized, was jesting and the other girls joined in her laughter, leaving Alice relieved.

"I know he is not the man my parents would have chosen given his lack of title and family, but one cannot help whom one falls in love with. It matters not that Henderson is not wealthy or titled. I love him anyway."

"But he *is* wealthy," Eliza said with nod.

Alice furrowed her brow. "He is?"

"You remember St. Claire. Nothing fascinates him more than strangers, and your Mr. Southwell intrigued him. As it turns out, his grandfather is quite well-to-do and Mr. Southwell has made a fortune for himself whilst in India. You didn't know?"

"We never speak of such things," Alice said, wondering what else she didn't know about the man she loved. She'd learned in the last few days that he could play the violin like a master and that he was probably far wealthier than Lord Northrup. "I wonder if my parents know."

"Do you think that would make a difference?" Harriet asked.

Shaking her head, Alice said, "I don't believe so. They care far more that he is untitled and comes from a family without status." The ugly word floating about the room—bastard—went unspoken, though Alice suspected everyone was thinking the same thing.

"However will you convince your parents if they are so opposed?" Rebecca asked.

Alice smiled. "I am confident I can convince them Mr. Southwell is more than worthy of my hand. And if I cannot, it's off to Gretna Green." The three gasped, not as much horrified as excited by the prospect of Alice hieing off to Scotland to get married.

"You wouldn't," said Eliza, the most proper of the four of them— at least she was now that Alice had decided to thwart convention so thoroughly. Alice had always been the one to stay on that straight line of propriety. "You have to think about what such an action would mean for Christina."

Alice made a face. "Of course you are right, Eliza. I hadn't thought of that, which tells you how very muddled my mind is these days. I will simply have to convince my parents that Mr. Southwell is the perfect choice for me. Then I'll have to convince my grandfather to attend the wedding and everyone will accept Henderson. I do wish my grandmother was still alive. I know she would have adored Mr. Southwell, if only to be contrary."

A small commotion outside the parlor door told them Harriet's parents and sister had returned home, and the women immediately took up their knitting, a shadow falling over the small group. Clara swept in looking fresh and pretty, wearing a gown that Alice knew must have cost a fortune. Her eyes went to Harriet, taking in her far simpler gown in a dull color that was completely unflattering, and she wondered if it was Harriet's choice to look drab or if her mother had chosen it for her.

"I don't know how you girls can sit and knit on such a glorious day," Clara said, spreading her arms out as if to capture the sunshine streaming through a window. "Come on, let's go visit Zennor Quoit."

"I don't know if I'm up for such a walk today," Eliza said, looking down at shoes, which were definitely not created with long walks in mind.

Clara sat down with a huff, chin in hand, and Alice was amazed at how pretty she looked even when miffed. Seconds later, she sat up, smiling, her bad mood gone. "Would you like to play whist in the garden?" She looked outside. "It is not very breezy today, so I think we could. I cannot bear to be inside on such a lovely day. I've already been entombed at the Fosters' all morning." She turned to Harriet. "How did you escape that dreary invitation?"

"Mother neglected to tell me about it," Harriet said simply, and Alice cringed inwardly. It was not the first time Harriet had been "forgotten" at home. This abandonment had hurt her when she was younger, but Alice suspected she quite liked the freedom it gave her now that she was older.

"Really, I'm beginning to suspect she does it on purpose to punish me," Clara said, wonderfully oblivious to the reality that she was the favored child.

Harriet gave her sister a long look tinged with disbelief and fondness. "I don't think Mother would bring you anywhere as punishment," she said, and Alice could hear the irony in her voice even if Clara could not.

Clara let out an inelegant snort. "Then why am I always forced to go and you are allowed to remain home?"

"Perhaps she hopes there will be a bachelor in attendance who can catch your eye," Eliza said, at which Clara rolled her eyes.

"I have no interest in marriage. Why should I when I'm perfectly content as I am?"

"What if you met the man of your dreams?" Eliza asked, then her eyes widened. "Who is the man of your dreams?"

"He doesn't exist," Clara said, and all the ladies laughed.

"The man of my dreams is tall and handsome and witty and adores children," Eliza said. "And he has to be rich and be fashionable. And a title would be nice, but not necessary. Oh, and he must love to read and have a dog, but not like to hunt because I think hunting is rather cruel when we can just go to the butcher for our meat."

"And have a clever little mustache above his upper lip. You've just described St. Claire, you ninny," Rebecca said, laughing.

"Have I?" Eliza asked with an exaggerated tone. "He is rather perfect, isn't he?"

"If you say so," Rebecca said, wrinkling her nose. "I could never marry anyone who dresses better than I. That's why he's perfect for you, Eliza."

She grinned. "He is, isn't he? Alas, he is leaving in just two weeks to head back to London. Perhaps I will see him during the little season. He has hinted as much."

All the knitting and pretense was put away, and the women carried on with their gossip for several long, wonderful minutes, until Mrs. Anderson entered. Her daughters must have sensed her presence long before the others, for they immediately straightened and schooled their features. Giving the group an assessing look, one that reminded Alice of the way a teacher will survey a roomful of naughty children, Mrs. Anderson walked to the mantel on the far side of the room and picked up a vase. It was such an obvious ploy that Alice nearly laughed.

"Rearranging, Mrs. Anderson?" she asked, pressing her lips together when Rebecca gave her an amused look that acknowledged her courage.

"I am, Miss Hubbard," she said. "Harriet, have you inquired for refreshments for your guests?"

"No, Mother. I didn't think so soon after luncheon—"

"Really, Harriet," she said, looking about the room for approval. "How many times have I told you that you must always offer your guests refreshment. How many?" She shook her head as the women sat silent, embarrassed for their friend.

"Too numerous to count," Harriet said with just a hint of rebellion in her tone, just enough to make Alice tense. It never worked out well when Harriet showed even the smallest bit of backbone, and she had long since stopped trying. Part of Alice wanted to applaud Harriet, but she knew her friend would suffer her mother's wrath unless she was in an unusually forgiving mood.

Mrs. Anderson gave Harriet a long stare, but Clara saved the day with her bright smile. "Mother, we were talking about who our perfect husband would be. When you were a girl, what did you believe you wanted in a husband?"

Fortunately, Mrs. Anderson was distracted by Clara's question and her face softened. "I married him."

If anyone else had said that, Alice might have sighed at the romance of it all. But Alice knew Mr. Anderson and disliked him nearly as much as she disliked The Termagant.

"Let's all go to the garden, shall we?" Rebecca asked. "I'm heartily sick of knitting at any rate."

Alice looked down at her scarf, realizing with a start that she'd neglected to complete even a single row.

* * *

Robert Bennet made up the entire constabulary of St. Ives. His office was in the town hall, a tiny space tucked next to the clerk, where he would spend most of his long days either reading or napping. St. Ives was not a hive of criminals, and it was often weeks between arrests. Most of his time was spent, if not reading or napping, trying to solve disputes between fishermen or sending someone who over-imbibed safely home. St. Ives had two small holding cells for the more serious criminals or those too drunk to make it safely home, and on most days, the cells remained empty. Indeed, one had become a bit of a storage room for the town hall, a fact that didn't bother Constable Bennet in the least.

But this last week had been trying. Bodies didn't turn up every day in St. Ives, and this particular one had caused a bit of indigestion, especially when he heard the rumor that the gentleman had been stabbed in the back before floating off into St. Ives Bay. Thankfully, that rumor was completely false. The wound in the gentleman's back had been a deep scrape, no doubt caused by one of the many jagged rocks along the bay.

It had been an especially trying week, so Bennet had resorted to long naps to relieve the stress of it all, and that was how Henderson and Lord Berkley found him the day they went to visit him with their theory that St. Ives was harboring a man they suspected of murdering as many as five victims.

A soft snore sounded from the office, and Henderson gave Berkley an amused look before knocking, loudly, on the door. From the sounds of a small commotion behind the door, Henderson suspected the knock had startled the constable nearly out of his seat. When the door was flung open, St. Ives' sole police officer stood there, all five feet of him, eyes bloodshot, hair askew, looking about as irritable as a man can look. Henderson suspected Bennet's day was about to get much worse.

After they'd carefully detailed what they knew of events, from the time the five boys were building that tree fort to the day Sebastian's body was found, Bennet sat back, looking rather ill. And then he swore, loudly. "That's a fine kettle of fish, gentleman, a fine kettle of fish. I knew I should have retired two years ago when we got that recommendation the department should be disbanded. Four men, you say?"

"Yes, sir. Five if you count Mr. Stewart."

Bennet closed his eyes briefly. "Do you know where this…" He looked at his notes. "…Mr. Grant resides?"

"No, sir," Henderson said. "When he was a lad, his parents lived on Trelawney Road, but I've no idea if he still resides there."

"Easy enough to find out. Clerk'll have that information. All right, then. Thank you both for coming in. I know how to reach you, Lord Berkley, but where are you residing, Mr. Southwell?"

"At the White Hart Inn at the moment, but I shall be leaving soon. I'm expected in London by the end of August, and after that, I plan to travel to India. I don't expect I can be of more assistance as I have told you everything I know. Would you mind telling me what will happen next?"

Bennet shook his head. "Likely nothing." At Henderson's sound of outrage, Bennet held up a placating hand. "Please, you must understand how very difficult these cases are. Every man died of accidental causes, all clearly documented and dismissed. I suspect that some were not investigated at all by my predecessors, and these deaths happened years ago. Mr. Hubbard's death, for instance. Witnesses saw him fall."

"Only Gerald Grant saw him fall. I don't know what the other lads saw, and now they are conveniently dead."

"No one else came forward to dispute his claim at that time, did they? You must realize that other than the very real coincidence that all four of the men were present when Mr. Stewart died and the only one left is the man who caused that gentleman's death, I have no evidence. I don't know if the magistrates would even agree to hear the case."

"They will hear it," Berkley said with a smile. "I can guarantee it."

Henderson looked over at Berkley and suspected his father must have something on at least one of the magistrates who would oversee such a case.

"Even so, there is scant evidence. I will pursue this, rest assured. Perhaps when Mr. Grant is confronted by the facts, he will confess. I can't imagine it has been easy all these years living with the guilt of such crimes."

Standing, Henderson said, "I have a feeling that a man capable of what Mr. Grant has done feels little guilt. I have come to realize over the years the depths of what a man can do to preserve himself."

* * *

The two men left the constable feeling only slightly satisfied with their accomplishment.

"It's in his hands now," Lord Berkley said, looking out over the fishing fleet that remained in the harbor. "At least now you know that even had you been there that night Mr. Hubbard died, you likely could have done nothing to stop it. I have a feeling Mr. Grant would have killed him, if not that night, then another."

Henderson came up short, his mind whirling at this possibility. For some reason, he'd silently counted Joseph's death separately, as a suicide that could not be tied to the other men's deaths. He'd kept the secret so long, it had become a part of him, a particular truth that he no longer even tried to dispute. Gerald had told him about that night—Gerald, who had likely killed Joseph.

"What's wrong, Henderson?" And when tears filled Henderson's eyes, Berkley clasped one shoulder. "What's wrong?" he repeated.

"My God, all these years I felt to blame for Joseph's death, not because he died, but because I thought it was suicide."

"Suicide?"

"That night Joseph died, I came upon Gerald in the White Hart Inn. He was clearly upset and he told me Joseph had killed himself, that they all agreed never to speak of it to protect the Hubbards and Joseph's memory."

"Jesus, man."

"I thought if I had been there that night, I could have stopped it or that Joseph never would have done it. And all this time, he'd been murdered and I likely wouldn't have been able to stop it. Sebastian and Tristan were there that night and they saw nothing. I know they would have told me if they had." Henderson gasped, in and out, as the enormity of what he realized hit him. "These last four years have been a living *hell* because of that man. By God, if they do not arrest him I do not know if I can stop myself from putting him in his grave."

Berkley squeezed his shoulder and dropped his hand. "A foolish thought, but one I completely understand. I'm afraid I cannot allow you to commit murder, but I swear I will do everything in my power to make certain Gerald Grant hangs for his crimes."

Chapter 17

"I am terribly sorry, my lord, but I'm madly in love with another man and cannot in good conscience allow you to continue to court me in hopes that we will marry." No, that wasn't quite what she wanted to say. "While I will continue to hold you in the highest esteem, my lord, I'm afraid I cannot marry you."

Alice smiled at her reflection and nodded. That was much better. She'd informed her mother of her decision when she'd returned from her knitting group, an announcement that was met with stony silence. While she did not exactly give Alice permission to end her relationship with Lord Northrup, her mother did not outwardly forbid her to reject his proposal, and so Alice chose to take that as implicit permission. This rift between herself and her mother felt odd and uncomfortable, but Alice had faith that her mother would come around and accept Henderson. After all, she'd accepted him when he was Joseph's best friend.

Northrup at this very minute was waiting in the parlor for her; she'd promised a game of checkers that morning and this meeting would be perfect for sending his lordship on his way. When she entered the room, he was sitting at a small table setting up the board, and Alice felt an unexpected twist of sorrow. He really was a good man and she did not want to hurt him, but she feared she was about to.

"My lord, I was wondering if we might talk."

Northrup looked up and immediately stood, his smile slowly fading as her words and tone hit him.

"Ah," he said, and there was so much unsaid in that single syllable.

"I am sorry. I do want you to know that I admire you and hold you in the highest—"

"Please," he said. "You don't have to continue. I cannot say I am surprised. I suppose I was holding out hope you would come to care for me as much as I care for you. That is it, isn't it? You do not love me in the least."

Alice shook her head, feeling horrible. "I wanted to. I thought we would suit, but so much has changed in the past few weeks. I have come to realize I would make you a terrible wife, that you need someone better, not as apt to argue or be cross."

He smiled sadly. "You would have made me a wonderful wife. Had you loved me." He swallowed, and for a fleeting moment Alice thought he might break down, but he gathered himself, straightening his jacket as if putting his emotions in order.

"Thank you so much for understanding. I do feel horrible and mean, but I know this is the right thing to do." This was far more dreadful than Alice had thought it would be; Northrup seemed truly distraught and Alice found herself fighting tears.

"The right thing for now," he said, and touched the tip of her nose with his index finger. "If you should change your mind, please do write me."

It was on the tip of her tongue to assure him that would not happen, but instead she simply smiled and said, "Thank you."

As Alice watched Lord Northrup leave the parlor, no doubt heading up to his room to pack, she was hit with a powerful rush of relief that left her nearly giddy. One chapter of her life was over, a very dreary and upsetting one, and now she could get on with the rest of it. Hugging herself to hold close the complete joy she felt, Alice slowly walked from the parlor, stopping suddenly when she spotted her mother descending the stairs.

"I just saw Lord Northrup," she said. "Oh, Alice, how could you? How could you throw away such a chance?" She shook her head, her eyes filling with unshed tears, dousing that fierce joy Alice had been feeling just moments before.

"I am sorry, Mama, truly I am. But I don't love him. I never have. I thought we would suit, that liking him would be good enough. It isn't. Now that I know what it is to love someone—"

Her mother let out a sound of exasperation. "A good marriage requires so much more than love, Alice. I thought you understood that."

"I do understand. It's about understanding and laughter. Sharing dreams and values. Henderson and I are friends, the best of friends, and we have been for a very long time."

Elda shook her head and looked so sad, Alice felt her heart wrench. "He didn't write for four years, Alice. And now he's suddenly in love?

How can you be so naïve? Do you think it's pure coincidence that he had to come to St. Ives? I like Mr. Southwell, you know I do. But I fear he's a bit more opportunistic that either of us realized."

Narrowing her eyes, Alice said, "Opportunistic? You think his secret plan all along was to somehow trick me into marrying him? That he returned to England for me and not for his relief efforts?"

"Perhaps."

"No. You don't believe that, Mama. I know you don't."

Elda let out a long sigh. "I don't know what to think anymore," she said, sounding weary.

"Then I shall do all the thinking for us," Alice said, making her mother chuckle lightly.

"Come here, my little sunshine," she said, using Alice's childhood nickname for the first time in more than ten years. Letting out a small sound, Alice threw herself against her mother and burst into tears.

"I dislike arguing with you, Mama. It is purely awful."

"I know. I do not care for it either."

Lifting her head, she asked, "Does this mean you are accepting Henderson?"

"Not yet," Elda said, but Alice leaned her head against her mother's shoulder and smiled.

* * *

That night, Alice went to bed feeling better than she had in days. Everything would work out—she just knew it. In her heart, she knew her mother would relent; it was her father who was her real worry. After all, her father was the one who'd asked that Henderson leave, who'd struck Henderson, who felt most keenly his obligation to maintain Alice's social rank. But he would come around. As she lay in the darkness, she fought that terrible feeling in her stomach when she recalled her father's anger, his ugly words, memories that only served to feed her doubt.

Her window was open, letting in the cool night air, and she gazed out at a nearly full moon, trying to push away her doubts. She really should get up and shut the window, for it was quite chilly, but instead she snuggled deeper beneath the covers and closed her eyes, only to re-open them less than a minute later.

Someone—and she had quite a good idea who—was tossing pebbles at the windows of the empty room adjacent to hers. Really, she thought, if Henderson was going to do something as foolish as come to her window in the middle of the night, at least he should have been careful about which window to hit. If he'd erred on the other side, he would have awoken Christina.

Throwing off the covers, she tiptoed to her window, making sure to stay out of sight of whomever was out there. Sure enough, Henderson stood in her garden gathering up more pebbles from the gravel path. Though it was full night, the moon cast a silvery light on him; she would have recognized his form anywhere. Alice grabbed her light robe and the blanket from her bed and hurried across her room and out the door, pausing only briefly to be certain no one was about. On silent bare feet, she padded quickly past her mother and father's rooms, hugging her blanket against her, breath held, heart beating madly, and made her way down the stairs and to the back of the house, where a set of French doors led to a small terrace and their back garden.

Henderson was on the far side and so did not see Alice as she slipped through the doors and down the stairs, taking the time to deposit the blanket on the top step. The grass was cool beneath her feet, and wet with dew. Picking up her skirts, she ran toward where Henderson stood. She was nearly upon him when he turned, and Alice launched herself into his arms, letting out a small sound of pure happiness. She wrapped herself around him, locking her ankles behind his back, until he was wearing her.

"Oh, God, it's so good to hold you," he said, his voice low and rough as he held her to him, squeezing so tightly it was very nearly painful, but wonderfully so.

She nuzzled her face against the crook of his neck, breathing him in, mad for him. Henderson nudged her head up with his and kissed her with so much need, Alice cried out and clung even tighter. It was a long, hot, drugging kiss, filled with love and lust and a need that left her light-headed and her core on fire.

Henderson spun slowly around, holding her tightly, kissing her insensible, for several long minutes, making up for the days they had not been together. Finally, he pulled back, kissed her again, and again, then let her slowly slide down his body until her toes once again touched the cool, wet grass.

"Not seeing you has been torture," he said, then leaned in and kissed her again, as if he couldn't get enough of tasting her. "How is your father?"

"Better. I've only spoken to him briefly. And I told my mother that I love you and that I plan to marry you."

He drew her against him and tucked her head beneath his chin. "What did she say?"

"It matters not. Either way, we are getting married."

"I'd much rather your parents be, if not excited by the prospect, then at least accepting of me. But I'm not certain it's possible." He stepped back until he was no longer embracing her, and Alice felt a coldness that was more than just the night air.

"What is wrong?" she asked, reeling at the idea that he had changed his mind about getting married. Surely he was not going to allow what had happened at the ball to sway him.

"I have to talk to you about something and I've no idea where to start."

It sounded so much like what she had just said to Lord Northrup, Alice found herself unable to speak, bracing herself for a pain she knew was coming.

Henderson began pacing back and forth in front of her, clearly tortured by whatever it was he was going to say.

"I'll understand if you no longer wish to marry," she said, the ache in her heart nearly unbearable. "You never did formally propose, so you have no obligation to follow through with—"

Henderson stopped pacing and stared at her as if she were speaking a foreign language. "You'll understand, will you?"

She wished it was daylight so she could better see his expression, but his voice sounded oddly...amused.

Shaking her head, she said, "Actually, no, I will not understand."

Henderson reached out with both palms and gently grasped her head, ducking his own so that they were looking into each other's eyes. "I love you. I am going to marry you. Now, shush and let me tell you what I came here to say."

"Shush?"

"Shush." He let out a long breath. "I fear the thing that has lifted a weight from my soul will only add a burden to yours."

"I don't understand."

"You will. I don't know where to start, but once I am finished, you will understand why I left four years ago, why I stayed away even though it nearly killed me to do so, and why I came back when I did."

Alice took his hand and led him to a small bench in the garden, the pebbles of the gravel path sharp against her feet. Once they were seated, she turned toward him, her hand still in his, needing his strength and warmth. "Tell me."

"It's all about Joseph. He is here, in this story, from beginning to end."

Alice shook her head in confusion. The last thing she'd expected him to talk about was Joseph.

"When Joseph was around fourteen years old, about a year before we met, he and a few of his friends were building a tree fort. One of those friends accidently dropped a branch on a Mr. Stewart, killing him."

Alice gasped. "I remember that. The entire town went to the funeral. It was the first funeral I'd ever attended. Joseph was there when it happened?" She sagged a bit as she was hit by the realization of the terrible secret her brother had kept, a terrible burden for such a young boy to carry.

"As were Peter, Tristan, Sebastian, and Gerald. All dead, except for Gerald Grant, who happens to be the lad who dropped the branch."

A chill enveloped her as she understood the implication of what Henderson was saying. "You think he killed them all? That he killed Joseph? But it was an accident. There were others there. Wouldn't one of them have said something?"

"I don't know what happened that night. As you know, I was not there and I carried the guilt of that for years. Joseph asked me to go, was angry when I wouldn't, but I had other plans."

"No doubt with a lady friend."

"Perhaps," he said with a small smile. "That night, I stopped into the White Hart and saw Gerald there. He looked bloody awful, and I knew something had happened. Alice, he told me Joseph had committed suicide, that he stood on that roof, said 'Tell Southie I'm sorry,' and fell back." Henderson's voice thickened on this last, and Alice gripped his hand even tighter. "It was all a lie, one made so that I would not discuss what happened. It was my idea not to speak of it, not to tell your parents, who would have been devastated to know their son killed himself. It was brilliant on Gerald's part, you see. By telling me that, I remained silent. I didn't question the other lads who were there, who most certainly would have disputed his story. I was silent and then I left, so filled with guilt, I could hardly live with myself. I couldn't bring myself to look at you or your parents; it felt as if I had pushed Joseph myself."

"Oh, Henderson," she said and pressed her lips against his beard-roughened cheek.

"I had to leave. I felt I was to blame for Joseph's death, that if I had been there, he would not have killed himself. All this time, I've suffered, unable to fully live knowing that I was responsible for my best friend's death."

"My parents, I don't know what I should tell them." Alice could feel the tears pricking at her eyes, recalling that terrible night when they'd been informed of Joseph's death.

Henderson scrubbed his face with his free hand. "They will find out at some point. The constable is fully aware that Gerald Grant is likely responsible for the deaths of five men."

"I can't believe so much evil lives within him. I know Gerald. I always thought he was a bit strange, but I never would have thought him capable of murder. All those men. It's overwhelming to think of." Alice let out a small sob, and Henderson gathered her against him, making low soothing sounds.

"I don't want you to cry, because there is something else I need to tell you."

Alice let out a watery laugh. "I'm not certain I can take much more of your news."

He chuckled and gave her a quick kiss. "This is good news— well, mostly. The night before he died, Joseph made me promise never to touch you."

Drawing back with surprise, Alice said, "He did? Why ever would he do that? And how could you possibly think that is a good thing?"

"At the time, it wasn't, of course. You were walking by and I looked at you and I suppose Joseph saw something in my expression that angered him. It might have been that I wanted to make love to you; it was all I could think of at the time."

"Truly?"

"Truly. Then he died, and I thought it was suicide and I left. And you kept getting engaged but never married. Think of it. What are the chances that one girl could have so many weddings called off? Why, one fiancé even died in the church. I think it was Joseph trying to bring us together. If he was looking down from heaven, he surely knew I loved you and that I falsely believed I was responsible for his death. I think he's been trying to right a wrong all this time."

Alice's eyes widened. "You think Joseph killed poor Lord Livingston?"

"Not in so many words, but I think it was fate and Joseph was behind it all. Everything has aligned to finally bring us together, and I'm convinced that Joseph has been watching and likely getting a bit frustrated in the process."

She smiled softly. "It is nice to think."

"There, see? I told you there was some good in all this. Now all we have to do is convince your parents to allow you to marry me."

"My mother is very nearly convinced already, but I fear my father will be a bit more of a challenge. I'd never realized how strongly he felt about society's rules. Then again, his father *is* a duke."

Henderson leaned forward, bracing his forearms on his knees. "I'm very rich, you know. I realize that does not matter in terms of bloodline, but I could give you the life you are accustomed to. You wouldn't suffer in that way."

Letting out a small laugh, Alice said, "I know. Apparently St. Claire was intrigued by you and did a bit of detective work. How wealthy are you?"

"Wealthy enough to make your father reconsider how worthy I am of you. I was a man driven after I left England. I worked endless hours and built a bit of an empire, only to see that very empire cause the deaths of millions. I couldn't have foreseen what would happen when England built all those railroads. If I had, I would never have made such investments. I sold my shares when I realized, of course, but the damage is done. That is why I feel so strongly about famine relief. Guilt is a powerful incentive, and it seems it has driven nearly all my decisions for years."

Alice gave him a small punch to the arm. "Don't you dare blame yourself for the famine. My goodness, Henny, you're just one man."

Rubbing where she'd hit him, even though it had merely been a tap, Henderson nodded. "I do realize that. I invested blindly in a railway company as hundreds of men have before me and I made scads of money, which was my only intent. It wasn't until four years later, after a terrible drought, that the full effects of what we had done became evident. I was like all Englishmen, thinking improvements to a country's infrastructure would lead to modernization, would help the natives become more civilized, more like us. It wasn't until I lived amongst the people for years that I realized the English do not know the true meaning of civilization. I'm afraid I've become a bit of a progressivist in the last four years."

Alice was quiet for a time, digesting all he had said, her admiration for him growing even stronger. "You are such a good, good man, Henderson. I think that perhaps I am not worthy of you. And I am going to do everything in my power to prove to my parents that to have you as a son-in-law will only reflect well on them."

"Thank you," he said softly.

* * *

Henderson was moved beyond speech by what Alice said, and he counted himself among the luckiest of men to have such a woman love him. He'd been sickened by the thought of telling her about her brother, about his small role in the famine in India, not knowing what her reaction would be. But there she sat, leaning her head against his shoulder, making him feel like a man worthy of such a prize.

"My mother was pregnant with Joseph when they were married." She said it quickly, as if it had been bubbling up inside her, straining to be released.

"Is that so."

He felt her nod. "I'm not certain what I shall do with that information, but I may use it during my argument to gain acceptance of our marriage."

"That would not be nice," he said, his voice tinged with amusement that she would consider such a thing. "And it would do nothing to remove their real objection, that I am not worthy of you."

She let out a small snort. "Then I suppose I shall have to tell them we must marry post haste because of certain possible consequences."

Henderson leaned back and looked at Alice in disbelief. "We cannot tell such a lie, Alice. I will not agree to such a tactic."

"It won't be a lie," she said, looking up at him with complete innocence, an innocence that belied the implication of her words. He knew what she meant, and his body reacted immediately, his cock springing to life. Suddenly, he was aware that they were alone, that she was wearing almost nothing, that it would be a simple thing to lay her down on the cool, sweet grass and make love to her.

Which was why he could not quite believe the words that came out of his mouth next. "We cannot."

Even with only the moonlight, he could see her smile. Was it his imagination or was that a provocative smile?

"We can. And it's not only because I want to force my parents' hands if need be. It's because ever since that night we were together, it is all I can think of. Something happened that night. Something woke up inside my body and now it's driving me a bit mad."

Henderson shifted uncomfortably, his arousal becoming nearly painful. What man could say no to such words? Ever since she was fifteen years old, he could never say no to her, even when he knew what she asked was wrong. Perhaps she hadn't realized all those quiet nights alone in the library were wrong, but he knew. And yet, one impish smile, one pleading sentence, and he would return, night after night, to read aloud and talk and pray that no one ever found out. If he were completely honest, the idea of making love to her, of creating a life inside her, was heady stuff.

"We don't have to if you don't want to," she said softly.

The sound he let out was much like that of a man being tortured. "Never think I don't want to make love to you, but I can hardly toss you down on the grass and have my way with you as if you're some milk maid. Not for your first time."

She leaned forward and gave him a soft kiss. "I have a blanket," she whispered.

"A blanket."

Nodding, she kissed him again. "I think lying underneath the stars atop my big soft blanket will be heaven."

When Alice rested her hand against his chest and kissed his neck, he was lost. In one move, he hauled her onto his lap and kissed her deeply, his hand finding the lovely curve of one breast, his palm pressing against the hardened peak. He heard her sharp intake of breath and smiled, then groaned when she wriggled her soft bum against his aching cock. "You little tease," he said, chuckling. "Where did you leave that blanket?"

Alice let out a delighted squeal, much as she used to when he would agree to whatever book she'd been begging him to read, and crushed herself against him, making him laugh aloud. "I fear I will be one of those husbands who is completely ruled by their wives."

"Of course," she said without hesitation, then stood, dragging him up with her. Tugging on his hand, she led him to the terrace stairs, where a small bundle lay, already damp from the night air. He grabbed the blanket and allowed Alice to bring him wherever she wanted. He was her slave, following her wherever she wished, doing her bidding for whatever she wanted.

Alice led him behind a hedgerow, which shielded them from the house should anyone look out, even though it was unlikely anyone would be able to see them from that distance. Other than the crickets, the night was silent. It was an unusually warm evening, the kind of rare night in St. Ives when winter and its colder temperatures seemed a lifetime away. Together they laid out the blanket, an astonishingly intimate exercise, then lay back, side-by-side, and gazed up at the infinite stars above them.

"We're going to make love," Alice said, sounding all breathy and a bit nervous.

"Yes."

"And tomorrow, I shall speak to my father, to see how violently opposed he is to our marriage, and then we can decide how to proceed."

He took her hand and pressed it against his mouth. "I'd rather not force your parents if we can at all avoid it. I fear their opinion of me will only lower further. Agreed?"

"Agreed. Shall I remove my clothes now?"

Henderson smiled, for she sounded so brave and he knew she must be a little nervous, despite the intimacies they had already shared.

"Not entirely, just in case someone should come upon us, I think it might be better to push your gown up a bit."

Alice tugged her skirt to just above her knees. "Like this?" she asked, laughter in her voice, and Henderson growled, reached down, and pulled her gown up, past her hips, her flat belly, the turgid peaks of her breasts, until a soft mass of cloth lay bundled just beneath her chin.

"My God, I'd forgotten how beautiful you are. How could I have forgotten?" he said, drawing his hand up her impossibly soft skin, from her hip to her breasts. Dipping his head, he took one hard nipple in his mouth and sucked softly, loving the sounds she made, and the way her hips began to move, a silent request for him to touch her. He skimmed one hand down her taut body, past her soft curls, until he rested his palm against her core and pressed.

"Please."

Henderson closed his eyes, that one word making him even harder. He found her slick opening, then pressed one finger inside, slowly, cautiously, ready to withdraw should she pull away. But Alice moaned and spread her legs, and he nearly let out a shout of joy that she was so responsive to his every caress.

"I shall put myself here," he said, creating slow a rhythm with his finger.

"Oh." Her breathy response sent another wave of lust through him.

"Do you remember the last time, how it felt?"

"Yes."

"I'm going to make you feel that again, before...before."

"Okay," she said, her voice small, making him think for just a second that he should stop. She sounded frightened.

"We don't have to—" He started to withdraw his finger and she clamped a hand over his to stop him.

"What? Why would you say such a thing?"

"You seemed frightened so I..."

She was giggling. "I was not frightened, Henny, I was so distracted I could hardly speak. Please, do not stop or I shall have to murder you."

With a low moan, he kissed her deeply, sweeping his tongue inside her sweet mouth, and commenced torturing her with his finger between her legs. Kissing his way down her body, pausing for long moments at her breasts, he found with this tongue the small erect bud between her legs, teasing and sucking until she was bucking beneath him.

"God, Henderson." She clenched her legs around him and laid one hand atop his head, and he reveled in the sounds she made, her soft words urging him on, until she let out a small scream, finding her release.

* * *

Wave after wave of delicious sensation coursed through her body, leaving her limbs boneless, her heart pounding madly in her chest. She was dimly aware of Henderson kissing her stomach, one breast, her chin before she heard the sound of him removing his shoes and trousers. Then she felt his manhood between her legs where his finger had just been. The effort to lift her hands to touch his shoulders, his back, was nearly impossible.

"I love you, Alice," he said, then thrust inside with one quick movement.

"Oh." It hurt a bit, a sharp burning, but it was such a glorious feeling to realize the man she loved was joined together with her, that this act was somehow sealing them together. He was still, his muscles taut, and his arms, braced on each side of her, shaking slightly.

"I hurt you," he said, his voice laced with concern.

"Only a little." She couldn't stop the grin. "Look at us. We've done it now, Henny. There is no turning back."

Henderson laughed and dipped his head to kiss her as he moved slightly back before pushing inside her again. "You feel so good," he said, his voice strained. "Impossibly good. Better than my imagination."

"You imagined this?"

"Every night." He laughed. "Every minute." He began moving, in and out, letting out manly sounds that told Alice he was feeling much the same type of pleasure that she had just felt. And then, a wonderful thing started to happen. That feeling, the warmth and tingling that told her a release was building, began again. Every time he thrust, the feeling grew, until her body began to react, until she was once again seeking that glorious feeling she knew was within her reach.

Her breathing changed, and when it did, Henderson's rhythm changed, became faster, harder, driving even more of those sensations through her body, as if he were completely attuned to her. When he reached down between them and touched her aching nub, Alice let out a sound she hadn't realized she was capable of making, a high keening that Henderson stifled with a kiss as her body convulsed around him. His thrusts quickened and then he drove deep, his entire body taut and hard, and he let out a deep groan of pure pleasure. It was the most beautiful thing Alice had ever experienced in her life. They were lovers and she was fiercely glad of it.

Chapter 18

Late the next morning, for she had overslept, Alice stood outside her father's door, gathering the courage for what she needed to say. No doubt her mother had already discussed Henderson with him, and she wondered what her father had said. Probably not very nice things, given how angry he'd been the night of the ball.

It had been five days since the ball, and from the laughter she occasionally heard from her father's room, he was doing much better. He might not be hale and hearty yet, but certainly he could have a candid conversation with his daughter without falling ill again. She hoped.

In the wake of her glorious night with Henderson, Alice felt nothing could ruin her buoyant spirit. Even her maid had mentioned that she seemed to have a glow about her this morning, and Alice could not stop the blush from forming on her cheeks. She could still feel him there, between her legs, a soreness that she'd never felt before, that reminded her again and again of what she'd shared with Henderson.

Alice could hear the murmuring of voices and thought she recognized her brother's chuckle, so she entered the room without knocking, still fearing that she would be sent away. Instead, her brother welcomed her with a smile and her father held out his hand for her to take. The relief nearly brought her to tears.

"Good morning, Oliver. Papa, you look nearly well enough to run to the village and back."

"I am much better, thank you, and looking forward to seeing the doctor later this afternoon so I can convince him I'm more than ready to get out of bed. All this lying about cannot be good for me."

"A couple days' more rest will not hurt, Papa," Oliver said, and Alice laughed at his stern voice. She realized with a twinge that Oliver had been small moments from being the man of the house, a position he fervently did not want. At least not yet.

"Oliver, would you mind giving Papa and me some privacy?"

"Of course." He leaned over and kissed her forehead, completely surprising Alice and making her eyes shine with unshed tears. Though she knew her brother loved her, he had never shown her affection, unless tugging ribbons from her hair could be construed as affection, and Alice was touched far more than he could know. Perhaps he understood how dreadful she'd been feeling about the entire episode.

After he'd left, Alice sat down in the chair her brother had occupied and took a bracing breath. "I don't want you to think ill of Henderson, Papa. I love him dearly and it hurts to think of you at odds with him."

To her disappointment, her father's smile faded and he turned his head away.

"I wanted him to kiss me. I knew when I went out on that terrace that he would. If you want to be angry with someone, be angry with me."

Her father gave her a quick look before turning his attention back to the ceiling.

"A gentleman would never have taken such liberties—"

"—without the benefit of marriage?" she finished for him, her tone rife with meaning.

It took perhaps two seconds for Richard to understand what she was saying. He stared at her for two beats, then, "Agatha." It was not a question, but a pronouncement, and Alice understood that he knew what she knew.

"I am sorry, Papa. I wasn't supposed to know but I do and I fear I must save you from hypocrisy."

He let out a sharp laugh, then quickly sobered and shook his head. "It is not only that," he said. "It is that Henderson's background is not what I would have chosen for you. You must realize how inappropriate a match with him would be."

"I don't care. I love him, Papa, and he loves me. And perhaps best of all, he already loves all of us, despite your awful snobbishness."

"So." He moved his hands atop the covers, smoothing them. "I thought you swore never to marry."

"That's because I'd never been in love before. It's easy to swear you will never marry if you've never been in love." She leaned over and kissed his cheek. "And if it makes you feel any better, Henderson is quite wealthy."

"So I've been told. By more than one person in this family. It appears you are all conspiring against me in this. Somehow you've even won over your mother."

Alice smiled. Her father's words were like seeing a slice of sunshine splitting the clouds after a long rain. Waving her hand dismissively, she said, "Mama was easy to convince. She's always adored Henderson. I think she just wanted to please you."

"Hmm." Alice held her breath, sensing that her father was about to make some sort of pronouncement. "You may have Henderson visit with me later today if you'd like."

"Oh, Papa," Alice said, leaning into him and giving him a long embrace. If he'd been well, she would have flung herself atop him, but she feared she might hurt him if she did that now. "You have no idea how happy you have made me."

He let out a grunt, and Alice chose to take that sound as one of pleasure, not regret. "I cannot wait to tell Henderson the news. Thank you, Papa."

She sailed from the room, and her father watched her depart, a fond look on his face, for it truly was impossible to remain angry at Alice for any length of time.

* * *

Henderson arrived in time for tea, and Mrs. Godfrey, having somehow learned he would be coming for a visit, served his favorite, cherry tarts. Elda, Christina, Oliver, and Alice sat expectantly when he entered the parlor, and used to being treated as a member of the family, he nearly laughed at the formal way they each greeted him.

"Thank you for inviting me," he said to Elda.

"Thank you for coming. Lord Hubbard is still not well enough to join us, but has requested an interview after we've finished with tea."

Henderson glanced over at Alice, who sat stiff and still, the oddest look on her face, as if she were bursting with some news but was unable to express it. The note inviting him to tea that afternoon had arrived at his hotel earlier that day, a cryptic message in the neat handwriting of Lady Hubbard. He'd studied the invitation for long minutes, not knowing quite what to make of it. Had Alice told her mother what had happened last night? Had something happened between the time he had left her standing on the terrace and the time her mother had written the note?

This formal greeting confused him even more. Everyone seemed happy enough to see him, and he could see no censor in Lady Hubbard's expression, but it was clear that something was up.

"Is Lord Hubbard well?" he asked, because he wasn't supposed to know he was doing much better.

"As well as can be expected," Elda said, and Alice gave her mother a look of disbelief.

"He's doing much better," Alice said. "Things are looking very positive."

Henderson was about to take his first bite of cherry tart, and he paused, staring at Alice, who pressed her lips together and looked at him with eyes full of what could only be described as pure happiness. He put the tart down, suddenly finding it difficult to breathe. "That is good to hear," he said finally, then sat back as the meaning of his visit fully hit him. He was here to ask Lord Hubbard's permission to marry Alice.

"Are you all right?" Oliver asked. "You look suddenly ill."

"Quite the opposite, in fact. I do not believe I have ever felt better in my life." He looked over to Elda, who'd been sitting across from him with a rather stern expression, and couldn't help but notice she was smiling at him fondly with that old look that had always comforted him, always made him feel welcome. By God, if he'd been alone, he just might have wept.

"Well, I'm done with tea," he announced, then glanced at his favorite treat, nearly untouched on his plate. "I expect I shall have a visit with his lordship now."

He stood and the small group all followed suit, staring at him expectantly. Christina looked especially adorable, for it was clear she also knew the purpose of his visit. Henderson left the parlor, and a footman led him to Lord Hubbard's room, even though he knew the way, another strange formality that only served to increase his nervousness. Surely he wouldn't have been invited to tea if Lord Hubbard was going to reject his suit.

The footman entered the room in front of him and announced him. "Mr. Henderson Southwell to see you, my lord."

"Send him in."

At least Lord Hubbard sounded well and strong. And when Henderson got his first look at the man, he was vastly relieved to see him looking as he always had. He was sitting up in bed, wearing a robe over his night clothes, his hair neatly combed and his face freshly shaved. Lord Hubbard had prepared for this meeting, it seemed, and Henderson was glad he'd taken extra care with his own appearance.

"It is good to see you well, my lord," Henderson said. "I want to apologize for any part I may have had in your illness. You should know it has been a heavy burden on me these last few days."

Richard waved a dismissive hand. "I am on the mend." Richard gave Henderson a hard, long look, and it took quite a bit of discipline not to squirm or look away. "My daughter believes herself in love with you."

"For which I am eternally grateful. And I very much love Alice. I have for a long time, sir. I realize I do not have the pedigree you wish for in a son-in-law, but I am here to ask your permission for your daughter's hand in marriage." He let out a small breath of relief that he'd been able to get out the words without stumbling.

"What of India?"

"I must go back and complete my mission there, but then I will return to England and stay. I would like Alice to come with me as my wife."

Lord Hubbard frowned at that, but he nodded. "Very well. You have my permission."

The relief at hearing those words was profound. "Thank you, sir."

"You have proven yourself a gentleman, more than once, Mr. Southwell. You have withstood my wrath, my disappointment in you, my doubts. And by doing so, you have gained my admiration. I think my daughter is a lucky girl to have found someone like you."

Henderson swallowed thickly. "Thank you, sir. You have been a good example to me over the years."

"Now go tell my daughter her father isn't the ogre she thinks he is."

Henderson grinned and held out his hand for Lord Hubbard to shake. "I will, sir. Thank you."

Never in his life had Henderson felt as happy as he felt at that moment. It was almost beyond belief that he would finally have his Alice, forever. She would be his wife, the mother to their children. She would lie with him every night and he would wake up to her soft smile every morning. To be accepted, finally, was a gift he'd never thought to own. He flew down the stairs, propriety be damned, because he couldn't wait to tell Alice the good news, even though he knew she suspected such a happy outcome. If he'd known what the tea invitation had been all about, he would have taken the time to purchase a ring. Having nothing, he stole a tiny white flower and stem from a flower arrangement and tied it into a small circle.

The family was still in the parlor, speaking in hushed tones, when he entered. He was grinning like a madman, so it must be evident that the interview with Lord Hubbard had gone well. As one, except for Alice, they left the room, Oliver patting him heartily on the back as he passed.

Alice had stood when he'd entered, but sat down with an audible *flump* as he approached. When he reached the chair, he dropped to one knee and she let out a small, happy sob.

"Alice Hubbard, I have loved you for as long as I can remember. Will you do me the honor of becoming my wife?"

With one hand pressed against her mouth, her eyes brimming with tears, she nodded. Then he took her hand in his and slipped on the silly little flower ring, making her giggle. "It's lovely," she said, gazing down at it as if he'd just handed her the largest diamond she'd ever seen.

Henderson stood, drawing her up with him, and pulled her into his embrace. "I shall get you the most beautiful ring I can find," he said, and he could feel her shaking her head.

"I like this one."

He chuckled. "Good, because that is all I have at the moment. This entire day was completely unexpected. However did you manage to convince your father?"

"I didn't have to. My mother did. And my sister and brother. He does like you, Henderson. It's just difficult for him to give up on traditions."

"I am heartily glad he came around." He bent his head and kissed her long and hard, sighing when he realized her mother could return at any time. He did not want either of her parents catching him ravishing their daughter again.

Chapter 19

The day of their wedding, Henderson made sure he arrived well in advance of the bride. His grandfather thought him ridiculous, but Henderson was taking no chance of worrying Alice. When she arrived, he sent his grandfather to tell her that he was already there, waiting in the wings, to see her walk down the aisle of the small church in the center of St. Ives.

Lord Berkley was his best man and Oliver his groomsman, and he knew Joseph was there in spirit.

"Are you ready, lad?" his grandfather asked gruffly.

"As ready as a man can be to wed," he said.

"You've done well for yourself, boy. Your grandmother and I could not be prouder."

Henderson knew everything he had in life was because his grandparents had made sacrifices on his behalf. He would not have gone to Eton, he would not have met Joseph, and he would not be marrying Alice if not for the love and support they'd given him his entire life. From his vantage point, he could see his grandmother, looking nervously about, no doubt feeling a bit out of place among some of the dignitaries in the room, which included the Duke of Warwick himself. Alice had tried to convince her grandfather that he need not attend yet another of her weddings, but the old duke insisted, saying that he would never forgive himself if he missed her actually get married.

"I want you to know how grateful I am for all you and Grandmother have done."

"'Twas nothing." His words were gruff, but Henderson could tell his grandfather was pleased. "Just don't go thinking you're better than you are."

Henderson had to laugh, for all his life his grandparents had made him believe he *was* better than he was, that he had every right to go to Eton, to Oxford, to spend summers with the aristocracy. "I will never be a better man than you, Grandfather, though I will try."

His grandfather chuckled. "I'll go sit with your grandmother and give her some courage. She looks about to faint."

Henderson watched him go, his heart swelling. He truly had been blessed with his grandparents, and that his mother wasn't there and he didn't even know who his father was meant nothing today.

When the organ began to play, Lord Berkley and Oliver came up beside him and Oliver slapped his back. "Are you ready?" his soon-to-be brother-in-law asked.

"I am."

"Don't die, don't run off, and I think we'll all get through this fine."

Henderson was laughing as he walked to the front of the church and waited to see his bride. The church was packed and outside in the street, he could hear the rumble of the small crowd of spectators who had gathered to wish the couple well—and to get a glimpse of a duke and an earl, the grandfathers of the bride.

It had been two months since Lord Hubbard had given his permission for them to marry, and since that time, Henderson had hardly had the chance to kiss Alice, never mind make love. While it had been torture, they had agreed to act like a proper engaged couple, though Henderson had managed to sneak in a few kisses along the way.

When Henderson got his first glimpse of her, he held his breath, she was that beautiful. Her gown was emerald green, the same green as her eyes, and was something a princess might wear in a fairy tale. Never had a bride looked as lovely as Alice did, walking toward him, a smile on her face that told him she was as happy as he.

Lord Hubbard handed over his daughter with a wink and a smile, and even that small gesture had Henderson fighting back tears.

The ceremony was short, the cheers afterward heartwarming. As they stood before the congregation, hand in hand, now Mr. and Mrs. Southwell, Henderson gave a look to heaven and silently thanked Joseph, who he knew was up there watching and probably cheering just as madly as the rest of them.

Alice leaned over, and he ducked his head so he could hear her whisper.

"My gown is too tight. Around the belly."

Henderson dumbly looked at her tiny waist, his brows furrowed. "You look lovely to me," he said, and was surprised when Alice laughed.

"Around my *belly*, Henderson." She widened her eyes as if to say, *Are you a dunce?*

Well, he must be because he had no idea what—

"No."

She nodded her head and her eyes filled with tears. "Yes. Aunt Agatha is going to have another interesting entry in her family tree in about seven months."

Then, in front of the entire congregation, who still stood and clapped and looked at them with smiles and misty eyes, Henderson kissed his wife senseless, propriety be damned.

Epilogue

Lord Berkley prepared for long hours for his first speech before the House of Lords, only to find out, not two weeks prior, that the monsoons had returned to India and now after two years of drought, the general feeling, even among those who supported relief efforts, was that it was no longer needed.

"I'm more relieved that I can express," Berkley said. He had invited the Southwells to stay in his home while he and Henderson were in London preparing for the speech. It was a moderate townhouse in Cavendish Square, and Berkley mentioned more than one time that he felt suffocated in London. "I spent too much time in the American West to feel comfortable in a city ever again. I cannot find enough air to breathe."

Henderson had left India before the monsoons had arrived, and was unaware that the long-awaited rain had returned. Even had he known, the news would not have altered his mission, for he knew, as the general population of England did not, that one year of rain could not help the ongoing starvation. Food prices remained high, and those with land had nothing to farm with, having sold off every animal, every bit of equipment, in a futile effort to keep their families fed.

As proof, he had a letter from Dr. Cornish, expressing his deep frustration with the government as millions of Indians continued to suffer. Their cause, he'd written with deep regret, was a lost one. Even Henderson realized the futility of asking for relief when the vast majority of people wholeheartedly believed relief had already come in the form of much needed rain. It was Dr. Cornish's letter, more than anything, that made the decision not to press the issue of relief to a group of men who were unlikely to change their minds, even had Berkley given his impassioned speech. Quite a large number of the House of Lords had attended the durbar pronouncing Queen Victoria Empress of India, a lavish and long affair that hardly bespoke a nation suffering from starvation. Nonetheless, it was the most difficult decision of Henderson's life.

"Will you be returning to St. Ives, then?" Alice asked Lord Berkley. "I miss it already."

Indeed, despite his disappointment that all his efforts were for naught, Henderson had been relieved to hear they would be staying in England, for Alice was already showing.

"As soon as physically possible. In fact, I will bid you good evening and farewell, as I plan to leave on the first train tomorrow morning. Stay here as long as you wish. In fact, buy the place, for I have no wish ever to return."

Henderson laughed uncomfortably, for his friend sounded unusually bitter and he wondered if his pronouncement had something to do with his late wife. The décor, he realized, was much the same as Costille.

Once Berkley had departed, Henderson drew Alice against him. He always found it difficult not to touch her and cursed the dictates of society that prevented him from constantly caressing her. After two weeks of marriage, he still could not believe she was his wife, that he could make love to her any time he liked, that she was as willing as he was to shed her clothes and take him into her. That she was carrying his child. How could a man be so blessed?

For so long, it seemed as though fate were conspiring against him, and now all was falling into place with frightening ease. A large and handsome house in St. Ives that Henderson had long admired, one overlooking the sea with an impressive plot of land, had become available, and Henderson's offer was immediately accepted. Gerald Grant, once confronted by Robert Bennet, confessed, then, sadly, took his own life, freeing Alice of any concern that he might harm Henderson.

"I'm ready to go home as well," Henderson said, dipping his head and stealing a kiss.

"I like the sound of that. Home. Our home. I still cannot believe we are married. Each morning I wake up and have to pinch myself."

Henderson chuckled. "When are you going to tell your mother about our little one?"

She bit her lip. "I suppose I'll have to say something when we return. It's getting rather obvious. Perhaps I can say I ate too much cake in London."

"You have been eating rather a lot of cake," he said, pretending to consider her idea.

She batted him playfully. "I cannot help it if my daughter likes cake as much as I do."

"Daughter?"

"Or son. You do have a bit of a sweet tooth yourself."

"We shall have to steal Mrs. Godfrey away so she can make tarts daily."

That night, after Berkley's efficient servants had packed their belongings, Alice went to her well-organized trunk and pulled out a large rosewood box, running her fingers over its surface lightly. With a small flick of one finger, a secret drawer opened up and Alice pulled out a key.

"This," she said, making certain he understood the importance of the moment, "is the key to my heart." With that, she opened up the desk and pulled out a neat stack of letters. "These are the letters I wrote to you after you left. You don't have to read them now, but I would like you to read them. Please keep in mind that I was just a girl."

He reached out for them solemnly, but she pulled back. "I need a promise from you."

Smiling, he said, "Anything."

"I want you to play for me."

"You mean the violin." She nodded. "I'm not very good anymore. I haven't played, really, in years."

"It doesn't matter. I'm sharing all of me with you."

"And you want me to share all of me?"

"Yes."

"Fair enough." He kissed her lightly, then looked down at the stack of letters in his hand, written by the girl he had fallen in love with all those years ago. Opening the first, he looked at Alice, then down to the words she had written just days after Joseph's death.

"Dear Henny," he read, then chuckled at the use of his nickname. "Without you here, it seems a part of me is missing. The large and hopeful part, the only part, really, that makes me smile." Henderson swallowed past a growing lump in his throat, and put the letter aside. "I don't believe I'll be able to read these aloud to you. Or read them at all without bursting into unmanly tears."

Alice let out a small laugh. "I wanted you to know that you've always been in my heart. Even when you were gone."

Henderson looked down, overwhelmed by emotion. To have someone love him so was astounding. "And now we have forever."

"To live happily." She beamed him a smile.

"Ever."

She laughed, she just couldn't stop herself. "After."

Read on for an excerpt from the next book in Jane Goodger's charming Brides of St. Ives series.

Preface

Long before Augustus Lawton saw Costille House, his ancestral home, he heard it. Loud strains of music flowed in the breeze, distorted and haunting, along with raucous laughter and the occasional delighted scream.

His wife was having a party, apparently. And to think she'd lamented to him in her last letter about how bored she was. How lonely. Her infrequent letters were no more than long lists of complaints that were entirely justified. Unhappy wife, unhappy life. A truer sentiment had never been uttered.

Lenore was deeply, unfathomably unhappy and had been since the day she'd married him. Their wedding night ended with her shouting, "I hate you. If you ever touch me again, I shall kill you." He'd obliged.

As he turned the bend in the long, tree-lined road that led to Costille, he pulled up short and had the ridiculous urge to double back to be certain he was on the correct lane. It had been nearly three years since he'd been home, after all. But no, that brilliantly lit Medieval castle was Costille, except the last time he'd been home they'd had no gaslights, nothing to modernize the old place, not even water closets. Augustus's father, the Earl of Berkley, had generously allowed Lenore to stay at Costille in his absence, mostly because he knew she would hate living there (they disliked one another intensely). Her stay was allowed with one caveat: She was to do nothing to change the house.

Trepidation filled Augustus as he urged his horse to move toward Costille, the sounds of the party getting louder the closer he got. Costille was a sprawling Tudor house, an addition to the original Medieval castle, with a square turret that dominated the back of the structure. When he'd been a boy, it had been a source of pride that the turret could be seen from nearly every place in St. Ives. He could never get lost, never lose his way, as long as he could see his home. His father, as strong and indestructible as this castle, shared only one thing with his son—his love of Costille.

Augustus rode his horse slowly beneath a smaller square tower with an arched entry that led to the courtyard just as a drunken reveler spilled from the home's main door. He was easy to spot because several large gas lanterns hissed in the courtyard, shedding a light so strong, Augustus was tempted to shield his eyes.

"Hey," the man called. "The stables are in the back, you dumb sod." He was wearing formal attire, but his tie was askew and his hair a rumpled mess, as though he'd been recently under the covers servicing a lady friend. Augustus wondered, without a hint of jealousy, if it had been his wife.

"As this is my home, I know very well where the stables are, sir."

The man squinted at him, swaying on his feet. "Lord Berkley?" he asked, clearly confused to see such a young man before him.

"His son, Augustus Lawton, Lord Greenwich." It felt strange to say his title when for the past three years he'd only been known as Gus. The American West was not a place where a man styled himself higher than another. His gun, his ability to shoot and ride a horse, those were the marks of a man's worth. When he'd decided to return home, part of him wanted to keep his beard, his long hair, his fringed, leather jacket and thick canvas trousers, just to see his father's reaction. But when Augustus made the decision to return, he did so wholeheartedly. It was time to grow up, to take his place in society, to try to be some sort of husband to the bride he'd abandoned. Someday he would be the Earl of Berkley and by God, he wanted heirs. Lenore would be horrified to know what had precipitated his return.

When Augustus told the man his title, he straightened and saluted, and Augustus couldn't help but smile. He wasn't one to stand on ceremony so wasn't at all insulted. His drunk friend wandered to the far side of the courtyard and pissed in some bushes as Augustus dismounted and tied his borrowed steed to a post. The noise of the party suddenly got louder, and the courtyard even brighter, and Augustus realized it was because the drunken fool had gone back into the house and left the doors wide open.

That was when Augustus let out a small sound, the type a man makes when he is stabbed or shot. It was difficult to breathe, to stand, to *see*.

For through that well-lit door, Augustus saw a nightmare. A modern Victorian floral nightmare.

"I'll bloody kill her."

Chapter 1

Harriet Anderson had long ago realized she would never light up a room with her bubbly personality, would never make a man's head turn with her beauty, would never provoke anyone's interest. She was a dimmer version of her sister, Clara, a shadow in the moonlight, not quite seen.

What a glorious thing that was.

Harriet knew that her friends felt sorry for her. Poor Harriet, so shy, so reserved. So *free*.

Just that afternoon, her parents and sister had climbed aboard a carriage for a three-hour drive to Plymouth to visit some distant relative who'd mentioned she was hosting Baron Such-and-Such. Harriet had been excused, much to her delight. They would be staying overnight at least, which meant Harriet had more than twenty-four hours of doing whatever she liked. Clara, ever cheerful, scrambled aboard the carriage and waved good-bye, completely oblivious to the unfairness of leaving Harriet behind. Harriet never complained, for the times her parents were gone were perhaps the most wonderful days of the year. Being dragged around whilst they showed off their elder daughter was something Harriet didn't miss in the least.

Truth be told, it was embarrassing the way her mother pushed Clara in front of every titled man she came across. Her parents and their ancestors had come from strong Cornish stock, working men and women, the sort who never would dream of putting themselves forward. But her father, through grit and hard work, had managed to accumulate enough money and enough position to buy one of the many tin mines in Cornwall. They were rich now, so rich that an impoverished lord just might be persuaded to marry a woman far below his station. Clara was beautiful and her dowry was impressive, and for those reasons she had garnered quite a bit of attention over the years, though her heart had never been engaged. At twenty-four years old, Clara was still lovely and youthful and stirred the heart of many a man.

Harriet, on the other hand, counted herself lucky if anyone asked her to dance at the limited balls she attended. On those rare occasions when she was asked, her mother would critique her the way a director critiques an actor's performance. *You laughed too loudly. You smiled too much. Why didn't you smile? Did he ask about Clara? You really mustn't dance the reel, you're much too clumsy.* And so, she was rather relieved when no one did ask her, for her mother would always make her feel stupid and silly. It used to hurt far more than it did now, but it did still hurt a bit, to be that unwanted child who never could match her mother's great expectations. She couldn't change her sex, she couldn't become another Clara. And that was enough for her parents to dismiss her as a being who lived in their house but had nothing at all to do with their lives.

Any time that hurt made her stomach clench, Harriet would push it down and remember that she had the afternoon free to do as she pleased. She could walk to the shore, work on her needlepoint, sing badly in her room, read a book. This time, Harriet had enthusiastically arranged a luncheon with her friends, something she was very much looking forward to.

Her closest friend, Alice, was recently married and just beginning to show her pregnancy. Such an odd thing to think about, that a little being was growing inside Alice, the same girl she used to make paper dolls with. Not a day went by that Harriet didn't thank God that Alice had fallen in love with a man who lived in St. Ives. She would never move away.

Looking in the mirror, Harriet stuck out her tongue at her reflection and laughed. Sometimes she would look at Clara, then into her mirror, and find it startling how much plainer she was than her sister. It was not self-pity, not every time at any rate, but rather a pragmatism that made her realize long ago she would never be a beauty like Clara. Perhaps it would have bothered her if Clara had been mean or vain, but her sister was kind and sweet and Harriet loved her dearly. Two years ago, Harriet stopped trying to be lovely, wearing the latest fashions, asking her mother to buy new gowns each year. Perhaps the worst of it was that no one even noticed.

Harriet smiled at her reflection, then tilted her jaw. She wasn't *ugly*. In fact, if she turned her head just so, she was actually pretty. Narrowing her eyes, Harriet studied herself objectively and came away moderately pleased with her appearance. Her dress was a dull brown, a stark contrast to her light blue eyes, and her hair, usually a frizzing mess, held a few soft curls. It was, she realized, the light oil the girls' maid had given her, and Harriet gave herself a mental reminder to thank Jeanine for her hair tonic. If she were going out, Jeanine would usually iron her hair, then take the stiff, coarse results and curl a few select strands. But with Jeanine completely occupied by Clara, Harriet had simply brushed out her hair, applied the tonic, and pulled it back into a tight knot.

As Harriet went to leave the house, she kept an eye out for their housekeeper, whom she suspected reported to her mother any transgression. It was easy enough to thwart the woman; Harriet had long ago realized no one, including her mother, could fault her for "going for a walk." And if Harriet happened to walk to St. Ives village and meet her friends, who was to be the wiser? Sometimes she wished she had something more adventurous to do, something slightly dangerous, so she could really feel victorious.

Today, a walk into St. Ives was enough adventure for her. It was a lovely day, with a brisk wind blowing off the Atlantic, making her cheeks pink. She huddled into her old woolen coat and adjusted the soft wool scarf around her neck. It was October, and though it never got too cold in St. Ives even in winter, it was a day that called for a thick coat and a soft scarf.

When she reached the cobbled streets of the village, her boots tapped loudly, a sound that made her smile, for it meant she would soon see her friends. Teague's Tea House was a favorite of the villagers, and on this day it was fairly crowded with patrons. Harriet liked going there because she always felt so sophisticated, taking tea in a shop rather than at home. The store held a half-dozen small tables with smooth white linen table cloths, and the delicate clink of silverware and china, as well as the soft murmur of voices always made Harriet feel a small rush of warmth.

"Hello, Miss Anderson," the proprietor, Mrs. Teague, called out. Harriet often wondered if the Teagues truly liked having a tea shop or if they felt it was necessary to take advantage of their last name, but she was too shy to ask.

In the far corner, she saw her friends—Alice, Eliza, and Rebecca. Eliza and Rebecca were staring raptly at Alice's tummy, slightly rounded, as if it were some sort of oddity. The first of them to marry, the first to have a child, Alice was a bit of a celebrity amongst them. When they spied Harriet coming toward their small group, they stood, smiling widely, happy she was able to come that day. When her mother was home, she was not allowed to go into the village without a chaperone—and one was rarely available, as her mother was always too busy to accompany her.

"I don't mean to be terrible, but I'm awfully glad your mother is traveling," Alice said, giving her friend a hug. Her belly got in the way a bit, and Harriet laughed at the feeling.

"You're so round," she said. It had been a few weeks since Harriet had seen Alice, who had recently been in London.

"I know. My mother is already admonishing me not to go out. 'No one wants to see that,' she says." Alice laughed. "If Queen Victoria could go out in public en famille, then I can too. That's what I told her anyway."

"And how did your mother respond?"

Alice wrinkled her nose, her green eyes bright. "She said Queen Victoria set a bad example for all women." This she said in a whisper, as if she were committing some sort of treasonous act.

Once they were all seated, they caught up on each other's news. Alice, of course, had the most to relay, having been recently to London and being newly married. For the first time in her life, Harriet was jealous of a married woman. Perhaps it was because Alice seemed so completely happy, as if a new and brilliant light shined from within her. Or perhaps Harriet was, for the first time, aware that she might never find what Alice had. Any awkwardness she'd felt over Alice marrying Henderson had long since dissipated. When Harriet was a girl, she'd had a terrible crush on Henderson. Though her friends had treated it as a lark, Harriet had truly liked him, had dreamed that perhaps one day he would return to St. Ives and realize he liked her too. Instead, he'd returned and realized he was in love with Alice. Harriet hadn't been *devastated* by any means, but it had served as a reminder to her that she might not find love.

When conversation lulled, Rebecca pulled out a silk scarf and said, "Let's play the game, Harriet, shall we?"

Harriet groaned, even as her friends expressed their support of Rebecca's suggestion. Despite her groan, Harriet was secretly pleased; her memory was the only singular thing about her. She would never be the most beautiful or talented or lively one in the group, but no one could recall details the way she did. As a girl, she hadn't realized she held any special talent for memorization. It was little things, like her sister misplacing a book, or a maid unable to find a particular hair piece that gave her the first clue. Harriet always knew where everything was, because the minute someone would mention a missing article, a picture appeared in her head of its exact location. Recognizing her ability, one day Clara blindfolded Harriet and started quizzing her. What color tie does the man in the painting wear? Is the blue vase to the left or the right of the statue on the mantel? It didn't matter how small the detail, Harriet knew it. And so was born the game.

Rebecca jumped up and placed the scarf across Harriet's eyes, and the three other women started peppering her with questions. Around them, the other patrons grew quiet as they watched the game unfold.

"What color flowers are in the vase on the counter?" someone called out.

Harriet started, realizing others were listening, but she smiled. "Come, now, that's hardly a challenge. Yellow."

More patrons called out their questions, and Harriet laughed. For a girl who did not like to be in crowds, this was somehow wonderful. Perhaps it was because she was blindfolded and could not see them gawking at her. Or perhaps it was because she was among her friends. Normally painfully shy, she felt almost not herself.

"On the shelf, there are three containers, each with a different picture. Tell me, in order from left to right, what picture is on those containers."

Harriet straightened, and beneath the blindfold, she furrowed her brows. That deep baritone, commanding and somehow tinged with something close to…fear? She knew that voice.

"Lord Berkley," she said, slightly louder than a whisper. They had met once, at the John Knill ball. Alice's husband had introduced them, and the earl had muttered a proper greeting, thoroughly distracted by the sight of Clara, who had been especially pretty that night. It had been a small moment, a snippet in time, but Harriet still remembered feeling suddenly more alive than she had in her life because he was just that beautiful. And then he'd walked away, without ever really looking at her.

Jane Goodger lives in Rhode Island with her husband and three children. Jane, a former journalist, has written and published numerous historical romances. When she isn't writing, she's reading, walking, playing with her kids, or anything else completely unrelated to cleaning a house. You can visit her website at www.janegoodger.com.

CPSIA information can be obtained
at www.ICGtesting.com
Printed in the USA
LVOW08s1436080617
537403LV00001B/78/P